SHROUDED DECEPTION

by

Michael J. Martino

Spinning Wheel Publishers

www.ShroudedDeception.com

Shrouded Deception

Paperback Edition

Cover designed by: Peter M. Martino

Produced by: Spinning Wheel Publishers
                      64 Spinning Wheel Dr.
                      Uxbridge, MA 01569

Shrouded Deception is a work of fiction. All Characters and incidences are the products of the author's imagination and are used fictitiously. Although historical data was researched, it is not necessarily accurate.

ISBN 978-0-9903921-0-1

Shrouded Deception

Shrouded Deception

Preamble

On September 14, 1578, a very unusual linen cloth was moved from a small obscure church in Lirey, France to Turin, Italy. Today, that same linen can be found in the Royal Chapel in the Cathedral of St. John the Baptist in Turin.

Over the years, there has been an ongoing debate as to what this linen cloth really is. Many believers claim the cloth is nothing less than the burial shroud that wrapped the body of Jesus Christ. They say the faint image which can be seen in the linen is that of Jesus Himself; burned in at the moment of his resurrection. However, many others believe that it is a clever forgery created in the Middle Ages. Disclaimers point to the radio-carbon dating that was done on it in 1988, which said the cloth's linen fibers were grown between 1260-1390.

This story is meant to reveal what may have happened and why the carbon-14 results were inaccurate. The one truth we can be sure of is that the Shroud is a very controversial artifact cloaked in mystery...

NB: Torino, Italy has been known as Turin, Italy to the English speaking world. For the purposes of this novel we have used Turin during the earlier periods and Torino for the contemporary time.

Shrouded Deception

Chapter 1

Feeling her stir, I rolled over towards Luiza and softly asked, "You awake?"

"I am now," she replied sleepily. Then, wiggling herself closer, she cuddled up against me.

"Why don't you go back to sleep? It's too early to get up," she said quietly.

"I can't sleep," I replied now putting my arm around her and tucking her in tighter, "I've been awake for a while. You know how I am just before leaving on a trip. I've started my twenty-four hour countdown."

"You need to try to rest. You've got a long day ahead of you," Luiza tried to say while yawning.

"You know my routine. In twenty-four hours, I'll be here. In twenty-four hours, I'll be there."

Luiza turned her head towards me so I could see her roll her eyes and say, "Martin Daniels, I just don't understand you sometimes. Is that why you were so distracted at dinner last night?"

"You could tell?"

"Could I tell?" she replied sarcastically. "You hardly ate."

"I'm sorry. You know me. All I could think about was being at the airport, waiting at the gate, debating on whether I should join the crowd hovering around the gate, or just sit and relax and be one of the last to board."

"I hope you'll just sit and relax. Flying is so stressful for you," she suggested.

"Why do people congregate around the gate anyway? Are they really afraid they're going to miss the flight? Or, is it they can't wait to sit in those cramped seats."

Luiza again turned her face towards me briefly.

"What? Those things bother me," I said. We softly laughed.

From our bedroom, the back window faces southeast, and it was just about this time the sun began lighting the room. The sky's colors were bright yellow and orange highlighting the black silhouetted horizon. Above that, bright reds and purples filled what I could see of the sky. As I looked towards the window enjoying the colors, Luiza asked, "So what about bedtime? I wanted to cuddle, but you were just lying there lost in your thoughts."

"Well, I was thinking we're in mid-flight, just about the time the turbulence begins."

She then rolled over facing me and wrapped her arm around my waist. Hugging me tightly, she kissed me and said, "I know a way to help you relax. After all, you'll be gone a week."

I kissed her on the forehead and said coyly, "I'm not distracted now. We landed a couple hours ago."

She chuckled and kissed me again.

Every trip back to Italy was a mix of excitement and anxiety. Lying in bed, I couldn't wait to see my relatives and old friends. Mostly, I couldn't wait for the flight to be over. As an eighteen year old, I had studied art and apprenticed at a stained glass studio in Milan. I lived in Italy for three and a half years before returning to Boston to later open my own studio, Martin Daniels' Stained Glass Studio. Over the years, I'd jump at any opportunity to create new stained glass windows for small village churches nestled in the Italian Apennines above Reggio Emilia. Their names are so familiar to me: Busana, Aquabona, Cavanella, and Ramiseto. This area's significance is more personal since it is where my mother's family originated. Luiza, my wife, is sure the windows were excuses to travel back to Italy. As other trips before, I expected this one to be more or less the same--a quick trip to install the windows, a few days to visit friends and relatives, and home again.

These opportunities to create stained glass in Italy started by accident. In the early '90's, a second cousin, Domenico, conned me into making a few windows for his parent's church, in

Nismozza. His parent's church was in a tiny village high in the Apennines. If you were to find it on a map, it's half way from Reggio Emilia to La Spezia. Once I did the first church, word got out and spread to neighboring parishes. Every few years I found myself doing a few more windows and personally delivering them in small wooden crates. I'd build the crates from plywood and bring them as part of my luggage. I never dreamed fifteen years later I'd have done several small forgotten churches.

The five small windows I had with me on this trip were going into two different locations. One was the figure of "Our Lady of Mount Carmel". It was going into a small village church down the road from where my mother was born, Camporella. The other four were for a convent located just outside of Torino. The four small windows for the convent were eight religious symbols. I salvaged them from old stained glass panels that were being discarded after a restoration project of a church just south of Boston. The symbols had to be a hundred years old. I centered them into the stained glass windows and made the whole window look old like the salvaged centered medallions.

*　　　　*　　　　*

It was two o'clock when we loaded up the car with my carry-on and the three wooden crates. Luiza got into the driver's seat and turned to me, "Are you sure you have everything? Your passport, ticket, money, wallet? The list I told you to make yesterday?"

"Yes. I have everything except the list you told me to write."

"Did you ever make one?"

"No, I forgot."

"Martin, you know you can't remember everything. That's why you need to make a list," Luiza half-scolded me as she started the car.

"I know you're right, but why do I need a list, when you do that so well."

She said, "True," as she looked over her shoulder and backed out of the driveway and pulled away from the house.

"In twenty-four hours I should be with Loretta in Torino," I mumbled under my breath.

Luiza smirked and shook her head. "Only you, Martin Daniels, only you," and smiled.

We headed for Boston's Logan Airport for my 6:30 pm flight to Milan, Italy. Fortunately the Mass Pike wasn't backed up. Nonetheless, Luiza made the most of the passing lane.

"Sweetie, I'm going to be on time; you're drivin' wicked fast."

"You know Boston's evening traffic starts by three. I don't want to take any chances," she leaned forward and gripped the wheel getting even closer to the car ahead of us; hoping they'd move over.

Several minutes later I could tell Luiza had something on her mind so I asked, "What are you thinking about?"

"I'm thinking about all the work you have in the studio and how it's not gonna get done."

"I made a few calls and let them know something came up, and I'd be gone a week," I replied.

"Yes, but did you have to decide to go now?" Luiza asked, even though she didn't expect a logical answer. She has come to patiently understand that I can be impulsive. I think she believes it's because of lead poisoning from my work. I prefer to think it's because of my artistic personality, and it adds adventure to our lives.

"I wish you were coming with me," I said.

"Unlike you, I have a commitment to work. You know I can't just call them and say I'm off to Italy," Luiza said.

"I would've called John, your boss for you," I said.

"Ya right, that's all I need."

Chapter 2

We arrived at Terminal D with plenty of time to spare. As Luiza grabbed my carry-on, I quickly scanned the area for an abandoned luggage cart. I spotted one with the front two wheels on the street and the back two resting just up on the curb. I excitedly ran over, snatched it, and brought it back to the car with a big smile on my face.

"You'd think you just won the lottery," she teased.

"What? It's like getting a front row parking spot or finding a dollar bill. It makes your day."

She smiled, "You're right." We always appreciate the little things in life.

As she helped me load the crates onto the baggage cart, I began to feel nervous and already started to miss her. With watery eyes, we quickly hugged, kissed and said goodbye before a state trooper rushed her away. As I headed into the terminal looking for the check-in counter, I tried to distract myself from how much I knew I was going to miss her over the next week.

Even though it was about two and a half hours before the flight, a pretty substantial line at the check-in area had already formed. I waited my turn, inching forward ever so slightly. Once the man behind the counter signaled me, I made my way awkwardly towards him pushing my cart and pulling my carry-on with its wobbly wheel. Once up to the counter, I handed him my passport and ticket. He looked them over for a moment, looked up at me, then signaled for his manager. As soon as she stepped up next to him, she looked at me and asked, "May there be a problem?" The agent, who had been checking me in, handed her my passport and ticket. She studied them and then said, "I'm sorry, Mr. Daniels. We looked for you last night. This ticket is for the flight that left yesterday."

With confusion in my voice I asked, "Are you sure?"

"Here, look. The ticket is for Monday, May 12th not Tuesday, the 13th."

I could feel myself beginning to panic as I asked, "What am I going to do?"

The manager replied, "Although tonight's flight is completely booked, perhaps somebody will forget to show up, just like you did last night, and there may be a seat for you."

Motioning with her hand, she said, "Why don't you go over there, sit down, relax, and in a couple of hours we'll know if there's a seat for you."

I sat quietly for a while wondering how I could have missed the correct date on my ticket. It took me a while to muster the courage to turn my cell phone back on to call Luiza.

Eventually, I hit *send* and Luiza answered the phone, "Hi, how did everything go?"

"Well, not exactly as planned," I reluctantly told her.

After a noticeable pause she asked, "Why? What happened?"

"I was supposed to be here last night." I replied.

"What? You were supposed to be there last night?"

"Yes. My ticket was for Monday's flight."

"For Monday? Did you ever look at your ticket?"

"I was sure I booked it for Tuesday."

"What's going to happen now?"

"The manager suggested I sit down and wait to see if there's a seat available."

"What are you going to do if there are no seats?" she had composed herself a little.

As embarrassed as I was to have to tell Luiza I had screwed up again, I could tell she was talking to me as she might one of her patients. Luiza is a nurse and works in a nursing home dealing with the elderly. Because of their dementia or just child-like state, she speaks with them in a manner a mother might to a child. That's how I heard her relaxed tone.

"I guess call you and ask you to pick me up at the Logan Express."

"Marty, only you get into these situations. How do you do it?"

"I guess I'm just lucky that way?"

"Marty, you can be so distracted sometimes and even impulsive; not finishing what you've started."

"What does that have to do with me missing my flight?"

"You're just a bit of a scatter brain sometimes."

"Sorry," I said a bit sheepishly.

"Well, call me if you need me to pick you up. Call me anyway, so I know you're all right," Luiza said calmly having been through these situations with me before.

Like the time I got on the wrong train at South Station in Boston. Not to labor the point, but we were working on the windows at St. Leonard Church in Boston's historic North End. We found it better to take the commuter train from downtown Framingham to South Station and avoid the Mass Pike traffic. The walk was only several blocks to the church on Hanover Street. Anyway, I took a later train than the others and I must have been particularly tired. I inadvertently got on the wrong train, nodded off and woke up in Abington, twenty miles south of Boston, Framingham is twenty miles west of the city. Luiza had to first pick me up and get me to Framingham so I could get my car. It was about 10:30 by the time we got home that evening.

We said goodbye, and I began to wait, hoping for something to open up. I watched the people coming and going through the airport and tried to relax. There was a mother with a baby in a carrier on her chest pulling another child alongside her. The toddler had a stuffed monkey on her back with a strap her mother held tightly. Unfortunately for the mother her daughter wanted to inspect every little thing she saw on the ground. With a diaper bag attached to a carry-on in her other hand, she kept telling the little girl to hurry but to no avail. I watched as she picked up the toddler and rushed into the security line. Before I lost sight of her, she was smiling and nodding to a fellow passenger who offered to help push her carry-on as they steadily crept forward.

As I sat there and watched more passengers moving through the terminal, the desk manager waved her hand to get my attention and signaled for me to come to the counter. "I am sorry,

Mr. Daniels, but the flight is completely full. There's not a seat for you."

"Not even a seat in First Class?" I asked.

"Not with this ticket. You don't think we're going to put you in First Class. Do you?" she replied.

"What am I going to do? I have these stained-glass windows I'm supposed to install into a church in Italy. They're waiting for me."

"We have looked to see if there are any seats on the flights for Wednesday, Thursday or Friday but our airline's next three flights appear to be completely full," she informed me.

"I can't believe I never noticed my ticket was for Monday night," I lamented.

"I need to help someone over there. Perhaps Enzo can double check to see if anything *else* is available." She gave Enzo a knowing look and walked away. I watched him hopefully. After about a minute of clicking away on his keypad and moving his head up and down, saying, "Si, si," he finally looked up and said, "You need to quickly get yourself over to terminal E and the Virgin Atlantic check-in counter. There, they will put you on their flight to London, where tomorrow morning you will catch a connecting flight to Milan. As it turns out, you'll probably arrive only a few hours later than the flight you were scheduled for."

All of a sudden my sense of despair changed to relief and even joy with tears welling up. With gratitude, I excitedly said to him, "Thank you. Thank you so very much. You have no idea how much this means to me." As I awkwardly moved away from the counter, I caught the eye of the desk manager and yelled, "Thank you," "Thank you," while waving my ticket just above my head. She raised her eyebrows as if surprised to know a flight had been found. She smiled and turned back to the customer she was helping. As I headed for terminal E, I thought, I feel like I've just been born again—*again*.

Without yet realizing it, I was not only off to London and then to Italy, but I was off on an adventure of a life time.

Chapter *3*

The Royal Palace, Turin Italy March 1943

"What have I done?" the King said nervously, while laying his hand over his forehead. "The deaths, the pain, the ruined lives, all because of my fears," he muttered in sorrow looking out a window over the palace gardens.

"If only I could atone for my sins," he lamented.

Looking up from the gardens on that clear night, a casual observer might have spied the King looking out from his chambers. They might have seen his bodily form silhouetted against his warmly lit room, but they would not have seen the anguish in his face, the proof of his tormented soul. Victor Emmanuel III, the King of Italy, had a lot to hide.

King Victor Emanuel III was the third king of Italy. He ascended to the throne in July 1900, because his father King Umberto I was assassinated. King Umberto I was shot four times by an Italian-American anarchist who claimed he was avenging the deaths of Italian protesters killed by the King's troops a couple years earlier. Victor Emmanuel III was thirty years old when he took the throne and reigned until May 1946. His most notable physical characteristic was his short height, which didn't even reach five feet. One of his most notable aspects of his personality was his fear of assassination, causing him to seldom be seen in public.

"But you are the sovereign King of Italy. It is your duty to protect and defend our great country. You understood how dangerous Mussolini was," encouraged his aide, Alessandro Grassi.

The King's aide on the other hand was taller and larger than the King. Being well fed, he had more of a stout round shape and bald head. Grassi stood almost at attention several feet away in the middle of the beautifully gilded and baroque styled room. He was alone with the King in his private residence at the Palace in Turin.

"No. Instead of defending and protecting my people, I cowered," replied the King. "I acted out of fear of Mussolini more than for the defense of our nation. I sent thousands of soldiers to their deaths. That maniac was drunk with power, and I was drunk with greed."

Grassi tried to comfort the King, "Please sire, be at peace."

"The day is coming when I will stand in judgment for my actions. I must be judged before *The Almighty King*. I believe that day is coming very soon."

"Your Majesty, why do you talk that way?" his aide asked with concern.

"Because it's true. I know it in my heart."

"Do you want me to call for the Archbishop? I'm sure he'll make himself available, if you believe you need him," Grassi asked hoping to help.

"Yes, please call Archbishop Maurilio immediately, encourage him to come quickly and offer me absolution for my sins," the King pleaded.

"At your command, your Majesty," Grassi retreated from the King's presence to summon Archbishop Maurilio Fossati.

Slipping down to the servants' quarters Grassi disguised himself by dressing in common street clothes. He then slipped out the service entrance door and headed for the Archbishop's residence. The disguise served to hide Grassi's identity. He feared, if he was recognized as the King's personal assistant, he would inevitably be singled out by the King's enemies. The political climate at this time made it necessary for the King's aide to take precautions. Rounding the corner onto a busy urban street, he began to make his way to the Archbishop's residence. With his head low and his back arched, he stood at a tram stop a few blocks from Palazzo Reale. Grassi felt reasonably sure no one would recognize him.

*   *   *

Grassi arrived at the front door of the Archbishop's stately mansion, and rang the doorbell. The maid, who answered the door, had never met Grassi. She tried to send him away seeing the pauperly way he was dressed.

"I am Alessandro Grassi, the King's private aide. Tell Monsignor Bertolucci I am here to see the Archbishop," he urged her. Reluctantly, the maid contacted the Monsignor on the internal house phone.

"I'm very sorry to disturb you, Monsignor, but there is a man here who says he is Signor Alessandro Grassi, the King's aide," the maid explained.

Grassi could hear the Monsignor's response, "Send him up to my office immediately."

The maid turned to Grassi and said, "Please follow me; I will take you to the Monsignor's office."

Monsignor Bertolucci waited outside his office and greeted Signor Grassi, "My dear Alessandro, it has been a while since we've seen you. I pray and trust the King is well."

Grassi gravely replied, "I am sorry to report the King is suffering another extreme bout of depression."

Immediately, Bertolucci ushered Grassi into the Archbishop's office.

Archbishop Maurilio Fossati rose from behind his desk, "I am so pleased to see you again, my son."

Coming around to the side, he offered Grassi the opportunity to kiss his ring. Grassi bent down on one knee, grabbed the Archbishop's right hand and leaned forward to kiss his ring.

"Your Eminence, the King is suffering from paranoia and depression again," Grassi reported. "He has sent me here to request you come and hear his confession. He believes he may be dying."

The Archbishop reluctantly replied, "I have been through this with the King before. But very well, I will visit him. First I must conclude my meeting scheduled one hour from now."

"Your Eminence, I am concerned he will suffer greatly if he is made to wait," Grassi insisted.

"My son in God, there are no emergencies. Please, go in

peace, and I will follow as soon as possible." Archbishop Fossati waved Grassi away with a halfhearted sign of the cross saying, "May the Lord bless you, my son. Go in peace."

Disappointed, Grassi left knowing he had done all he could.

In order to make sure he wasn't being followed, Grassi took a roundabout route back to the Palace. He eventually returned arriving at the service entrance more than an hour later. Grassi made his way back to the King's private residence and could only wonder in what state he would find the King. Unfortunately, his fears were realized when he entered the room. He saw the King pacing nervously and crying out, "My soul, my soul is damned."

Grassi tried to reassure his lord. "Your Majesty, the Archbishop is on his way."

"When will he get here, how much longer do I have to wait?" the King asked with sadness.

"I'm sure he'll be here shortly," reassured Grassi. The King of Italy seemed to calm down a bit.

*   *   *

It was more than two hours later when the Archbishop finally arrived at the Royal Palace. As they approached the main gates to the Palace, the Archbishop and his entourage were immediately allowed access. The Archbishop didn't arrive in his usual regalia and princely garb. Instead, he came in a simple black clerical suit with a traditional priest's collar and a red zucchetto on his head. During this turbulent time in Italy's history, even the Archbishop, a prince of the Church, might be vulnerable to assassination attempts. Once ushered into the King's inner chamber, Fossati swiftly walked towards the King with his arms open wide and said, "My son, may your soul be at peace."

"Your Eminence, you have finally come. Please pray for me, hear my confession, and absolve me of my sins," pleaded the sovereign of Italy.

"Of course, but why are you so troubled?"

"Because that maniac Hitler will soon take over Italy, to try and prevent the British and Americans from gaining control of southern Europe," his Majesty insisted. "We cannot keep the

British and Americans out of Italy. I am forced to yield to the power and will of the Allies." The King added, "Once I do that, the Nazis will not leave peacefully, but will take control of the country. You know how ruthless they can be. They will be merciless against our people."

The King nervously paced around the room unable to calm himself down. It was obvious that he was in a state of paranoia induced panic.

"I now see why you are so troubled," his Eminence said with concern in his voice.

"I also fear for our sacred treasure...the holy relic must be protected," insisted the King.

"What are you saying?" the Archbishop asked with concern in his voice.

"I am talking about the only article that remains from Our Lord--His burial cloth. The sacred linen that wrapped His tortured body… I fear it will be stolen by the Nazis."

The Archbishop, now understanding the intense concern of the King asked, "What are you proposing to do? What can be done?"

"I am thinking of protecting the sacred cloth the same way I protect myself."

"But how?" asked Fossati, now wondering where the King was going.

"By having a duplicate made," announced the King.

"What are you saying?" inquired the Archbishop, now even more concerned.

"What I am saying is I have a man who closely resembles me to protect me from assassination. Even Hitler himself has a double for safety's sake. These extreme measures need to be taken. I am going to have a duplicate made of the original linen cloth Our Lord was laid in," the King explained.

After the King had paused to reflect on this action, he added, "I must do this before it's too late. I have already ordered my aide Grassi to begin to find a method to make an exact copy." He looked up at the Archbishop, his face fraught with anguish. "Please, I need you to pray for my soul."

With that, Fossati took a purple stole out of his jacket pocket, kissed it, and put it around his neck. He sat in an arm chair off in a corner of the room and motioned with his hand for the King to come and kneel at his left side. Victor Emmanuel III, King of Italy, went over to the side of the armchair, knelt on a pillow beside his confessor and as he made a Sign of the Cross said, "Bless me father for I have sinned…"

Chapter *4*

There was perhaps only one person who could closely replicate the Shroud. Grassi knew how to find him. He was renowned scientist Dr. Carlo Darius, a brilliant professor of Applied Sciences at the Polytechnic University of Turin. Grassi believed he could coerce Darius to help, so he secretly summoned him to the Royal Palace in Rome.

"There must be a scientifically feasible technique for counterfeiting the image on the Shroud, and you must find out what it is," Grassi demanded of Dr. Darius. After attempting to dissuade Grassi from continuing with the plan, Dr. Darius finally succumbed to Grassi's threats and agreed to help. He began the experiments in his university laboratory back in Turin.

Grassi had control over Dr. Darius, for the latter was well known for his anti-Fascist views. In fact, over the years he was persecuted by the Fascist Party for his political activities. At times they even considered assassinating him. Because he was considered important for the country, Mussolini's Fascists instead preferred to harass him. On a few occasions the Fascist police arrested, detained, and tormented him in different ways. One such way was to force him to drink a liter of castor oil. Once the laxative properties began to work, they'd send him home fully soiled. With the threat of death to him and his family, Dr. Darius gave in to Grassi's demands.

In spite of running experiment after experiment to replicate the image on the Shroud, the results never looked authentic. Dr. Darius realized the horror of what must be done. In order to make the cloth look genuine there would need to be a reenactment of what was done to Jesus on the day of His execution. Reluctantly, Darius requested Grassi find him an unfortunate victim, who would unknowingly assist in reproducing the figure in the Shroud. With only a copy of the famous 1898 negative of the face on the Shroud, the King's personal aide and now confidante, ordered Captain Cipollini, an officer in the Italian Army to look throughout the prisons around Italy to see if they could find someone who closely resembled the physical features on the cloth. Cipollini started in and around Turin passing from prison to prison and cell to cell trying to find someone who not only had similar facial features but also the right height and build. It took some time, but they finally discovered the unfortunate candidate in a prison near Genoa.

Very little was known about the selected prisoner. His prison number was 32764. He was Libyan by birth, and he had lived in the general region of Genoa for a few years. The prisoner had smuggled himself into Italy aboard a cargo ship that transported agricultural products grown in Libya for Italian produce markets. Even though he had a fairly strong Arabian accent, he spoke Italian fairly well. It was supposed he worked closely with Italians who immigrated to Libya, which had been one of Italy's colonies. He was arrested for helping to kidnap young women who were eventually sold to wealthy Arab men as sex slaves in and around North Africa. This practice was not uncommon in those days. White women were considered very desirable.

At the appointed time, Captain Cipollini and two of his conscripted soldiers arrived at the Genoa prison. Slipping in through a back entrance, they entered the dungeon-like stairwell, where they were stunned by the putrid smell. The prison's overwhelming stench was from the dampness in the prison mixed with human sewage and smells of bodies left to die. They covered their faces and descended the stairs to prisoner 32764. Awakened by the heavy steps of combat boots and the metal clanging of the cell door opening, the solitary prisoner was surprised to see them entering his cell. The two soldiers grabbed, gagged and shackled him without a word. They forcibly removed him from the prison, dragging him up the stairs. Once the captain assured the alley was clear, the two soldiers tossed the prisoner into the back of their truck and covered him with a heavy canvas.

Cipollini secretly transported the prisoner to an abandoned factory in the Piedmont region of Italy near the city of Turin. It was there that Captain Cipollini and his two soldiers re-enacted the torture and crucifixion that happened to Jesus during his passion. This included ripping out parts of his beard, lashing him with a Roman flagellum, piercing his forehead with shards from a make shift crown, digging spikes through his wrists and feet and finally piercing his right side to replicate the spear in Jesus' side.

After dragging him into the old factory, they threw him onto the cold concrete floor and then tied him to a post at one end of the building. They then went back to the truck and returned with a large box and opened it. He looked up bewildered as one solider pulled out a three stranded whip with metal shards on its end.

"What are you doing?" he sputtered, trying to free himself from his bonds. "Why me?"

"Because you're the right fit and won't be missed. Now say a final prayer then shut up," sneered Cipollini standing with his arms on his hips as he watched his soldier take practice swings.

The Libyan victim screamed out in agony as they whipped him over and over again, forty times, careful to replicate how the wounds are seen in the Shroud. The brutal treatment tore the skin on his back. He kept waiting to pass out, but never did. Finally, the whipping ceased. He noticed the box being opened again and saw one soldier bring over what looked like a crown made with spikes and wires. This was forced onto his head. The excruciating pain brought momentary relief as it distracted him from his torn back. Once untied from the post, he lay on the concrete in a pool of his own blood.

The two soldiers lifted him up and dragged him over to a wooden beam that supported the building. They had already attached a cross board about six feet off the floor, in preparation for what they would do next. They held his arms out precisely to where Dr Darius instructed them. They hammered spikes through his wrists and feet, just as the Shroud shows. He screamed in agony only able to ramble in his native tongue. Eventually, with a choke and gurgle as his final sound, the prisoner hung lifeless. Once he was finally dead, Cipollini made the final blow by slicing a spear through the prisoner's side. The three men stared at the limp mass of flesh and blood that no longer looked like a human being.

Ironically, even though the Libyan prisoner deserved to die for the heinous crimes committed against women, his ultimate capital offense was he too closely resembled the image in the Shroud who many believe to be Jesus'--the Prince of Peace.

It seemed like hours had passed, when the sound of another jeep on gravel stirred the soldiers from their daze. "It must be the King's aide and his scientist. Go get them," Captain Cipollini commanded. The soldier returned with Grassi and Dr. Darius following directly behind.

"Is it finished?" Grassi asked Cipollini.

"It is finished."

Grassi, Darius, and Cipollini and his soldiers proceeded with the next step in the process of forging the Shroud. The body was laid out in an oversized crate they built which measured about seven feet wide, four feet deep and ten feet tall. In the dead center on top of this crate was installed an optical glass lens. Several feet above the top of the crate were two sheets of plate glass. Also, to make the forgery look real, they found amongst the drop-cloths used to cover the palace's furniture, a linen cloth about the size they needed. This cloth was already very old so it had that certain patina only time could create. They trimmed it to measure the size of the original Shroud—14ft.x 3½ft. Half of the cloth was stretched tightly between the two pieces of plate glass, insuring it would not wrinkle. Before being laid between the plate glass, the cloth itself was sprayed with silver nitrate and other photosensitive chemicals.

Once the prisoner's body was positioned properly in the base of the crate, strong lights mounted on the ceiling and sides of the tall crate were turned on. This projected the image of the victim through the glass lens onto the chemically treated linen.

After forty-five seconds of exposure, the cloth itself became a huge negative. The body was turned over and the process was repeated to create the second half, which was the rear portion as seen on the Shroud. Once the exposures were completed, the cloth would only need to be developed as any negative would be. This hopefully would create the image that was seen on the original Shroud.

A dark room, lit with only a red light, was prepared for the developing of the counterfeit. First the entire cloth was immersed into a large vat of warm water to wash off the silver nitrate. Then several predetermined steps necessary to develop the image were carefully followed. Lastly, the cloth was soaked in a drum of urine collected from several soldier's barracks near Turin. The urine worked as a fixative, which caused the colors not to run.

Once the image was successfully fused into the cloth, they needed to add the burn marks. These marks were originally singed into the Shroud when it suffered damage in the Chambery Chapel fire of 1532. To accomplish this, they brushed on hydrofluoric acid, which precisely burned the areas necessary. Mysterious reddish bloods stains which are evident in the original, were applied using natural dyes. The water stains which occurred when the fire was doused were also created. The real Sacred Linen was seldom displayed in public and very few people knew exactly what it looked like, so they believed the forgery would easily go undetected.

The following evening, Grassi and Cipollini returned, to the old abandoned factory. Dr. Darius, having completed his part, was not with them. The two men carefully folded the Shroud in the same manner in which it was kept in the Royal Chapel. Grassi took the cloth and waited for Cipollini in their vehicle. Cipollini doused the factory and all of its remains in gasoline. He lit a match and walked out to Grassi. As the two men drove away, the burning building lit the road in front of them.

The King's aide and the captain drove directly to the Royal Chapel. Grassi used an acquired set of keys to unlock the chapel and the glass case holding the real Shroud. Carefully removing it, Grassi took the original Shroud out, and Cipollini laid down the forged version. Once the case was locked, each man walked over to the altar, lit a candle and genuflected, perhaps more out of habit rather than any sense of reverence. From there, the two men parted ways. Grassi brought the real cloth to the King. After taking a moment to inspect it, the King had Grassi place it in the rear of a storage closet in his private residence. This location they were sure would not be found. Grassi said goodnight to the King and retired.

Instead of going directly to his room, he decided to go for a walk outside the palace to try to shake off the smell of smoke. For that brief moment, he was satisfied to have done what his King had commanded. He thought about the cost, torturing the prisoner and burning the old factory—all this to appease a paranoid King. With the lighting of a match at the factory, he hoped to erase the evidence and with the lighting of a candle in the Royal Chapel, he hoped to erase the guilt.

Chapter 5

Just knowing our plane was approaching Milan's International airport my spirits rose. Even though I was exhausted after flying several hours to London, then waiting at Heathrow for another couple hours, I found a sense of expectancy. As the pilot lowered the plane's altitude making its approach towards Malpensa Airport, I began to think about how I came to live in Milan for the first time so many years ago.

While staring at the snow-capped Alps out my window, I thought of how my mother and her family immigrated to the US in the years just before World War II. My grandfather was accused of being a Communist who openly criticized Mussolini and his Fascist Party during the twenties. Eventually he was forced to either leave or find himself persecuted by the Fascists. Because my mother's parents thought it best they prepare the way first, in their new country, she and her sister remained in Italy for several years after their parents left.

My grandparents wanted to first get themselves established and when they could safely bring their daughters over, they did. In the meantime, my mother and her sister were put in a boarding school and cared for by nuns. The school and convent, *Convento del Buon Pastore,* could still be found on Vialle Umberto I in the city of Reggio Emilia up until twenty years ago. Today a church stands there in its place with the same name as the old convent. At this boarding school, all the children slept in bunk-beds. My mother's bunkmate was Tamira Grappelli. While at school they became close friends.

Just as World War II began, my mother and her sister left Italy to join their parents. Because of the war, she lost contact with her friend Tamira for several years. They reconnected and re-established their friendship later on as adults. They both liked writing letters, so they corresponded fairly regularly. At times, after receiving a letter, my mother would tell us about her friend and any recent news from Italy.

Because of the devastation in Italy after the war, my mother would at times send Tamira a bundle of items to help. I still remember as a young boy walking with her to the Post Office. She'd put together "care packages" in a cloth-bound bundle sealed by hand-stitched seams. When I eventually got to meet Tamira and her family, they told me how much they appreciated those cloth-bound bundles, especially with the shortages of pretty much everything. As we grew out of our clothes, mom would send them over with other items. Some of the clothes were baby clothes, the kind with snaps to make diaper changing easier. These styles were nonexistent in Italy. Tamira's neighbors would marvel at her baby's American clothes, and how well made and practical they were. When my mother heard Tamira had another baby, she sent the Baptismal outfit worn by us. The Grappelli's showed me that same outfit when I was there years later. It is still being passed down through their family.

Shortly after I finished high school, I decided I wanted to study art in Italy, perhaps roam around Europe and see what living in youth hostels would be like. I asked my mother to write Tamira to see if I could stay with them for a short while, which she did. Two years earlier Tamira had lost her husband suddenly. For that reason, I wasn't sure if they would be able to help me. To my delight, they graciously invited me to spend several months living at their home which was then in Segrate, a suburb of Milan.

*   *   *

Arriving at Malpensa Airport for perhaps the tenth time still excited me. Our plane approached its position stopping in the middle of the tarmac. As soon as the passengers deplaned, we were ushered into courtesy buses. I followed the herd of people heading for Passport Control and got into the Non-EU citizens line. When it was finally my turn to show my passport, I stepped up to the counter. "Business or pleasure," the agent asked. Attempting humor I replied, "It is a pleasure to do business in Italy." The agent stared at me, slapped my passport on the ledge, and slid it back to me. He nodded for the next passenger to move forward. As I got out of the way, I thought to myself, "Someone doesn't like his job."

Arriving in Baggage Claim and looking for the carousel which would deliver the luggage, I positioned myself in a perfect spot. I was not too close to the front rail where people were prepared to elbow one another, but a few feet back. I claimed my position, or so I thought, until someone decided to squeeze themselves directly in front of me. *"Che stronzo!"* I thought to myself, which was one of the first Italian swear words I learned.

After a while, a red warning light began to blink and an ugly squawking sound alerted us our luggage had arrived and was on its way out. I waited for all the suitcases to come out, but none of my wooden crates were among them. Nearby, a porter waited to help passengers with their luggage. In Italian I asked the *facchino,* "I have three wooden crates. Do you know where they might be?"

"You should go to the *Bagaglii Smarriti* (Lost Luggage) counter or first check just outside the door with a sign *Bagagli fuori misura,*" (Oversized Luggage) he explained pointing in the direction I should go. Sure enough, my crates were resting against the wall just outside the doors with the oversized luggage sign. Great! My crates had arrived. A luggage cart was what was needed. Since I couldn't see any abandoned ones waiting for me, I went over to the ones you can rent. I inserted my one euro coin and wrestled it free. Now it was off to Customs, hoping and praying all the way.

The tax on imported goods was 10%. The stained glass I had was worth thousands of dollars. If the customs official chose, he could charge hundreds of dollars for importing art objects. Along with my passport and ticket, I had a letter from Don Luca, the pastor of the churches in Ramiseto, Pieve di San Vicenzo and Camporella. The letter explained the stained-glass windows in the crates were a gift to a poor church from their American friend. He asked for the windows to please be allowed to enter Italy duty-free. I arrived at the counter and handed the letter to the uniformed customs agent standing at an inspection table. He instructed me to see the person in the office. I presented the letter to the woman sitting behind the desk. She read it and with typical Italian hand gestures asked, "What do you want from me?"

"I've made these windows to give as a gift to the village where my family came from. It is a small mountain village up in the Apennines. Don Luca[1], the Pastor is hoping you'll see they don't have a lot of money and will be kind to them," I explained.

"How much are they worth?"

"That depends," I replied. "To this village they have an incalculable value, but as scrap metal and glass they are nearly worthless."

The customs official asked, "Are they glass?"

"Yes," I replied.

"Then I will charge you as glass," she replied.

After looking up glass in her rate book she asked, "Is €30 too much?"

"No, of course not, thank you for your kindness," I replied handing her the amount. Then the custom official filled out a receipt showing the paid tax of €30.

---

[1] "Don" is a title of respect used for Pastoral priests, like our use of "Father"

Chapter 6

"Italy at last. I've arrived," I thought with relief after making it through Customs. However, there were still a few things needed to complete before I could leave the airport. I passed café-bars, car rental areas, money changing stores, and other tourist related shops as I weaved in and out of the airport crowds. Spotting a cell phone store, I decided to get my phone activated. Leaving my cart just outside the entrance, I got in line. When it was my turn, I stepped up to the counter and handed the clerk my cheap little red cellphone.

"I purchased this on a previous trip. Will you still be able to activate it for me?" I asked hopefully. She turned it around in her hand inspecting it.

"That should be no problem. I just haven't seen this model in a few years," she explained and smiled politely.

"Is there an electric outlet where I may charge my phone when you're finished?" I asked.

"Sure." She pointed to an outlet on the lower part of the wall near the floor. "You may plug it in and leave it on the floor there." I thanked her and waited for her to finish activating my phone.

I'd say, the woman behind the counter appeared to be in her mid thirties. Her hair was dark, and pulled back into a bun. She wore a smart uniform with the company logo over the left breast of her mustard colored blazer. Underneath the blazer she wore a light blue blouse. Because of the counter, I couldn't see if she wore a skirt or pants. Although she wasn't gorgeous, she definitely was attractive. While looking at her, or perhaps I was staring a bit, I began to think why I find Italian women so attractive. I decided it's because they take care of themselves. What I mean is their hair is combed neatly, they wear a bit of make-up, and their clothes fit well and are stylish. Perhaps it portrays self-respect or a feminine confidence. I think Italian women believe their blessed to be women…but I digress.

"May I see your passport?"

I took out my passport and handed it over the counter. "Do you mind if I ask why you need it?"

"Here in Italy you need identification for everything," she explained smiling again.

After a couple more minutes, she reassembled my cell phone with a new sim-card and phone number.

Handing it back, she explained, "It may take up to forty-five minutes for it to be fully activated."

"*Va bene, grazie*," I replied putting away my passport and credit card. After I plugged in the cell phone to charge, I announced to her, "I think I'll go find a café and enjoy a cappuccino while I wait."

"Yes, the cappuccino in Italy is very good."

Just beyond the cell phone store, I noticed a café-bar a short distance away. I left my cart just outside café, and walked up to the cashier.

"*Un cappuccino, e un brioche con crema per favore*,"

"*2.50.*"

I handed him the money; he gave me my change, a receipt, and my French crème filled brioche.

"*Grazie.*"

"*Prego.*"

I walked over to the bar and gave the barista my order, "C*appucio*," I said using the Milanese dialect. She immediately put a larger saucer and spoon in front of me to remind her I'm having a cappuccino. She then tore my receipt as is the custom.

Because of the crowd at the bar, the barista went nonstop, constantly pulling out the handled coffee holder, hitting it against a draw below that collects the used grounds. Then two whacks at the coffee grounds dispenser to refill it and back up to the espresso machine. A flick of a switch, two more cups were being made. I'm fascinated how quickly so many little cups of espresso and cappuccino can be made. Not like in the States, where they make a pot of coffee sometimes in a three gallon urn. If you're lucky they add the cream and sugar.

When served, with cappuccino and brioche in hand, I moved away from the bar and stood at a cocktail table to keep an eye on my cart. There, I added my sugar and took my first sip. I closed my eyes and breathed in deeply the delicious coffee aroma, fully enjoying the sweet and roasted flavor. Placing my cappuccino down, I looked around the café and soaked it all in once again. "I'm finally back in Italy," I thought to myself. The sights, the Italian being spoken around me and the flavors of my pastry and cappuccino, caused me to reflect back to my very first day here.

I had arrived in Italy for the first time, more than thirty years ago at Malpensa Airport. It also happened to be my first time flying, which I have never enjoyed. The cramped and close quarters, being surrounded by people I didn't know, the turbulence—I still hate turbulence. Flying more than nine hours the first time in a plane was quite the white-knuckle experience for me. The plane touched down early in the morning after flying across the Atlantic all night. About the only thing I remember from that first time in Malpensa Airport was walking through the Custom's doors. They opened out into a common area where friends, family and the occasional limo driver with a sign were waiting. As I came through the doors I saw Tamira Grappelli in a bright red coat. I recognized her right away. A year earlier she had sent us a family picture in which she wore the same red coat. Her neighbor Giancarlo accompanied her to the airport, since she didn't own a car.

I vaguely remember the drive back to Tamira's home in Giancarlo's strange Italian car. I sat in the front seat and Tamira took the back seat. Giancarlo's car was quite small and as I remember it was white. The thing I remember most was how he had to shift gears. Although it was a standard shift with the clutch on the floor, he would change gears by moving a handle just right of his steering wheel. It wasn't on the column, but instead stuck out of the dashboard. He would push it in or pull it out and twist the handle left or right to change gears. I guessed this allowed the front seats to be a bit closer since there wasn't a shifter on the floor.

The city of Milan was congested with vehicles of all kinds including trams, and big electric buses. Some of the buses were double long with a joint in the middle to get around corners, something I had never seen before. The city had a unique smell to me. It was more than the exhaust; I think perhaps it was mixed with aromas from bakeries and restaurants. Another thing I noticed, which I had never seen before was all the buildings had these roll up shutters. Some half way up some all the way down, they were everywhere, over all the windows. What also stood out was that quite a few of the apartment buildings had shiny colored glazed ceramic tile on the exterior as its siding. They were about the size of red bricks, and also staggered but vertically and not horizontally as bricks are.

We drove immediately to Tamira's home in Segrate, which is just beyond the city limits. Because Malpensa Airport is about thirty miles north of the city and Segrate is southwest of Milan, it took us well more than an hour to finally get to their townhouse. It was close to noon by the time we arrived. The house they lived in was at the end of a cul-de-sac, at the far right end. It had a wrought iron metal fence covered with well trimmed bushes.

They immediately brought my luggage upstairs to what became my bedroom. We greeted some neighbors who wanted a peek at the American, and shortly after we arrived they began to prepare lunch. I remember it was *brodino*, a light chicken broth with small pasta. They understood my stomach didn't need anything heavy after flying all night. As soon as lunch ended, they brought me up to my bedroom and encouraged me to take a nap. I eventually woke up just after three and made my way downstairs to finally meet Tamira's two children, Loretta and Massimo who had just come home from school. Loretta was older about eleven and Massimo was about nine. Loretta was excited to meet me and even tried to use her English with the encouragement of her mother. Massimo on the other hand was not excited at all. I'm not sure if it was because he was shy or felt another man was threatening his home. My difficulty with the language didn't help. Massimo and I never really got to know each other during those months I was with them. Loretta on the other hand was eager to have me to help her with her English.

Along with Tamira, she was always eager to help me with my Italian.

Shortly after four, we all squeezed into a small car and left for Selvapiana, a tiny village where Tamira's family originated from. Their village is just beyond Parma in the Apennine foothills. With Tamira's brother, Gianni, driving, I sat in the front and Tamira and her two kids squeezed into the back.

The trip to Selvapiana took a few hours to get to. From Segrate we were soon on the highway that heads towards Rome until we exited at Parma. From there we worked our way around the city to the outskirts, which was all flat farm country. Later I found out they grew grass for hay to feed the cows that produce the milk to make Parmigiano-Reggiano cheese, affectionately known as "*Grana*".

Once we arrived in Ciano d'Enza a town ten miles beyond Parma, we turned left and immediately began to climb a narrow road that took us up to Selvapiana. While switching back and forth on the hairpin turns, Gianni tried to avoid falling off the steep embankments, which at times had no guardrails. It was well after dark by the time we finally reached the village. We were greeted at the door by Tamira's sister Piera and her husband, Orlando. They had been watching for headlights out the kitchen window. Because there weren't any street lights in Selvapiana, at night, the only light seen came from the few houses in the village.

I can still remember the fresh smell of the surrounding hay fields as we entered the house. The old fieldstone building had walls about two feet thick and was hundreds of years old. The doorways were arched and the stairs that led up to the second floor were stone treads, well rounded after centuries of use. The exterior of the house showed the field stones, but all the interior walls were plastered smooth.

They had no inside bathroom toilet, which I found out after dinner. Understanding I needed to go use the bathroom, Tamira's brother, Orlando, gave me a flash light and gestured to follow him outside. We went around the house to the rear to where the barn was. There, a small room had been added on the side of the barn. Upon entering it, he pulled a cord attached to a light bulb dangling from the ceiling. The light revealed a flush toilet and a roll of the coarsest toilet paper I've ever felt.

After my thoroughly rustic experience, we watched TV on a small black and white television. I didn't understand anything except that it was the evening news. Shortly after, they noticed me nodding off in the chair. Tamira got up, took my arm, and lead me upstairs to my bedroom, where I found out about the *prete e suora* (priest and nun) when she removed the pan of hot coals and surrounding cane rack that had been warming my bed. The cane rack protected the blankets from catching fire. Although I was never told which was the priest and which was the nun, they certainly warmed up my bed. Tamira handed me my pajamas and motioned for me to put them on and climb into bed. She left me alone in a dark room with the only visible light peeking through the door left ajar. After changing into my pajamas and climbing into the coziest bed I've ever been in, I fell asleep; unaware I was falling in love with Italy, her people, and especially the Grappelli family.

*   *   *

As I finished enjoying my cappuccino and pastry, I looked around discreetly to see if anyone was watching. I ran my finger around the inside edge of the cup hoping to grab the last bits of foam. Now I was ready to roam around awhile before I checked back in to get my phone.

As I approached the cell phone store, I noticed they also sold tickets for the busses to "*Stazione Centrale,*" Milan's main train station. Since I intended to take the bus into the city, I decided to purchase my ticket now.

When I entered the cell phone store, I noticed there were now two women behind the counter; perhaps a shift change. There was no one else in the small store at this time, so they were making small talk. I greeted them politely and pointed to my cell phone on the floor. As I reached down to get my phone and charger, I overheard one of the girls congratulate her colleague on how much thinner she looked. The colleague, who had recently come to work, said she had been on a diet for about two weeks and had lost about two kilos. At this point, I stepped up to the counter and checked them both out. I told them I can't see why either one of them would want to be on a diet. I also added that through these middle-aged eyes, they both look quite good and were very attractive. The first girl, who had waited on me earlier, asked to see my phone. She said she wanted to see if it was working yet. She turned on the phone which seems to take about a minute and then she called her own cell phone, which rang. As soon as her phone started to ring she said "Very well you're all set." She then pressed the "End" button and handed it back to me. I thanked her and let her know that I would like to also purchase a ticket for the bus to Milan's central train station.

"That will be ten Euros please. The bus leaves every twenty minutes."

The conversation had only been in English up to now. So as I was leaving, I said in Italian "Whenever possible, I prefer to allow the woman to speak to me in English; it is such a pleasant accent." Then I quickly added, "Now that I have your cellular phone number, I would have called you this evening and asked you to dinner, if my wife would have allowed it." With that, she smiled as I left the store and headed for the exit.

Out in front of the terminal, I showed my ticket to an elderly gentleman standing on the sidewalk.

"Excuse me, sir. Do you know which bus I need?"

"That one there," pointing to the second bus in line.

"*Grazie.*"

He nodded, and I headed towards another man who seemed to be the bus driver. He took my ticket and loaded my luggage into the belly of the bus.

"*Quando partiamo per Milano?*" I asked hoping to know how soon before we would leave for Milan.

"*Fra cinque minuti.*"

After I boarded the bus, I moved closer to the back, and sat in a window seat on the left side. I took a deep breath and started to relax. My mind replayed the day's events: being put on a flight to London, the unfriendly passport control officer, the girl in the cell phone shop, and Luiza back home probably still asleep. The start of the bus engine, stirred me from my thoughts. As we pulled away from the curb and headed for the highway to Milan, my eyes grew heavy and I nodded off to sleep.

Chapter 7

As the bus began to enter the city, I awoke from my nap. I started to see the apartment buildings, trams, and the general city traffic of Milan. While the bus driver maneuvered his way through the morning congestion, towards the station, I started thinking about the next leg of my trip.

I was looking forward to seeing Loretta, Tamira's daughter.

Since having lived with the Grappelli family more than thirty years ago, I have kept in touch with Tamira, Loretta, and her younger son Massimo. Loretta and Massimo both moved from Milan to Torino because of their careers; they have lived there for about ten years now. I decided to call Loretta and let her know I'd be at the train station soon.

"*Sancarlo Viaggi, Bongiorno,*" answered the receptionist.

"May I speak with Loretta Grappelli?"

She connected me.

"*Ciao, Loretta sono Marty.*" I said letting her know it was me.

"It's so great to hear from you."

"Yes, I'm very happy to be back."

"How was your flight? Everything go well?"

"I'll tell you all about it when we meet. I'm about to arrive at *Stazione Centrale*, and I'll be taking the next train to Torino. I'll let you know which one and at what time I'll arrive."

"*Va bene.* I've asked for the rest of the day off. I'll meet you at the station," she replied.

"*Ciao, ciao.*"

"*Ciao.*"

We arrived at the bus stop and pulled up alongside the station, which is a huge building done in Neo-fascist style. We exited and waited for the bus driver to drag our luggage out from beneath the bus. Once my three crates were on the sidewalk, I wasn't sure what to do with them.

"May I help you?" a young man asked in English while approaching me.

"You speak English?" I asked surprised.

"A little."

"How much for you to help get these crates up to the train?"

"€2 each?"

After several seconds of considering if I should save the money and just wrestle them up to the platform alone I said, "Sure, why not."

He nodded to two friends and directed them in a language that sounded Arabic. They each grabbed a crate, and we began to work our way into the station. As I headed for the ticket counter to purchase my ticket, my new friend got my attention, "No, no. This way, it's faster." He motioned for me to follow him and led me over to the newsstand where they sold books, magazines and Metropolitana tickets. "Here, It is much better—no line," he motioned with his hand towards the newsstand.

I nodded and stepped up to the counter. *"Biglietto per Torino, solo andata,"* I said requesting a one-way ticket.

"€12."

I paid, and the clerk slapped a ticket down on the counter, looking for the next customer. I grabbed my ticket, and we headed up the escalator to the platforms. At the top, I looked at the large black board displaying Arrivals and Departures. The next train to Torino was on track seven and didn't leave until 12:15 p.m. I knew I must first validate my ticket. I found a yellow timestamp machine at the beginning of a track, stamped my ticket, and worked my way over to track seven.

"This is good enough," I indicated to my companions as we approached the mid-point of the train. I handed a €10 note to the one who spoke English. "Here's a little extra for teaching me how to buy tickets from the newsstand."

Before leaving me, they insisted on helping get my crates

up onto the train. We found a suitable area just inside the door on the floor. Standing in the doorway of the train, I smiled and thanked them. They waved and quickly departed to find someone else to help. I had more than thirty minutes before the train actually pulled out, so I found a seat where I could keep an eye on my crates and relax. As soon as I was settled, I called Loretta.

"Ciao…Yes, I'll be arriving at Porta Nuova station just after 2:00."

"*Va bene.* Let's meet just outside the station. Turn left at the end of the platform and exit out the side entrance. You'll see signs for via Sacchi. There will be a lot of busses parked alongside the station. Cross the street and stand on the sidewalk in front of the *Turin Palace Hotel.* I will pull over and you can jump into my car."

"But I have three wooden crates about 70cm by 70cm each."

"*Uffa,*" she replied. "*Ci vediamo più tardi,*" assuring me we'll see each other later.

"Okay," I said. "Ciao, ciao for now."

I looked at my watch again and wondered if it was too early to call Luiza. Because of the six hour time difference, it was about 5:40 am back home. I decided to wait until I got nearer to Torino.

I sat back, closed my eyes, and listened for signals indicating we were leaving the station. I don't know what it is, but I love when the train pulls out of the station--first the warning whistle, then the slow movement as the train makes its way out of the station, and finally the jolts from switching tracks as the train slowly works its way out onto the right track.

The first stop beyond Milan was Rho, then Magenta. Before we even reached Magenta I was asleep again, still exhausted from my travels and the time change.

      *   *   **

By the time the train stopped at Vercelli, I was awake again. I looked at my watch and realized we were about halfway through the almost two hour trip to Torino. Several passengers stood in the doorway and a few more stood in the aisle, waiting to get off. I saw my crates were untouched. As the train came to a complete stop, someone pushed the exit door button, and the doors opened with a pneumatic swoosh. The passengers exited swiftly. Once the ten or so passengers got off, new people began to file in looking for an empty seat.

An elderly couple decided to sit in the group of four seats where I sat. I was next to the window, so they sat facing each other in the aisle seats. We greeted each other politely. Shortly after we pulled out of the station, they began to open their lunch bag of sandwiches, cheese, and fruit. Perhaps because they noticed me looking at their food or more likely being kind and generous, they offered me a sandwich. In typical Italian custom, I first refused with a wave of my hand and a *"No grazie."*

They continued to offer, so I finally said, "If you insist. Thank you... Just a small sample to try it."

While enjoying the sandwich which had prosciutto and cheese, I asked about their travels, "Are you heading to Torino?"

"No, only as far as Chivasso. Our daughter lives there," the man replied. "Our granddaughter needs to be hospitalized for a kidney infection, so we're going to see them and help watch the house."

"I hope she'll be okay," I offered my concern.

"We think so," he said as he opened a bottle of Fanta orange soda. He poured some into a plastic cup and offered it to me. We exchanged small talk for a while. I could tell by the cadence of their speech, they originally came from southern Italy. After several more minutes of chatting and two or more cups of Fanta, I asked them to excuse me, since the conversation had now faded. I stepped out by the exit doors where my crates were and called Luiza.

"How did everything go?" she asked, anxious to hear how I was.

"Better than I expected. Everything went through Customs smoothly. My crates made it from London, and now I'm on the train to Torino."

"Oh, good, I couldn't sleep last night, worrying there might be something else you forgot."

"You know it's not like I'm trying to mess up. I just get distracted with all I have to do," I explained defensively.

"Yes, I know. I just think lists could help you stay

organized. So what are your plans when you get to Torino? Will you go by the convent later today?" Luiza asked changing the subject.

"I hope so. I'd like to at least drop off the windows."

"What else are you planning?"

"Besides meeting up with Loretta, I'm also hoping to see Massimo and Dani this evening," I replied.

"Call me soon and let me know how everything goes."

"Will do," I said and hung up.

Chapter 8

A few weeks after the switch had been made, the King summoned Grassi to his private residence on a Sunday afternoon.

"I want to thank you for a remarkable job," said King Victor Emmanuel III to his aide Alessandro Grassi.

"You're welcome, Your Majesty. It was a privilege to help rescue your family's most precious possession."

"Yes it is. It truly is a precious possession," the King responded thoughtfully. "How can you put a value on the burial cloth of our Lord and Savior?"

Grassi understood this meeting, in the King's private residence, wasn't just to have small talk. He wondered what the King might have on his mind. The King was pensive and slow in his manner, Grassi stood motionless and waited. The Seventeenth century Baroque style Palace was extremely ornate, with sixteen foot high frescoed ceilings, mosaic tile floors, and tapestries on most walls. It reflected the exalted position of Italy's King.

"Actually, there is a matter which will need your most discreet attention," the King finally spoke in a soft voice.

"My lord, you know you can count on me."

"As I have been thinking about it, it has become clear to me the sacred linen is still not safe. There are those who know the replica exists," the King said while looking directly at his aide and rubbing his chin.

"What are you suggesting?" queried Grassi.

"What I'm saying is, in order for the Holy Shroud to be truly safe; we must silence those who know the copy exists."

At this, Alessandro Grassi's expression changed. He began to sweat and panic thinking the King just informed him of his own impending death. Grassi had reason to fear for his life. It had now been almost eighteen years since Grassi first met the King. He had become well aware of his moods and actions. There were always the rumors that swirl around powerful people. With alarm in his voice, Grassi began to reassure the King of his devotion. "But your Majesty, I've always been loyal to you."

"Why are you acting afraid?" interrupted the King.

"Because I am afraid for my safety," pleaded the King's aide.

"Alessandro, I am not talking about you," brushing aside the thought. "I need you. You have always been true to me."

"I assure Your Majesty, my heart's desire is always to serve and assist you."

"Yes of course, I know of your faithfulness. You are almost like a son. I could never think of harming you," the King tried to reassure his aide.

"However, I warn you, when I'm gone you will need to be careful. I don't believe my son will be as kind to you as I have been." The King warned Grassi

"Thank you for that, Sire."

Wanting to get back to the important matter at hand the King said, "Now this is what I called you here for."

"Dr. Darius, for one, knows about the replica and also Captain Cipollini. I have a plan only you can carry out for me," the King said.

The King moved over to the window. Looking over his beautiful and expansive gardens, he pondered for a moment and then explained, "I have a very secret group. No one alive except me knows they exist. They take care of very sensitive matters for me. I want to put you in contact with this special group."

The King believed every now and again, it was necessary to eliminate any personal threats. For this purpose, he had a discreet group of men trained in the art of assassination. Their method of eliminating threats always varied. At times, they would get rid of someone in a dramatic way, such as blowing up their house and family while they slept. This would be done to send a signal to the King's enemies. Other times, this secret squad would do their work in a manner that made it seem like a natural occurrence. At times, they would poison their victim with an undetectable drug which wouldn't raise suspicion. In fact, they were quite proud of their many varied techniques. Regarding those who helped produce the forgery, the King felt the need to eradicate them, but decided this time a quieter way would be best.

"Your Majesty, why have you decided to involve me?" Grassi asked looking quizzically at the King.

"Because I need you to understand how much I trust you," the King tried to reassure his aide.

Continuing he said, "I also want them to only contact you from now on. I will soon need them to deal with their own commander. I have recently learned he is aligned with a group plotting against me."

Grassi began to panic again, now realizing his King was so paranoid that at any moment, he too could be in the King's crosshairs. This time however, Grassi did all he could to hide his fears.

The King tried to further reassure Grassi when he said, "Of all my counselors, aides and deputies, only you have proven trustworthy." This statement did little to calm Grassi's fears.

"Please come over here and sit," the King said as he raised his hand and motioned towards his desk. He then handed Grassi a piece of his stationery and said, "Fold this paper in half. Now rip off the lower half." This was done to remove the royal seal embossed on the top of the paper.

The King handed Grassi a fountain pen and asked him to write "Dr. Carlo Darius, Professor of Applied Sciences at Polytechnic School of Turin—Captain Guido Cipollini stationed at Caserma Vittorio Dabormida."

"Now please also write—'Show mercy to them'," he said this while pointing to the piece of paper.

After writing those last few words, the King reached down to his desk and picked up the note Grassi had just hand written. Folding it twice he said, "Give this to them," and handed it back to Grassi.

"Here is how you will be able to contact them." The King gave him a second small piece of paper which he took out of his vest pocket.

"After you have contacted them you must destroy these pieces of paper."

Understanding the King did not want him to review the note until he was alone; he slipped the two pieces of paper into a side pocket of his jacket. Alessandro Grassi bowed his head saying, "If that is all, Sire."

"Yes it is," he gestured with a wave of dismissal. "Please take care of it soon. We will never speak of this matter again." Bowing this time from the waist, Grassi began to move backwards towards the door being careful not to turn his back on the King until the door closed after him. For Grassi it didn't take a long private debate to decide if and how he would act. It was a long time ago he crossed the point of no return. He made his decision to never challenge the King and to fully carry out his orders and requests, because he believed his life depended on it.

As soon as Grassi was safely in his private residence, he took the small note out of his pocket and read what the King had written. It read, "At 21:15 Dial 49576 and say 'signal' to the person who answers—follow his instructions." While pacing in his room, Grassi repeated the phone number to himself several times, afraid he might forget it. Also, rather than destroy the note, he tucked it away in his personal journal and returned it to the shelf in his room.

Chapter 9

When I returned to my seat, the gentleman who shared his lunch with me said, "When passengers opened the door, I could hear a bit of your conversation. Where are you from?"

"I'm from a town just beyond Boston. I'm an American."

Obviously surprised, he said "I thought you were from Milan."

"Many years ago I lived in Milan, and that is where I first learned Italian."

"Are you going to Torino?" he asked me.

"Yes, I'm visiting with some old friends."

"Are you familiar with the city?" he asked.

"No, it's been a few years since I was there and only briefly."

"Torino is a beautiful city, rich with history," he assured me.

"It's unfortunate but in America Torino is known as the Detroit of Italy, because it is where Fiat has its headquarters. However, Detroit for Americans means an industrial city with large run down sections. Not many visit there as tourists."

"I see," the elderly man replied.

"On my one last trip to Torino, I found it quite interesting, especially the center of the city with all the porticoes and Baroque style buildings. Torino seems to resemble Paris to me in some ways," I said.

My new friend informed me it was the first capital of Italy, right after the unification of the country under Garibaldi, which is why it's such a rich looking city. The Savoys were the first royal family of Italy. Although the family originated from central France, they also ruled Sardinia and the Piedmont region. When the monarchy for the whole country was established, they became the first ruling family of Italy.

"If you do, you must visit the Mole Antonelliana," he insisted.

"Mole Anton?...How do you say it?" I fumbled.

"*Antonelliana*, it has become one of the most recognizable structures in Torino."

"Isn't it a tall domed building in the center?" I asked.

"Yes it is. Then there's the Royal Palace, and right around the corner from the palace is the beautiful cathedral. Attached to the cathedral is the Royal Chapel where they keep the *Sindone*."

"Sindone?. What's that?" I asked.

"Why it is believed to be the burial cloth Jesus Christ was wrapped in after his crucifixion."

"Oh, the Shroud," I said in English not realizing that *Sindone* is Italian for Shroud.

"I thought it was at the Vatican in Rome."

"No, no, it belonged to the Royal Family, so it has always been kept in the Savoy's private chapel."

"I never knew that," I said.

"We are getting near Chivasso," his wife informed him, pointing out the window.

"Yes, I see we are...Well, we hope you enjoy your visit to Torino," he said.

"Thank you. I hope I get to see these places you mentioned," I said.

A few minutes later the couple was on their feet and standing near the exit door. As soon as the door opened, he tipped me his hat and his wife smiled gently as they moved towards the steps down onto the station platform. I watched them as they headed for the stairway that would take them under the tracks closest to the station.

It wasn't two minutes after the train continued beyond the station, when a woman sitting in the group of seats across the aisle from our group moved over and sat diagonally across from me. While looking up at her, we made eye contact. Leaning slightly forward and towards me, she said in English, "Excuse me, but I couldn't help overhearing that you're an American."

"Why yes, I am," I replied in English.

"It's not often I get to speak to an American. Do you mind?" she said while adjusting her pocketbook in the seat in front of me. "I was a bit cramped across the aisle."

I noticed she was neatly and smartly dressed. She wore a light weight dark blue full-length coat, colorful silk scarf tied loosely around her neck. Her coat wasn't buttoned so when she sat, it opened. I could see she was wearing a beige skirt that covered most her legs and a printed blouse mostly covered by her half buttoned sweater. She was slender and I'd guess in her mid fifties. Her hair was still naturally dark. I knew this because of the several random strands of gray hair speckled throughout.

"I overheard them telling you about Torino and its history," she said. "I also noticed you struggling with the word Antonelliana, one of Torino's most recognizable landmarks, the Mole Antonelliana."

"It's going to take me a while to get it." I said smiling.

After a good pause she added, "The fascinating thing is the building was a hollow shell," she said.

"What do you mean?" I asked.

"It was built to be a synagogue by the large Jewish community that lived in the city."

"You mean it's not a Catholic cathedral?"

"No, it's not."

She went on to explain the building project got so expensive the Jewish community abandoned the project and moved into another building. It happened back about one hundred and fifty years ago when Torino was the first capital of Italy. Unfortunately, the architect, Alessandro Antonelli kept increasing the cost of the construction with changes and modifications to the design until it became too expensive to complete. Since then, for more than a hundred years it had been an empty hollow shell. Today it is a very interesting museum dedicated to the movies and cinema. In fact it's the largest museum of its kind in the world. She further told me the building has glass elevators that go up through the center of the building. Until you get to the top, you're suspended in the middle of nowhere with only glass and cables near you."

"Thanks for warning me," I said.

"Yes, but if you can make it to the top, you get a beautiful view of the city."

She then continued, "Also, for anyone interested in the movies and history of the cinema, it is quite the place."

"Do you live in the city?" I asked.

"Yes, I teach at the University of Turin. I'm a professor of Cultural History," she smiled. "And you? What kind of work do you do?"

"I'm a stained-glass artisan," is all I said. I wanted to continue telling her about my studio, the windows I had brought with me, and some of my recent projects. I wanted to brag about myself until she was impressed.

"Do you mind if I ask what brings you to Torino?"

"Not at all, in those crates out there by the bathroom, I have stained glass windows. I've been commissioned to do them for a convent in Beinasco. I also will be visiting dear friends who live in Torino."

Chapter *10*

"How interesting. How does an American artisan get to do stained glass for a convent in Italy?" she asked, perhaps now thinking she's talking with an internationally known artist.

"Purely by accident."

"Really? I'd like to know how," she said, her interest peaking.

Eager to explain, I related my story, "A couple of years ago, a priest hired me to restore some of the stained glass windows at his church. While chatting and making small talk, I told him I've done a few churches also in Italy. He told an American friend about me. This wealthy friend from California, who is financing the restoration of this convent in Beinasco, contacted me and asked if I would make stained glass for their small chapel."

"What a great story," she replied. "Your Italian friends, will they show you around the city?" she asked.

"I'm sure Loretta will. She works for a travel agency," I said smiling to myself, knowing Loretta's passion for her job.

As I glanced out the window, I could tell we were now in the outskirts of the city. No longer were there cultivated fields, but we were traveling behind old stucco homes, small factories and businesses.

"By the way, your English is excellent," I added.

"I lived and studied English literature in Ireland many years ago," she said.

"Ireland? I would think most Italians who want to learn English go to England to learn British English," I said.

"As a young woman, I had this fascination with the Irish.

Who knows why? I still go there on summer holiday now and again."

"That's funny; I have a thing for Ireland too. My wife thinks it's because I find Irish women attractive. I say I have an unfilled dream to visit several pubs there."

We sat there silently and gazed out opposite windows as our conversation trailed to an end. I began thinking about Luiza and about her morning routine. She was probably up and dressed now. Unlike me, she is organized and goes through her chores until she's done. I also started thinking about what happened the previous week, when we had friends over for dinner. Perhaps because of the wine that evening or more likely because I love my wife, I was hoping she would come up to bed real soon. But no, instead she had to clean the kitchen, load the dishwasher and scrub the pots and pans. She made sure everything was done to the point of getting the coffee pot ready for the morning. By the time she finally made it upstairs, I was gone, in a deep sleep and no doubt snoring.

My curiosity got the better of me so I asked, "You mentioned you are a professor of Cultural History." She nodded.

"I never knew Italy's line of kings were from Torino."

"Ah, yes, they were from the House of Savoy," she informed me.

"I remember learning about them but don't remember the details. Before I begin my tour of Torino, what pieces of history do you think I should keep in mind?" I asked.

She began to smile. I decided it was because as a professor she enjoyed teaching, and I was her attentive student. Some of what she said was in 1861, about the time of our Civil War in the United States, Giuseppe Garibaldi led a rebellion against the French and began unifying Italy into one country. Beginning with Sicily in the south, the city states of Italy were unified. Once unified under one flag, the monarchy ruled over the Italian people. The House of Savoy, ruled Piedmont and Sardinia before the unification. First they ruled Italy from Turin and later Rome. Four kings from this line reigned in Italy until 1946. Then in June 1946, Italy abolished the monarchy and a Constitutional Republic was formed.

She further explained, like other European countries, Italy

embarked on colonial quests to conquer lands in northern Africa. Eventually Italy also became involved in World War I. As a result of World War I and the cost of colonial expansionism, Italy's economy fell into depression. Poverty increased and political unrest spread throughout the country. This gave rise to extreme political views such as Nazism in Germany and Fascism in Spain and Italy. The leader of the Italian Fascist party, Benito Mussolini, not only demonstrated
for political change, but like Hitler and the Nazis in Germany, used violence to force his issues.

"So, Benito Mussolini drew you towards this subject?" I asked skeptically.

"No," she laughed. "Rather, the circumstances that led to his involvement and the consequences thereafter. In 1922, fearing further unrest in the country due to the economic depression, Victor Emmanuel III, King of Italy, appointed Mussolini as Prime Minister. Mussolini wasn't satisfied to just rule the country as Prime Minister. He had international ambitions and aimed to create a revived Roman Empire. Ultimately, aligning with Adolf Hitler and Emperor Hirohito of Japan, Mussolini joined the Axis powers in June of 1940. This plunged Italy into another destructive World War. Then, in early September of 1943, the King of Italy signed an armistice with the United States and Great Britain ending Italy's involvement in World War II."

"I can understand why Italy abolished the monarchy shortly after the war." I said wanting to add my two cents.

"Yes. There was a lot of distrust of the King and how he handled the country," she agreed.

"Thanks for the insights," I responded.

She nodded and softly said, "You're very welcome." She then looked out the window to gauge where we were.

A couple of minutes later she let me know she'd be getting off at the next station, Porta Susa, which was the last stop before we reached the end of the line.

As the train pulled into Porta Nuova Station, all the passengers began to get on their feet and head for the doors. Since I had the three small crates, I decided to wait and let everybody get off the train before I wrestled the crates down onto the platform. I dragged them off one by one and stood them together several feet away from the train and began to look for a porter to help me with them. I saw one more than a hundred feet away, which I thought to be a young man with longer hair. I yelled and waved my hand over my head, *"Facchino! Scusa, ma ho bisogno un facchino!"* I said calling for a porter to help me. When the porter turned around I realized she was a woman. With me waving my hand over my head, she noticed me. As she moved her cart closer to me, I thought about what I just yelled at the top of my lungs in the middle of a train station. I chuckled to myself and mumbled under my breathe, "Wait 'til I tell Luiza."

I asked her to please help me get the crates out onto the sidewalk. Of course, she obliged and informed me that it's €1 per piece.

"Si, va bene," I said.

I explained to her, "I have to get my crates over in front of the *Turin Palace Hotel.*" With hand gestures and very few words, she indicated to me that she was not able to exit the train station beyond the exit area. As we got to the side entrance, I saw it was a very busy street and noisy with jackhammers from the street construction. It was also where a lot of buses converged at the train station. In the middle of the road was a metal barrier to prevent jay-walking. The *facchino* pushed the cart with my crates to the sidewalk, which led out to the bus area. She unloaded them onto the sidewalk and said, *"Quarto Euro."*

Chapter 11

I replied, "I'll give you 5€ if you wait here with my crates while I drag each one across the street." Again with hand gestures and few words, she indicated she would wait for me to drag them across the street. I grabbed the first two crates and started my way down the gauntlet of traffic. First, I dodged between the buses pulling out, next between the metal fence barrier in the middle, across the two-lane one-way street, and finally between the taxis at the taxi stand and up onto the sidewalk. Running back to the porter, I gave her €5. This time I proceeded with the last crate and my carry-on. This actually proved more difficult to balance, because the wobbly wheels made it tricky over the road paved with cobble stones. Finally, on the other side, I began to wait for Loretta.

After less than five minutes, I heard a horn beeping and saw a hand waving out the car window. It was Loretta. She pulled up behind the last taxi, quickly jumped out of her car and had her arms wide waiting to hug me. I dragged a crate and my carry-on to get to her as quickly as possible. Giving her a big hug, I began the traditional kissing each cheek routine. Loretta, like most women, feigned to kiss my cheeks. What I mean is she turns to allow me to kiss her cheek, then puckers, and even makes a soft kissing sound, but makes no contact. Why do women do that, not wanting to smudge their lipstick? While I went to retrieve the other two crates, Loretta opened her hatchback and removed the cover attached to the top of the back seat. I put my first crate into the car, and it just made it. The next two slid on top and she could barely close the hatchback. We decided I would have to ride with the carry-on in my lap.

At the end of the busy one way, she turned right, traveled down Corso Victor Emanuelle II (named after the first King of Italy) to the end of the road where we came to the Po River. As we turned left and drove along the Po, Loretta said, "This is the Po River, Italy's Mississippi…It's very small not like the huge rivers you have in America." While explaining the size of the Po, she held her right thumb and index finger together repeating in English now "very small." In spite of how cramped I was, I realized she had decided to take me on a tour of the city.

Although Loretta speaks excellent English, when we are together, we communicate in Italian. It just has always been that way, since Segrate when I arrived at her home more than thirty years ago. After driving up the road that parallels the Po River, we took another left and passed close to the large domed building that has become the recognizable symbol for Torino, La Mole. I mentioned to Loretta what the elderly couple and professor said about it. We continued up to the end of via Po, and came to Piazza Castello. Loretta decided to drive past the Royal Palace. Of course, being the consummate Turinese tour guide, she started telling me all about the history of the Royal Palace and how the Savoy family built it in the late 16th century to early 17th century. I commented on how large and impressive it is. She then pointed to the red brick building that looks kind of like a fort to one side and let me know that it's now an antiques and art museum. She pointed to an armory museum. In fact she informed me there are forty-five museums throughout the city. Loretta went on-and-on with the private tour.

Working our way around Piazza Castello and the Royal Palace, we came to the cathedral, St John the Baptist. She pointed out to me there is a famous chapel on the side of the cathedral, known as "The Royal Chapel," which is where the Holy Shroud is kept. I told her I had just heard about the Shroud on the train coming here and always assumed it was at the Vatican. She explained to me up until recently the Savoy family actually owned it. They acquired it from a French nobleman back in the 15th century, but now it belonged to the Catholic Church.

"Do you believe it's the real burial cloth of Jesus?" I

asked, wanting to hear her take on it.

"I'm not sure what I believe, but I think it could be His burial cloth." Loretta went on to explain back about twenty years ago carbon-14 testing done on pieces of the cloth. These tests concluded the Shroud to be from the Middle Ages. Many believe it probably is a fake. Some have even speculated Leonardo DaVinci had something to do with it. Then again, there are people who say the carbon-14 testing could have been flawed and the results were not accurate."

After passing by the cathedral, I asked Loretta if we could please get to the hotel so I could take a shower and perhaps rest. She apologized for being distracted and not realizing how tired I must be from traveling. We headed over to the *Principi di Piemonte Hotel.*

Once in front of the hotel, she stopped the car in a no parking spot and said, "We must quickly unload before anybody comes." We jumped out; I put my carry-on on the sidewalk and went around to the back where we unloaded all three crates. Loretta said she could take the car into the parking garage. I said I'd be fine and not to bother. I could check in myself. Just as she was about to climb into her car, she turned and said, "Call me when you want me to pick you up. Tonight we will go to a very good pizzeria to eat a very special pizza and enjoy each other's company."

Chapter 12

Several restless hours passed while the King's aide waited anxiously to make the dreaded phone call. He waited for the hours to pass, which seemed like days and watched the minutes pass which seemed like hours. As soon as the minute hand touched 9:15, he picked up the receiver and dialed the five digit phone number. After one ring, he could hear the phone being answered, but no voice replied. Because of his nervousness, it took Grassi several seconds to say "signal." In a monotone low voice he heard the person on the other end say, "Giuseppe's Trattoria on via Corsica #14. Sit at the last table in the back left corner with your back to the wall. Order nothing but a *mezza Barbera (half liter carafe of Barbera)*. Be there within a half hour." Then he heard the click of the phone being hung-up. After a pause to consider what just happened, Grassi realized he had little time to get to the trattoria. As at other times, he disguised himself and made his way to the nearest tram stop. He kept a set of clothes that he got from a used clothes shelter not far from the Palace. They included worn pants, shirt, sweater, hat and overcoat.

Once on the main street, he had to decide to wait for a tram which may come in one minute or not for twenty. After waiting at the stop for less than a minute, Grassi decided it would be safer to walk twenty minutes to via Corsica rather than risk the tram not arriving for fifteen. Because of the miles of porticoes throughout the city of Turin, Grassi briskly walked from shadow to shadow, virtually going unnoticed. The night was drizzly and raw so few people were out, making his brisk walk even more unnoticed.

He walked up to the trattoria at 14 via Corsica and saw the storefront had windows mostly covered with curtains. Etched in simple lettering across the front window was "Trattoria di Giuseppe". On the lower right-hand corner of the window about three feet off the ground was a menu, which offered several *Primi Piatti* and only a few *Secondi Piatti*.

The Trattoria had a simple entrance door just to the right of the window. The wood panel door had an Art Nouveau style stained glass window in the upper third. Just above the door's handle and below the glass was the word *Tirare*. Grabbing to pull the door handle, Grassi paused a moment to think about whom he was about to meet. He whispered under his breath, "Lord, forgive me for what I'm about to do." It was a private prayer perhaps, more for self-absolution, rather than Divine.

Pulling open the door to the small family restaurant, he stepped inside and noticed only two couples dining. An elderly man with an apron around his waist greeted him with a warm, "*Buona Sera*." He motioned for Grassi to sit at a table for two near the front window. Instead, Grassi insisted he would prefer to sit at the table in the back left corner. With a puzzled look and shrug of his shoulder, the waiter, who was also the owner, replied, "*Si, dove volete*," inviting him to sit wherever he wanted.

The interior of this small dimly lit restaurant had a cozy atmosphere with warm homey smells coming from the kitchen. At a quick glance you would guess it had no more than ten tables. There were a few tables along the left wall and a couple more in the front with two chairs each. The rest of the tables had four chairs around them. In traditional Italian style, there were two table cloths on each table, a larger white one that almost reached the floor and a smaller red one with only the corners draped over the sides. On the wall to the right a mirror covered most of the wall, making the restaurant seem larger. The open spaces on the other walls were decorated with randomly scattered pictures of some of Italy's famous landmarks. Some of which were Rome's Coliseum, Pisa's leaning tower, and Venice's Rialto Bridge. At the back right corner, the open door to the kitchen allowed Grassi to look inside. He could see the cook, probably Signora Giuseppe, busy at the stove. The pasta was never precooked and the sauce improved as it slowly simmered.

One of the couples, who had finished their meal, wanted to pay and leave. Signor Giuseppe asked Grassi to excuse him for a moment while he allowed them to settle their bill. As soon as he put their lira into his pocket, he grabbed the two demitasse espresso cups left on their table, brushed off any remaining crumbs, and placed the cups and saucers on a tray near the kitchen door. Before Giuseppe could even place the hand-written one page menu on Grassi's table, he ordered *"Una mezza Babera per piacere"* as prearranged by the voice on the phone. Signor Giuseppe replied, *"Va bene, subito."*

Signor Giuseppe had just filled the glass with the Barbera wine when a man opened the door. Without taking off his hat or coat, he walked directly to the back of the restaurant. Never looking left or right, he sat in the chair in front of Grassi with his back to the two patrons and Signor Giuseppe. In the same voice as the man on the phone he said, "You are the one who called?"

With a small hesitant nod, Grassi took the note he had written on the King's desk and slipped it across the table. He said, "This is your assignment." The stranger and presumed assassin opened the piece of paper, read it, and put it in his pocket without saying a word. Without hesitation, the stranger got up and briskly walked out of the restaurant, being careful not to look at anyone as he left.

After a couple of minutes, Signor Giuseppe came over to Grassi's table and with a gesture asked, *"Per il primo signore?"*

Instead of ordering Grassi said, "I've decided not to stay."

Signor Giuseppe not wanting to lose a customer, it being a quiet night, began to say, "But signore, we have such a fine homemade *tagliatelli con funghi*. I know you will enjoy it."

Before the restaurant owner could continue Grassi raised his hand and said, "No, no, please. I've lost my appetite. How much for the wine?"

"Cinquanta centesime."

After putting the coins in the owner's hand, Grassi reassured him he would return another night and hopefully soon. Exiting the trattoria, Grassi noticed a tram down the street heading in his direction. It was beginning to rain, so he picked up his pace and just made it to the back entrance of the tram. With only the driver in the front and ticket taker in the rear, he chose to sit in the middle of a tram—farthest from anyone. As he returned to his residence, he pondered the fate of his two accomplices. Although Grassi felt sorry for Doctor Darius and Captain Cipollini, he was more concerned about his own future as the King's aide.

Chapter 13

Once back in his private room at the Palace, Grassi still upset and fearful wondered what might happen to him. He reflected, "How does a poor city boy from the streets of Turin end up in the Palace serving the King?" He thought about how the King, instead of being, a well counseled and strong leader concerned for his people; he was instead not only small in stature but weak, paranoid, and out-of-control. He realized it was the price he had paid for ruling in a Machiavellian manner rather than with honor and compassion.

He looked out his living quarter's window and noticed it was raining more steadily now. He thought about the innocence of his youth and how he had liked to kick a soccer ball around with his friends in an abandoned field not far from his home. How the worst thing he had ever done was to steal some fruit from a fruit merchant's cart. He thought about how guilty he had felt after peeking in the window of the young widow in his neighborhood, when he was about thirteen and curious about women. Now, again, Grassi looked out his Palace window. At one point he noticed a young couple embracing under an overhang. He looked away and then back. This innate curiosity reminded him of how he felt looking in the widow's window as a boy. He thought about his years at the Salesian Technical School. The brothers who taught him had recognized his cleverness and helped get him into Turin University, where he studied political science. After graduating, his connections and a bit of good fortune helped him obtain a position as a palace page, assisting one of the King's deputies.

While staring out of the window, he noticed several pigeons finding shelter under the eaves of the opposing wing of the Palace. As he continued to reflect, he remembered the first time the deputy had sent him with a message to the King's office and how nervous he was when speaking to the King. He expressed his excitement in the letters he wrote home. After a while, the King had taken notice of him and requested he be assigned to him personally. It seemed like a lifetime ago. Because of the demands of his work, Grassi never married even though he once discussed it with the one love of his life. He thought about her now, Donatella, a maid in the Royal Palace with whom he had a relationship so many years ago.

Grassi's mind wandered about the events of the past few months, how he had been asked to contact Dr. Darius and assist him with the experiments on how to recreate the Holy Shroud. It had taken several attempts just to transfer a faint image onto a linen cloth. They discovered it was better to put photosensitive material directly onto the cloth itself, using the cloth as a negative. Grassi reflected on how impressed he had been with Dr. Darius and his genius and how he figured out how to even re-create watermarks that had stained the Shroud from the time when they had doused the cloth to put out the chapel fire of 1532.

Grassi thought back to the search through the prisons which had started in Turin, and how they had worked their way through the prisons, finally finding that Libyan prisoner in Genoa. Reading the Libyan's file and learning about the heinous crimes he had committed, he thought about those poor women and where they were today—probably all dead. He felt his guilt assuaged believing that monster had deserved to die. He recalled how the prisoner was brought back to Turin and along with Captain Cipollini and Dr. Darius they reenacted step by step the torturous punishment suffered by Jesus. Grassi thought about the agonies the prisoner suffered. All this was done, because the King feared the Nazis would steal a linen cloth from him. Finally he remembered when he and Cipollini slipped into the Royal Chapel and switched the original with the forgery. Now to think, this precious relic was still hidden in an unmarked box in the back of a closet in the King's private residence. As Grassi continued to brood and reflect about their fate, he decided he would check the obituaries daily.

It wasn't even two weeks later, when scanning *La Stampa*, Turin's daily newspaper, Grassi came upon this obituary:

Professor Dr. Carlo Darius born 1877 died Tuesday. It appears Dr. Darius died in his sleep peacefully. Cause of death is unknown. He leaves behind his wife of forty-two years, Maria Castalana, their three children Paolo 38, Angela 36, and Lorenzo 25. They also have five grandchildren. Dr. Darius was professor of Applied Sciences at the Polytechnic University of Turin. He had taught at the school for the past thirty-one years. Dr. Darius graduated magnum cum laude from Polytechnic University of Milan, as a member of the class 1902. A funeral Mass at 10 AM will be celebrated and a grave site memorial to follow immediately after.

Grassi decided he would secretly attend Dr. Darius' funeral Mass.

Chapter 14

A few hours later, I called Loretta to let her know I had rested and would be waiting for her in the lobby. She said she would come by as soon as possible, but it would be at least a half hour, perhaps longer. I also wanted to contact the mother superior of the convent where the stained glass would be installed. I called Sister Mary Boniface, who calls herself Sister Bonny and told her I was in town with her Chapel windows. I later found out the nuns at this convent were nurses who worked in a couple of hospitals in Torino and helped minister to the city's poor. Sister Bonny was very excited to hear from me. She said she'll send Signor Gianni by to get me in the morning, and I should make sure I plan to stay for lunch. She explained that Signor Gianni Paltrineri is a retired gentleman who helps the nuns with odd jobs around the convent and would be available to pick me up.

Rather than sit in my room and watch TV, I decided to go down to the lobby and see if I could use the Internet, which I found off in a corner. It had a flat-screen monitor, keypad and barstool, where guests could have free Internet access. After checking e-mails and shooting Luiza a quick note, I Googled "Holy Shroud." My curiosity made me want to find out more, having just learned it was here in Torino. I read the Wikipedia article about the "Shroud of Turin." The article explained its mysterious history, and how it was owned by the "House of Savoy", Italy's formerly ruling family until 1983. According to the article, it was photographed for the first time in 1898 and that's when they discovered that the image is seen clearer as a negative. The Carbon-14 testing done on it proved it came from the Fourteenth Century, so I concluded it must be a hoax of some kind. It was about this time that Loretta found me in the lobby at the computer terminal. With a sweeping wave of her arm up over her head said, *"Andiamo."*

All I replied was, *"Vengo,"* letting her know I was coming.

Massimo and his wife Dani arrived at the pizzeria a few minutes after we did. It was great to see them again and of course our greetings were warm. The restaurant was quite busy this night and thankfully Loretta had made reservations. As soon as we were seated Massimo and Dani were curious to know how my trip went. I explained how I had missed my flight from Boston because I arrived a day late. We all had a good laugh. After shaking his head Massimo commented, "Marty, I remember even when you lived with us you were always losing things."

"I know. Your mother would say I'd lose my head if it wasn't attached to my shoulders," I added, still chuckling.

While still laughing over the story, our waiter arrived with our menus and asked what we wanted to drink. Since we were ordering pizza, we all decided on beer. Instead of a known bottled beer, we got the house draught beer—*dalla spina* (from the tap). Both women had *media chiara*, (medium size, light) Massimo and I had *grande rosso*. While waiting for our beers, we continued to get caught up. Even though I have seen Loretta and Massimo seldom over the past thirty years, after a few minutes it was almost like I never left.

The pizzeria was attractively decorated in a contemporary but rustic style. It is located on one of Torino's larger avenues, which is tree-lined and under a portico. One of the things I love most about Torino is that so much of the city is protected by miles of porticoes, sheltering one from the weather.

Settling in to look at the menu, Dani said she wanted to try the arugula pizza. Loretta said she wanted the *quattro formaggi*. When I read the menu, I realized that their pizzas had no tomato sauce. While trying to decide which pizza I wanted, I commented, "At home we order one pizza for three or four people each. It arrives sliced into eight or more wedges."

"Yes, we've seen it in your movies," Dani said.

"Americans seem to eat a lot with their hands," Loretta added.

"The size of our large pizza is about as big as a car tire," I told them.

"I've always found it a bit crude to eat food like that," Loretta admitted.

"I'm still getting used to eating my own pizza and not having to share it," I said. I decided I would have a *Quattro Stagione,* which has black olives, ham, artichoke hearts, and mushrooms. Massimo decided on a *Napoletana,* which is similar to a cheese pizza in America.

While waiting for our food, Massimo filled me in on what had been happening at work and with their family especially their daughter Alessia. He told me about her lastest interests, which included reading 'Teen Magazines' and discussing her last teeny-popper crush with her girl friends. I asked if I could mail her a few 'Teen magazines' in English when I get home. Massimo and Dani thought it would help her English. I promised I would send them to her.

Loretta told us about her recent trip, which involved taking a tour group to Sharm el-Sheikh, Egypt on the Red Sea. She also filled us in on some of the office gossip, mentioning one colleague in particular who tries to dress very sexy.

"Even with her uniform on she dresses provocatively," Loretta said.

In my mind, I immediately envisioned fishnet stockings, perhaps a black choker around her neck and of course a lot of make-up.

"Her name is Paola and she talks about her involvement in a strange form of witchcraft called *Stregheria,*" Loretta added. "She claims she can cast spells and says having sexual encounters with different people increases her power by connecting her spirit with theirs."

She continued. "Everyone in the office is intimidated by her. If it wasn't for the fact she is a good travel agent and books a lot of vacations, they would probably try to get rid of her."

This brought up other topics of religion, which Massimo had little patience for. His only comment was, "Religion is for the gullible who are afraid of dying."

I mentioned, "While I waited for Loretta to pick me up this evening, I googled 'Holy Shroud' because I never realized it was here in Torino." I asked them what they thought about the Shroud. Dani shrugged her shoulders and said, "How can anyone be sure?" Massimo added, "I think Leonardo DaVinci made it as a prank on the Church."

Loretta on the other hand was less convinced, "I believe it could be the burial cloth of Christ. I have read it is possible the Carbon-14 testing may have been done improperly or purposely rigged." She agreed with Dani that nobody can really be sure.

Wanting to tell a joke I said, "Because we are talking about religious stuff and we are here in a pizzeria, it reminds me of something I recently heard." Once I had their attention I continued. "The Dali Lama went into a pizzeria and asked the pizzaiolo, 'Is it true you can make me one with all?'"

Massimo and Dani getting the joke began to chuckle while Loretta said, "I don't get it." Trying to explain it I said, "One with all...Dali Lama...get it?"

While composing ourselves and trying not to laugh too loud our waiter brought our four pizzas. What is it about pizza? Sometimes I think it's the perfect food. What does it lack? From the delicious aroma of a fresh baked pizza, to the crispy crust, then the variety of toppings. I think if I was a bachelor I'd live over a pizzeria. I would be there every lunch time and probably for dinner too. I could work my way through the menu, just so that I'd have a variety in my diet...but I digress.

Getting back to our discussion, I said, "My faith is in Jesus and not the Shroud." Massimo said nothing, but I could tell he'd like to change the subject.

Loretta finally said, "Yes, it is Jesus whom I pray to, but for me the Shroud puts a face on Jesus and makes him more real." After a pause she added, "I think it also shows how severely he suffered."

"It reminds me of conversations about 'Who killed President Kennedy?'" I said. "I find the opinions about whether Oswald acted alone or whether there were others involved, reflects more on the person's personality rather than the true facts, since we will never know *all* the facts." I went on to explain, "I know this fellow back home who worked for the government and later as a private eye. He can be somewhat cynical, especially about the Kennedy assassination. He believes that there must have been other shooters on the grassy knoll to create a 'kill-zone'." Then I added "His insistence only speaks to me of his personality rather than the facts since he wasn't there."

After dinner, we went for a walk around the center of the city. Loretta again slipped into tour guide mode and explained why all the porticoes around the city. She told me that there are about fourteen kilometers of porticoes around the city, mostly found in the center. Apparently, the Savoy King of Piedmont back in medieval times had them built so that even during the rainy and winter seasons he could go out for a stroll unhindered by the weather.

We also stopped for gelato at a Gelatoria. The shop's décor was very modern with white Carrara marble, chrome and thick glass everywhere. Apparently, the chef, yes I found out this shop has an ice cream chef, uses only the freshest milk directly from the farms, only natural ingredients, and simplest recipes in his gelato. He has developed some very different flavors, which made us want to experiment. One gelato I sampled was 'Farina Bona', which translates to 'Good Flour' and it does have flour in it. I was amazed at how good it actually was. We asked for a few samples before we ordered. They had these tiny plastic spoons for samples and whatever you asked for they'd give you a taste. I think I over did it and sampled almost all of them. Finally, Loretta said, "Un Americano," while rolling her eyes, shaking her head and smiling. I ended up with a double wide cone that had, "Nocciola" (Hazelnut), "Crema all uovo" (egg nog) and I asked them to throw a little "Pera" (pear) on top. I think they obliged me because of Loretta's comment.

It was close to midnight by the time I got back to my room. Before I went to bed I called Luiza to tell her about how much fun I had that night.

Chapter 15

About three months after Dr. Darius' death, in September 1943 Italy, signed an armistice with the Allies ending her involvement in World War II. However, the war raged on for almost two more years until the Soviet and Polish troops marched into Berlin. World War II finally ended on the 8th of May, 1945.

Once the armistice was signed and the Italian army no longer controlled Italy, the German military became Italy's occupiers until the bitter end of the war. With Italy devastated by war, feeling betrayed by her leaders, especially the ruling royal family, there was a decision to hold a general election to see if they wanted to abolish Italy's monarchy. In June 1946, a plebiscite election was held which abolished the Monarchy. Shortly after, a new constitution was ratified setting up the form of government which still rules Italy today. In fact, as part of the new constitution, all male members of Italy's royal family were banned from their country. It was therefore necessary for the former King Victor Emmanuel III to seek refuge, which he found in Egypt. Because of the fear of assassination, the royal entourage slipped out of Rome under the cover of night and headed for Ostia, where a ship took them to Egypt. Nineteen months later, he died in Alexandria, Egypt, while in exile.

*   *   *

It was Christmas 1947, when a servant came to Grassi and said, "Senior Grassi, the King has requested to see you in his private residence."

Grassi made his way up to the King's room, on the second floor of a secluded villa just outside of Alexandria, Egypt. The villa had been given to the King as a place where he and his family would be safe. Entering his room, Grassi noticed the King still in bed and not looking well.

"Your Majesty, why aren't you up and dressed? Aren't you feeling well?"

The King replied in a soft and weak voice, "No, I'm not feeling well...I have no strength...I have no desire to get out of bed."

"Is there anything I can do for you, Sire?"

"No there isn't...I have no desire to live any longer...For years, I feared my inevitable death. Now it draws near, and I welcome it as a relief."

"Your Majesty, it makes me sad to hear you talk this way."

"To think of all the hours I anguished over my soul," recalled the King. "My only prayer now is history will be kind to me. I hope my countrymen will eventually understand and consider the circumstances I found myself in," the King tried to explain and justify his actions. "There were forces greater than any king's power, and these forces moved us in a direction I could not stop nor prevent."

Although it was still a few days before Christmas, the baker was already preparing the desserts to be enjoyed Christmas Eve. The sweet smells from the kitchen filled the villa and now the King's room. The contrast was noticeable from the acrid stench of death to the sweet preparation to celebrate Christ's birth.

"How may I help you now, Sire," inquired his longtime aide.

"Dear Grassi, the reason I have called you here is because of the way our lives have worked out. I fear you will soon be without a position and alone in a foreign country. The best I can do for you is to give you this letter. I hope it will help you find a new position." Reaching across the bed, taking hold of an envelope then giving it to Grassi, the King's last words to him were, "You have truly been like a son to me. I pray your future improves."

"But Sire, please. What can I say?... I never wanted things to end this way."

He always knew this day would eventually come. With a faint wave of his hand, the King motioned for Grassi to leave. He left the King's room and never saw him alive again.

Grassi made his way over to his room which was now on

the first floor in the back part of the villa. Closing his bedroom door behind him, he sat on the side of his bed, opened the letter written in the King's own personal handwriting and began to read:

To whom it may concern,

This letter is to inform you Signor Alessandro Grassi has served me for almost twenty years as my personal aide. He was proved to be knowledgeable, cooperative, and above all trustworthy. It is my personal request you consider these qualities and take him into your service.

Respectfully,

King Victor Emmanuel III

It was difficult for Grassi not to feel bitter and angry. He had known the King always saw him as a servant, even though at times he said he saw him like a son. He had hoped a monetary reward would be granted to him. He had hoped for enough money to peacefully retire back in his home village of Roletto, a quaint town in the foothill of the Alps.

Instead of a King's reward or perhaps a good piece of property or even a small sack of gold coins, all he got was a letter of reference. A letter from an unpopular King, whose country believed he had betrayed them.

"How am I supposed to find employment with this?" Grassi bitterly lamented aloud to himself.

Grassi avoided any Christmas Eve festivities at the villa but instead decided to stay in his room, avoiding contact with anyone and contemplating his situation. He wasn't even seen at the Christmas Mass the next morning. In fact, very little was seen of him for the next few days.

In the early morning hours on December 28, word began to filter through the Egyptian villa that the King had died. Although wailing and weeping could be heard, Grassi decided to roll over in his bed and go back to sleep.

They buried the King at St. Catherine Roman Catholic Church in Alexandria, Egypt. St Catherine's was established primarily for expatriate Catholics who lived and worked in Alexandria. The King's funeral Mass was not well attended. Italian government officials who attended the funeral, out of respect for the deceased King were commanded to keep a low profile. The King's family could not attend because they were scattered throughout Europe since the Monarchy had been abolished. As Grassi reflected on how the King's life had ended, he understood the futility of power. Once the King was buried, Grassi found himself with very little money in a foreign country and a useless letter in his possession.

A few days later, Italy's ambassador to Egypt came to the villa and met with the staff and servants. He offered them safe passage back to Italy, if they wanted it. Grassi decided to take him up on his offer and asked for help to get back as far as Turin. The ambassador, who knew Grassi as the King's personal aide, took him aside to ask how he was doing. He informed the Ambassador that a week before the King died he had given him a reference letter. The ambassador asked if he could read the letter to see if he could help. Several days later, everyone in the King's household was ready to leave and return to Italy. Before being taken to the ship, the ambassador asked Grassi to meet with him briefly at his office. He informed him he had made some inquiries on his behalf. Because Grassi had wanted to return to Turin, he had made his inquiries in that direction. As it turned out, for the next few months there would be a position available at the Royal Palace in Turin that would involve archiving and putting the King's belongings into storage. Because of Grassi's knowledge of the King's office and private residence, he would be of great assistance to them. Grassi quickly agreed and thanked the ambassador for his help. He hoped after this short-term employment ended, other opportunities would present themselves.

Chapter 16

The returning members of the King's household and staff boarded a ferry ultimately bound for Bari, Italy. Grassi made his way to his cabin having no desire to mingle with the other passengers. The ship's route took them first to Crete and finally landed in Bari, Italy almost five days later. Once he exited the ship and cleared Customs, Grassi grabbed a bus that took him to the train station, *Stazione Bari Centrale*, which is located in the center of the city. With his one suitcase in hand, Grassi purchased a ticket for Turin. After boarding Train Number 8346, he found his compartment and settled in for the journey home.

Once beyond the 'spur of Italy', the train traveled up along the Adriatic coast towards Ancona. With the Apennine Mountains on the left or port side and the sea to the right or starboard side, this leg of the train trip was quite beautiful. In several sections of the trip the mountains came down to the coast, where at times the tracks ran literally along the beach by the Adriatic. From Ancona, the train continued across Italy's fertile and flat land to Bologna where at Bologna Centrale Grassi caught a different train bound for Turin. It took another several hours to get back to his home city, arriving in Turin late that evening. Because he had little money, Grassi decided to find a hostel where he could get a bed for the night. The traveler's information desk at the train station informed him that several blocks away there was a shelter at a church. The tram just outside the station took him on this bitter cold January night to a church that welcomed homeless men with a free bed for the night.

*   *   *

Waking up at the shelter was damp and depressing for Grassi. There were perhaps twenty other men who had taken a cot for the night. The large room was sparsely furnished. There was one window on the far side of the room and the walls were made of stucco. One light hung from the center of the ceiling. The beds provided were arranged in two rows lining the two opposite walls, heads towards the wall, feet towards the center of the room. They were clean with two sheets, a blanket and one pillow each. The small bathroom which contained a sink and a toilet was located at the end of the hallway.

On the opposite wall to window was the entrance door. Above the door was a good size crucifix. While Grassi lay on his cot waiting to nod off to sleep, he looked at the crucifix. It caused him to reflect back to the days the King had him with his helpers create the fake Shroud. He thought about the pain and agony the Libian victim suffered before he died. To Grassi it seemed like a lifetime ago instead of just a few years. It also made him wonder what may have happened to the fake. Was it still in the Chapel? Was the real one still in the King's closet?

In the morning, the Capuchin monks who ran the shelter had caffé-latte and stale bread, ready for the men. There were clean toilets and sinks with warm water, where in turn the men could wash and shave. After this meager breakfast, Grassi sat in the church contemplating his life up to now. He realized at sixty he was alone, unmarried and penniless with little else other than frustrating and nightmarish memories. Although he believed in his heart his desire had been to serve his King, he also knew that life was unpredictable and often cruel. While sitting there in the church, one of the monks approached him.

"May I sit and visit with you for a while?" the monk asked.

Grassi, who would have preferred to be left alone, only shrugged as if to say, "If you'd like."

The monk hoped Grassi might open up to conversation. "How long have you been here in Turin?" the monk asked.

"Since last night," Grassi curtly replied.

"May I pray with you?"

Grassi declined, "Don't waste your prayers on me. They will do no good."

The monk realized Grassi was not yet receptive to his attempt to help, so he left him alone.

At about 8:30 Grassi got up and left the church to head for the Palace. When he arrived at the front gate, he introduced himself to the guard and explained he was there to begin a new position assisting with the archiving of the deceased King's personal effects. The guard gave Grassi a pass and pointed him to the curator's office. On his way to the office, he ran into some old familiar faces. He paused briefly to exchange salutations. He still was in no mood to explain how things had been for him, since the last time he was there. The curator, Signora Bucci, a large and rather busty woman expected Grassi and knew of his former position as the King's top aide. She had already determined to make sure he knew she was in charge now. Their initial greeting was congenial but cold. She informed Grassi of what his responsibilities would be and how he would be expected to follow their cataloging procedure to the letter. Furthermore, she told him she would not tolerate any insubordination. Grassi, understanding his situation, did not want to antagonize her.

After their brief meeting, one of Signora Bucci's assistants brought Grassi up to the former King's private residence where another assistant was busy inspecting the King's personal belongings. As he entered the room, Grassi's thoughts rushed back to the countless times he had been alone there with the King talking over various matters. Most of the time they discussed his schedule and meetings the King needed to attend. Once in a while the King would even discuss matters of state, but there were also those times when the King had suffered his fits of depression and paranoia. It was those times Grassi knew he had been his only confidante. He wondered how such a powerful man could have been so extremely lonely.

Finally, he turned his attention to the business at hand as the two assistants began to explain the procedure to him. They showed him how they archived and cataloged the contents of the room. Essentially, they would either stick on an identification numbered sticker or tie an identification tag onto the items. It was an alpha-numeric ID number. Then they entered the ID into the catalog with descriptions of the item. Grassi was asked to add any remembrances he had about any given item. They hoped Grassi would add background info about the King's belongings, such as how the King used it or if it was a gift did he know who gave it. The rest of that first day was fairly uneventful.

Because of Grassi's financial situation, he decided to return to the shelter for another night. He arrived at about 6:30 that evening. The same monk, who tried to speak with him earlier that morning, greeted him. The monk informed him that at eight o'clock they would be serving the evening meal, and Mass would be offered at seven. Grassi declined the offer to attend Mass wishing instead to rest before dinner. While he lay on his cot he thought to himself how he would have liked to have answered the inquisitive monk: "Frankly, I believe I am beyond salvation. If only you knew what I had to do for the King," he would have lamented.

Chapter 17

The next day at work, one of Signora Bucci's assistants, Silvio Fontana approached Grassi and asked him if he had a place to stay. Grassi replied, "I have so little money, I am unable to get a room."

The assistant informed him, "Where I am living, there is a comfortable room available for an affordable rent. The rooms are small but comfortable and clean. You would have some privacy," He quickly added, "If you'd like, I'll introduce you to the landlord."

"I need to find a place. I can't stand this shelter," Grassi gratefully accepted the offer, and said he would be very happy to speak with the landlord. That evening after work Grassi and the assistant arrived at the rooming house and met with the landlord, The room was clean but small. Against the wall to the right was an armoire with a small mirror hung above it. It also had a small eating area near the window, which included a two door cabinet, a hotplate on the table, and a solitary chair with four wooden slats for a back, chair. The single bed was pushed against the opposite wall with a small wooden crucifix above it. There were even a few pictures hanging on the wall. One had a scene of the Piedmont countryside with terraced hillsides and a village at the crest of the hill.

The rent was reasonable and Grassi informed the landlord he could only take the room if he could wait until he received his first week's pay. With Silvio's encouragement, the landlord finally agreed. Grassi breathed a sigh of relief and was grateful not to have to stay at the shelter any longer.

A few days later, Grassi approached Signora Bucci and asked her if he might visit his old room to get a few of his personal belongings left there years earlier. He explained to her when they exiled the King he was unable to return from Rome to collect his items. She said she understood the situation and was willing to allow him to collect only his things.

It felt strange for Grassi to be back in his old room. Aside from a light periodic dusting, he found the room had been virtually untouched since the last day he had been in Turin which seemed so long ago. From the bookshelf he collected several of his books including his journal. From the nightstand drawer he removed his pens, a few family photos, and several miscellaneous items. In his closet he found his old clothes and an old carpetbag made from the remnants of a woolen tapestry. He filled it with all the items he gathered. Taking the bag to Signora Bucci's office, she inspected it to make sure what he had taken was considered personal and not the property of the Palace.

Later that evening at his new living quarters, Grassi went through what he had collected. Thumbing through his books, he began to find the old slips of paper he had periodically slipped in as mementos. One of the pieces of paper Grassi stumbled upon was the note the King had given him regarding Captain Cipollini and how to contact him. This stirred up all the old memories again of when the King asked him to approach Dr. Darius and Captain Cipollini and how the three of them re-created the forgery of the Shroud. Another note was from Dr. Darius questioning the moral ramifications of murdering someone. How could they obey the King's request? Grassi recalled how he felt at the time of the whole endeavor. As much as he hated the thought of murdering someone, he believed he had no choice. He knew he had to do the King's bidding, even if he thought it was morally wrong. In a soft voice he whispered to himself, "How do you say no to the King?"

Grassi began to wonder if the authentic Shroud was still tucked away in the back of the closet where they had put it, more than four years earlier. He recalled how first he read about Dr. Darius's death and then a few months later, saw a notice about Captain Cipollini, who died in Russia on the battlefield. The obituary stated he had the unfortunate honor of being one of the very last Italian officers to be killed in the war. It happened the day before the Armistice went into effect. He wondered if he could have been the victim of the King's assassins or just an unfortunate victim of the war.

Suddenly an overwhelming desire to get his hands on the Shroud came over Grassi. His spirits lifted for the first time in a long time just contemplating this. He thought about the possibility of stealing it from the Savoy family, their one true sacred possession. He saw it as justifiable retribution for all he had been through on behalf of that family. He grew more determined. "But how?" he mused. The next day he would look to see if it was still stored away in the back of the closet. If it was then he would find a way to remove it from the Palace and make it his possession.

Grassi knew that during their lunch time, most the Palace workers were in the lunch hall eating. Very few people would be roaming around the Palace. The next day during lunch he excused himself from the table with an excuse to use the bathroom. Instead he slipped away from the other assistants who expected he would be back shortly. Knowing his way around the Palace, Grassi slipped into the King's private residence and into the storage closet where he knew he had placed the real Shroud a few years earlier. There, in the back of the closet carefully buried under some other items, he found it. He remembered how after the war ended and Nazi Germany was defeated, the King had always intended to return to Turin. He would have had Grassi put the real Shroud back into the Royal Chapel and destroy the forgery they had made. However, the King never returned to his preferred Palace in Turin, leaving it abandoned and forgotten. Grassi placed the folded linen in the bottom of a trash bin, and returned to his fellow archivist without being missed.

Once back to work he made it seem as though he was eliminating papers Mrs. Bucci had determined were unimportant. Hiding the Shroud in a simple canvas sack and placing it carefully behind the stone wall near the back entrance to the Palace, Grassi waited until the end of the day when he could retrieve his treasure.

Once in his room Grassi sat on the side of his bed with the Shroud next to him. The sense of power and vindication began to overwhelm him as he considered the fact he was now in possession of the House of Savoy's most treasured artifact. He thought about how the Savoy family had been exiled from Italy while he sat in their city, Turin. Needless to say, Grassi got very little sleep that night thinking about how his fortunes had changed.

*   *   *

Archiving the King's possessions continued under the scrutiny and leadership of Signora Bucci. Progress was slow, but Grassi persevered with an inner contentment. A few weeks into the project on a particularly cold, winter morning, snow had fallen during the night and about an inch covered the ground. Grassi got himself dressed to go to work. He left his room and made his way over to the tram stop accompanied by Silvio his co-worker.

The night before he had felt slightly ill and uncomfortable wondering if he had the flu or was it something he had eaten. Just as the tram arrived, Grassi took a few steps forward raising his foot to step up onto the tram and suddenly collapsed. Immediately, people waiting to get on the tram began to gather around him. One woman, apparently a nurse, bent down to see what she could do. Grabbing his wrist, she checked for a pulse. The sardonic smile with its relaxed cheeks exposed most of his teeth, the limpness of his body, and the stench of his own excrement alerted all those who stood around that he was dead. The tram conductor concerned more about keeping his schedule said with a curt briskness, "Quick, move him out of the way." Two men grabbed Grassi. One man held his wrists and the other grabbed one of his ankles dragging him to the back of the sidewalk, where they left him. Silvio stood there in shock not knowing what to do.

Grassi's body lay there in the snow waiting for the authorities. Signore Fontana returned to their rooming house to report what happened to Grassi to their landlord. Grassi's landlord helped arrange for his body to be buried and gathered up all his personal possessions, which he placed into an old used wooden trunk. Put into the trunk were his books, all his clothing, some letters and jewelry along with a few photographs. Unwittingly, also included with his belongings was the Shroud of Turin. Knowing he came from a small town called Rolleto, the landlord was able to find and contact Grassi's only sister. She agreed to take possession of her brother's belongings.

Chapter *18*

It was about 9:30 the next morning when Signor Gianni met me waiting in the hotel lobby with my two crates. He was an elderly gentleman probably in his early seventies, a slight build with a mustache, gray hair and a bit hunched forward. He also spoke and gestured in a lively manner, excited to meet me and looking forward to helping me install the new chapel windows.

As he approached me from his double parked car, he subtly waved and said, "Hello, Joe."

"My name is Marty Daniels. Are you Signor Gianni?"

"I know who you are. I just like to call Americans, Joe." Signor Gianni mumbled and chuckled while now shaking my hand.

He then, looked at the crates, grabbed his chin pensively, and said, "We can work it out." I wasn't sure exactly what he meant until we reached his car. It was an old Ford Escort, two-door sedan with the backseat already covered with gardening and carpentry tools, as well as miscellaneous junk. Circling around his car in the middle of the street, he began pulling items out of the back to make room for the two wooden crates. Moving everything around, he managed to position the crates up onto the backseat; squeezing his belongings into his trunk and putting some of his tools back on the floor behind the front seats. In order to get it all to fit, he relocated some of the excess gardening implements out the passenger side window. When I got in, he instructed me to 'buckle my seatbelt, stick my right arm out the window and hold onto the spade, hoe, and rake'. Then off we went to meet Sister Bonny.

Driving through the streets of Torino to Beinasco, a suburb just outside the city limits, turned out to be an adventure in itself.

Although Signor Gianni was elderly, he certainly didn't act it. He was so full of life he reminded me of a twenty-year-old. In typical Italian fashion, he drove aggressively, regularly switching lanes to get around slower vehicles, and commented on every person who didn't drive the way he thought they should.

Another part of our adventure was he needed to fill up with *Metano*. This meant finding a station that sold liquefied methane. We located one near the entrance to the Autostrada. Also, since his gas gauge didn't work, Signor Gianni had to keep track of how much fuel he used. He did this by keeping a small notepad clipped to his dashboard. Once he finished writing down his odometer reading and calculating how far he could go on this purchase, he returned his notepad to its handy magnetic clip. Just before pulling out of the station, he decided to light up a cigarette, an Italian variety called Nazionale. After lighting the smelly cigarette, he turned to me and in English said, "Let's go, Joe," which by his chuckle told me he thought he was pretty funny.

When we arrived at the convent, Signor Gianni shut off his engine, and allowed his car to coast the final twenty feet, which I presumed was an attempt to save gas. Once at a full stop he jumped out of his car, ran over to the side door, and rang the doorbell. He then immediately ran back to the car and began to help me unload the crates.

The convent was undergoing very extensive renovations, which is why it took the nuns a while to descend from the second floor living quarters to reach the side door. The restoration project was being funded by a generous American family from California. They were the ones who commissioned me to create these windows for the chapel. This benefactor contacted me and asked if I could also do a few windows for the chapel. Without hesitation, I agreed and here I was, finally installing them.

Sister Bonny was the first of three nuns to come out to greet us. She was also the tallest of the women, elegantly deliberate in her movements and appeared to be well educated. To my surprise, I discovered she was not Italian, but rather of Nigerian nationality. I had always assumed she was an Italian, having only spoken to her a few times over the phone.

She greeted me in English with, "Maestro Daniels, we are so excited to see what you have created for us."

"Yes, I'm excited to finally be here."

"How may we help you?" Sister Bonny asked.

"Oh, I think Signor Gianni and I can handle it. I trust he'll have any tools I might need."

The convent of sisters were all very excited to finally have new stained-glass windows for their renovated chapel. Once we got the crates into the chapel and straddled them across two pews, Signor Gianni pulled out his cordless screw gun and began to unscrew the covers. By this time, we not only had the three nuns, who met us at the door but a couple more who curiously came by to see what was going on. I took the covers off the crates. It was the first time I had seen the windows since crating them a few months ago at my studio. I was relieved to see they arrived in good shape.

The windows consisted of two sections of stained-glass for each of the four windows. One was installed above the other. In the middle of each of the eight panels was a round religious medallion about seven inches in diameter. They were easily a hundred years old when I acquired them. I had salvaged them from some old stained glass windows that we had removed from an old church slated for demolition. These medallions originally made part of a foot wide border that surrounded ten foot tall figures of saints. The figures were restored and moved to another church. The borders were no longer needed, so I had kept them and was able to use some of them in these windows. Most of the symbols represented Christ, such as: INRI with three spikes in one. Another had a lamb with a white and red cross flag. Another had a quarried cornerstone with an Alpha and Omega on it and so on. The background pieces that surrounded these medallions were rectangles and were shadowed with black enamel paint in such a way to make the windows look old and distressed. We had even cut crooked lines across some of the rectangles and added lead channeling to give the appearance they had been repaired. The two inch wide border that went around the perimeter of two stacked panels was also made up of old salvaged glass. To me, there was a great deal of pleasure looking at what had been created from so many sources.

Signor Gianni hovered around looking enthusiastically for a way to help. In a short time he was able to anticipate my actions and had the tools necessary in his hands before I even asked for them. It took us a little over an hour but we were able to successfully install the windows without much difficulty. The sisters came in and out pausing for a few minutes to watch us work. When they were finally installed, someone went and called Sister Bonny. She entered the chapel with tears in her eyes, and both hands on her cheeks saying, "My my, Maestro Daniels, they are so beautiful." After all of the compliments were given and the excitement waned, she reminded me that lunch would be in about a half-hour. This gave us plenty of time to finish our touchups, cleanup, and wash for lunch.

The convent had approximately ten nuns living there; four were from Nigeria and the rest were Italian. Some were at work in the hospital and in fact I understood Sister Bonny herself had worked the overnight shift the previous evening. When we were called for lunch, we went into a large open kitchen with a dining area. They had two long tables put together in such a way that the table was almost square, and everybody sat along three of the four sides. Across the room and in the corner was a television which was turned on to the noontime news broadcast.

They first served us a decent portion of spaghetti, with a meaty ragù. They then had prepared a stove top chicken dish that had the chicken parts cut smaller, with potatoes and green beans all sautéed together. It was very tasty.

Perhaps in an effort to make small talk, I asked Sister Bonny, which language she prefers to speak in. The few Nigerian nuns seated near her quickly said English as they nodded and smiled. Sister Bonny instead said in English, "I have now been here in Italy almost thirty years, so Italian comes more easily for me. My sisters here have not been here as long, so they are still learning the language, which is why they asked me to speak to you in English."

She then asked, "The stained glass windows, they are new, right?"

"Yes, most of it is. I mean the rectangles that make up the background were cut and painted by us. I purposely made them look old. Not having seen your chapel and only knowing the convent was under reconstruction. I pictured it to be an older building."

"As you can see it is." She interjected.

"Anyway, I thought it would be more interesting to do a somewhat traditional design, but paint the glass as though it showed wear and age. The small round religious symbols I salvaged from parts of old church windows I had. They were left over from a project we were involved with several years ago." I said.

"How did you come to have them? May I ask?"

"In the Boston area we have too many Catholic Churches. What I mean to say is that a hundred years ago during the great immigration to America, every ethnic community had their own church and priests. There was an Irish church for the Irish, a Polish church for the Polish, a French church for the French, etcetera. Of course there were the Italian churches too." I explained. "Today everyone is pretty much assimilated and are now Americans and so many churches, especially the older ones have very few parishioners and needed a lot of repairs. Consolidating parishes has been going on for years."

"Today here in Italy there is a shortage of priests, so one priest oversees several parishes." Sister Bonny said.

It was about this time, we had already finished lunch, when one of the Italian nuns, a Sister Grazia who perhaps had just arrived from the hospital, came into the kitchen very upset. She was obviously distressed and needed to speak with Sister Bonny. Rather than go to another room, they went off to the side. Without them realizing it, I was able to overhear the startling news, perhaps due to her agitated tone and elevated voice. As it turned out Sister Grazia had a brother who worked in the *Curia Arcivescovile di Torino*. He had phoned his sister to ask her and the other nuns to pray and intercede. The Archbishop and his office had just discovered the "Shroud of Turin" had been switched with a fake copy almost sixty-five years ago. The one in the Royal Chapel was believed to be the fake.

Since we had finished lunch, Sister Bonny and some of the other sisters said goodbye. As Signor Gianni and I packed up our things and got ready to leave the convent, I noticed all the nuns filing into the chapel for a special time of prayer. I was told that the reason for this special time of prayer was related to the phone call Sister Grazia had received from her brother.

While we drove away from the convent, I thought about the nuns in their chapel with their new stained-glass windows. I also thought it was curious they were praying for the recovery of the "Shroud of Turin," an item that the day before I thought was in Rome in some Vatican Museum, not realizing that it had been owned by Italy's former Royal family for hundreds of years.

Chapter 19

It was a warm Saturday morning when Bruno Russo's wife, Maria, asked him to go down into the cellar and begin to remove the furniture that had been stored there. More than ten years earlier Bruno and his family moved back to the small village of Roletto shortly after Maria's mother died. Because of her father's age, declining health, and need of more assistance, they decided it would be better to give up their apartment in the city and move back into the home of her youth to take care of her "Papa." Unfortunately, Papa lived only a few years after the death of his wife. This left the house to the Russo family: Bruno, his wife Maria, and their only daughter Elena.

Elena was getting married in a month. She and her fiancée had found an apartment in Torino which needed to be furnished. The Russo's knew this day would eventually come. They were glad they had chosen to store their old furniture, which now could be passed onto their daughter. The cellar stored a dining room table with six chairs, a hutch, and a queen-sized bed with beautiful inlaid woodwork on the headboard. There also were two bed stands, a good size armoire, a bookcase and even some old china.

Once the furniture was removed, loaded onto the moving truck, and headed for the new apartment, the Russo's thought it would be a good time to organize their cellar. While cleaning it out, Bruno discovered an old wooden trunk he had never seen before, buried under clutter. Bruno could not say exactly why his curiosity took hold of him, but he decided rather than just throw out the old trunk, he first wanted to investigate its contents. The locked trunk had no key. Unable to find anything in the cellar to pop it open, he went out to his car and got the tire-iron, which had a tapered end for prying off hub caps.

Once he popped the lid, he discovered artifacts that went back many years. In the top of the trunk were some old clothes, a man's gray wool overcoat, a few pairs of pants, several shirts and even some men's underwear. At first Bruno assumed they belonged to his father-in-law, but he quickly realized these clothes never would have fit him. These obviously belonged to someone taller and larger. Below the clothes were several books, a few novels, a political science book, and even one leather-bound handwritten journal. While rifling through the pages of one of the books, he discovered several pieces of paper tucked in between the pages. Bruno picked out one of the handwritten notes. Examining it closely, he became even more intrigued by what he read. The note had a curious message scrawled on it:

"Meet me at the bar at the corner of via Milano and Garibaldi at 8:30 tonight. Captain Cipollini."

On another piece of paper he read:

"I have considered your offer and realize my only option is to trust you will keep your word if I comply, and my family won't be harmed. I have been considering several techniques that might give us success. I will need to experiment. This may take some time. Please meet me at my office as soon as possible.
Dr. Carlo Darius."

There were other pieces of paper tucked in the pages of his books. Bruno wondered what these cryptic messages meant. He also found a small handful of letters, which were addressed to Signor Alessandro Grassi presso: *Palazzo del Quirinale* Roma. He realized the trunk belong to his wife's uncle, rarely spoken of. The letters were in the same type of envelope and had the same handwriting on the front. He opened one of these letters, and realized it was a love letter from a woman named Donatella. It was quite passionate and most intriguing. There were other letters addressed to Alessandro Grassi that came from the Russo's village, Roletto and two were from Bruno's mother-in-law. Lastly he found one final letter which had the royal seal of the King at the top of the stationary. Once having read the letter, he realized this was a letter of reference given to his wife's uncle by the King, dated December 22, 1947.

It was about this time that Bruno's wife Maria called him up for lunch. Responding to her call, he closed the trunk and decided after lunch he would investigate the trunk's contents more. At lunch, Bruno turned on the television to listen to the noontime news broadcast and weather report. Clicking it off, he commented to his wife, "It's more than two years since the twin towers were struck down in New York, and I can still remember that day vividly." Then he began to ask his wife about her uncle. "Didn't your uncle, Sandro, work for the King at the Royal Palace?"

"Yes, we knew he had worked at the Palace, but we never knew exactly what he did." Maria replied.

"Why is he so seldom mentioned?" Bruno asked.

"He had very little to do with our family. He very rarely ever visited. I guess after his death, we abandoned him and his memory," Maria said.

"Why didn't your mother ask him about his activities?" asked Bruno.

"On the few times, when my mother talked about him, she said, he was always secretive about his work," replied Maria. "When we wondered why he never got married, she told us he claimed there had been a woman in his life, but because of his responsibilities, he would never be able to live a normal life."

After telling his wife he had discovered a trunk in the corner of the cellar, Maria expressed her surprise and said she vaguely remembered her family got it shortly after his death.

"I think you should throw the whole thing out. There can't be anything in there of value, just a bunch of junk—the last memory of a person better forgotten," Maria said while getting up from the table to get Bruno a little more pasta.

After lunch Bruno returned to the cellar. Instead of throwing everything back in the trunk and hauling it off to the dump, he finished going through everything just to see what the life of his wife's uncle might have been like. Below the clothes, the letters, the books, and a few knick-knacks, he found a gray canvas sack that had a folded linen cloth wrapped inside. Bruno decided to remove the cloth and investigate it more. Initially, it just looked like an old tarp. He wondered why anyone would wrap an old drop-cloth up and put it in a canvas sack. Upon further investigation, he saw it had been scorched and patched at the scorch marks. He also noticed faint brown markings on a cloth but couldn't make out what they were. His curiosity made him want to open it up fully to see what it was. Climbing out of the cellar through the bulkhead to the backyard, he stretched the cloth out across the yard and stepped back to get a better view. It startled him to discover what lay before him.

Bruno remembered a few years earlier in September of 2000, he and his family had traveled to Torino to visit the "Holy Shroud of Turin," which is seldom ever displayed. The Archbishop decided to exhibit it for several weeks to celebrate the new millennium. Bruno wondered why Grassi would have a replica of the Shroud kept in Torino. He wondered how Grassi would have come to be in possession of it.

Chapter 20

By the time Signor Gianni returned to my hotel, I decided to give Luiza a call. It was after 8:00 in the morning back home. She would be up and about. It took four rings before she answered the phone. She answered with a quizzical, "Hello, who is this?"

"Why it's me!"

"Oh, it's you; I didn't know who was calling me because the caller ID said 'Unavailable.' I thought it might be a tele-marketer," she said half kidding.

"Well, I guess in the future you'll have to answer any 'Unavailable' calls or at least until I get home," I replied.

"Guess so."

"Luiza, I have some good news for you and some bad news. Which do you want first?" I asked.

"Marty, why do you play these games?" she retorted.

"Which do you want to hear first—the bad news or the good news?" I asked a bit more emphatically.

"I guess I'll take the bad news first," she said.

"I've fallen in love with another woman," I said.

"Yeah right, good luck...I hope she'll put up with you like I have had to," she said with a half mocking tone.

Quickly I added, "That's the bad news, but the good news is she's a nun, Sister Bonny, the mother superior at the convent,"

"Marty, how is that good news?"

"These nuns are the sweetest women I've ever met. They giggle all the time and they are just so excited to have their new stained-glass windows," I said.

"But what's this about Sister Bonny?" Luiza asked.

"You've got to meet her. She's the most amazing woman. I

know you'll love her too."

"Hopefully, someday I will meet her."

While chatting with Luiza, I turned on the television in my room, hoping to find something interesting to watch. As I scrolled through, I stopped for a moment at an infomercial. An attractive woman was selling a fancy multi-purpose ironing board, which also converted into a small step ladder. The woman used it to get something out of a tall cabinet.

"Luiza, I've got to tell you about something else that happened." I said in a tone as though I was about to give her a juicy piece of gossip.

"Yeah, what's that?"

"After we finished installing the windows, they invited me to stay for lunch. Just as we were finishing lunch, one of the nuns came into the dining room area visibly upset. I'm not sure she even realized I was there. She began to take Sister Bonny aside and tell her about a phone conversation she just had with her brother who works for the Archbishop here in Torino. She told Sister Bonny how he had called her and asked her to get the nuns together to pray. The Archbishop's office had just found out the *Shroud of Turin* they possess is a fake. The original one is missing, and now they don't know what happened to it."

Luiza, who had been silent up until now said, "You sure it's true?"

"What do you mean am I sure if it's true?" I asked.

"All I'm asking is did you understand what she was saying? They were speaking in Italian, weren't they?" Luiza asked.

"Yes, of course there were speaking in Italian. *Anche, Io capisco Italiano.*"

"I know you understand Italian, but I was just curious, if in all the excitement and the way she might have been speaking, you clearly understood what she said."

"Yes, I understood," I said.

"This *is* startling news. Let me know if you hear anything more," Luiza said.

"I will."

I started scrolling back to find the infomercial about the ironing board wondering how I might bring one home for Luiza.

By this time the woman was using it to help paint the high parts of a wall in a room.

Then, my wife said, "Marty, before I forget, I got a call yesterday from Dan Carlson."

"Really?" I questioned.

"He called to ask where you were in Italy."

"Ok, what did you tell him?" I asked.

"He said he thought visiting Darla's relatives in the Netherlands might help him bring closure to his aching heart. Instead, he found them half blaming him for her death. He's decided he'd rather get away from them. However, his ticket is for two weeks and he still has another ten days to go," Luiza said.

"What does that have to do with me?" I asked, already knowing something was coming.

"He wanted your cell phone number. He is thinking of traveling down to visit you."

"I hope he doesn't intend to spy on me," I complained.

"Marty, I don't know if you are nuts or just kidding sometimes," she said.

"I guess I'm half kidding, but I'm not excited about babysitting him and having him tag along while I go up to Ramiseto."

"I'm sure you'll be fine," Luiza said.

The infomercial demonstrator was now showing how quickly it converted back into a usable ironing board. I decided it probably wasn't the best gift to bring Luiza from Italy.

I said, "Massimo is picking me up here at the hotel, and I'm going over to his apartment for dinner. Tomorrow I'm planning on grabbing the train and heading down to Reggio."

"How early are you planning to leave Torino?" she asked.

"There's only one direct train that leaves just after 8:00. It will get me there by 11:00. If I miss that train, I will have to travel first to Milan and then catch another train down to Reggio. I'm hoping to get the early train," I told her.

"Call me tomorrow and let me know how your plans work out."

"Hey, hey there's one more thing," I said, stalling her good bye.

"What's that?" she asked.

"Over here they call me Maestro...I'm called Maestro Daniels."

"Oh great, that's all I need," Luiza jokingly lamented.

"Why, what do you mean?" I asked.

"Now you'll expect everybody to call you Maestro," she said.

"Why not, what's wrong with that?" I asked. "They call people who are doctors, Doctor So-and-so or Pastor So-and-so. What's wrong with me being called Maestro Daniels?"

"Yeah right...Ok, My-*aass*-tro, call me later," Luiza joked.

"I always wanted to be called Maestro...I miss you," I said and ended my call.

I decided to lie down for a while. The jet lag was still causing me to feel tired at strange times. Since I had some time to kill, I hoped to be able to sleep.

I dozed off watching an Italian soap opera. I think I was asleep about an hour, when I was awakened by the ringing of my cell phone. It was Dan Carlson calling from Amsterdam. "Hey Marty, it's me, Dan. You'll never guess where I'm calling you from?"

"Amsterdam?" I said.

"I see you spoke with your wife," he replied.

"She told me you would be calling."

"I'd like to catch a plane tomorrow for Milan. I'd arrive at Bergamo Airport shortly after 3:00 pm."

"But I'm not in Milan. I'm in Torino," I said.

"Should I fly to Torino?" he asked.

The soap opera was over and now the news was airing. Apparently, there had been a kidnapping of a young boy. They found him left at the entrance of a cave in the mountains in Sardinia. I reasoned, the family must have decided to pay the ransom.

"Why are you arriving at Bergamo Airport?" I asked.

"I want to grab a cheap flight, and they fly to the Bergamo not Milan," he said.

"Then, I'll meet you at Milan's central train station," I said.

"How?" Dan asked.

"When you arrive in Italy, they'll have buses to the main train station. Take the bus to *Stazione Centrale* which is Milan's main train station," I informed him.

"Why at the train station?" he asked.

"That's where I'll be arriving in the afternoon. Call me as soon as you're on the bus and let me know what time I should expect you," I said.

"Did my phone number come up on the caller ID?" he asked.

"Yeah, it did," I said.

"Good, so you'll call me if there is any change in your plans. Otherwise I'll call you when I get on the bus to Milan," Dan said.

"Keep in touch...I'll see you then" I said and hung up my phone and tried to get back to sleep.

Because Dan and I have never been close friends, spending the rest of my time in Italy with him was not the most pleasant thought. I considered just calling him back and suggesting he not bother coming to Italy now, or at least not to plan on tagging along with me. Eventually, I decided against it thinking to myself, "Oh, what the hell it won't be that bad."

Chapter 21

Bruno decided he needed to go through Grassi's journal and hopefully find an answer to these questions.

The journal, which was grouped with the other books, was leather-bound with a red bookmarking cord. Opening the journal Bruno began to read the first entry dated October 12, 1925. Grassi's entry into what must have been his private diary was made on his first day at the Palace. It read, "Today is my first day after having been assigned to be one of King Victor Emmanuel III's personal aides." Russo read how excited Grassi was to find himself in this position. For the first twenty or so pages Grassi wrote in his journal daily, but then it became only every week. He could see it was not as exciting a position any more. He began to write about the King's quirky little habits: his ritual before he ate, how he wanted his desk to be kept in a certain way, and how he would notice if anything was moved even slightly. The most unsettling thing Russo read was the King's fits of paranoia and his belief that his own people wanted to have him assassinated. Bruno read about how wearying and tiring the job had become. Thumbing through the journal, Bruno noticed the entries were no longer weekly but instead, just every now and again, with even several weeks and months having passed. In fact, he realized unless something significant happened, Grassi wouldn't bother keeping any notes.

He investigated further searching for the reason this replica of the Shroud of Turin was amongst his belongings. Finally he stumbled on an interesting entry dated March 5, 1943. This entry mentioned how one of the King's fits of paranoia was so severe, the King made him fetch the Archbishop of Turin. When the

Archbishop arrived at the Palace, the King informed him he had decided to reproduce the original Shroud. Bruno continued to read what Grassi had written about the King fears of what the Nazis would do to Italy once Italy surrendered to the Allied forces. A later entry talked about his meetings with Dr. Carlo Darius and Captain Cipollini. These entries talked about their secret experiments to re-create the original Shroud. His journal explained how Captain Cipollini searched for a man who resembled the beaten and bruised face of the man in the Shroud. Later entries documented how Grassi and Captain Cipollini had switched the cloth in the Royal Chapel and hid it away in the King's private residence.

Bruno continued to read about the turmoil in the Royal Palace after the end of the war and the decision made to get rid of the monarchy. He read how upsetting and distressing the whole series of events turned out. Grassi wrote about how soon they would be secretly leaving the Palace in Turin to make their way back to Rome. They all feared, after the vote to remove the Monarchy, they may need to flee the country or risk being murdered themselves, as had happened to the Royal Family of Russia during the Bolshevik Revolution. Grassi even wrote that he wondered if they would ever return to Turin to restore the real Shroud back into the Royal Chapel. Towards the very end of his journal Bruno read a cryptic entry that caused him to shout, "I can't believe this." The entry Grassi wrote was, "Their most Sacred possession is now mine." It was dated January 28, 1948. With that entry, Bruno Russo realized what he had in his possession was the authentic Shroud of Turin and not a replica.

*   *   *

As Bruno Russo walked out of the doctor's office, he had a blank look on his face. He stared off into space, not conscious of where he walked. The devastating news the doctor had just given him turned out to be a death sentence. Bruno had just been informed he had Stage Four cancer and his prognosis was very grim. His doctor had told him without another aggressive round of chemotherapy and radiation treatments, his chances of living more than several months were unlikely. Because this was not the first round of treatments Bruno had gone through, he knew how sick he would be the next few months. All that suffering would perhaps give him only an extra year or two. As he left the doctor's office, he contemplated whether or not he could endure further treatments.

Russo arrived home that evening about a half-hour after his wife. She was already in the kitchen preparing dinner. Between the sauce simmering on the stove and the pork cutlets roasting in the oven, the wonderful aromas filled the house. Signora Russo had known about Bruno's appointment with the doctor and anxiously awaited his return home. It took her all of a few seconds to know the news was not good. The way her husband entered their house with his head lowered and his brown eyes fixed in a stare said everything. Quietly just sitting there, his wife sat next to him, took his hand and asked, "What did the doctor say?"

While staring up at their ceiling Bruno said, "He wants me to go through it again."

"Oh, Bruno," Maria cried softly.

Slowly and quietly Bruno said, "I am not sure I can go through it again. I don't know what to do." Dinner that night was quite somber. Later that evening Maria wanted to head up to bed after one of their favorite TV game shows finished about 11:00 o'clock. Asking her husband if he would be up soon he replied, "I'll be up later. I'm really not sleepy."

About 2:00 AM Signora Russo woke up and realized Bruno had not yet come to bed. She could hear the television going and assumed he must have fallen asleep on the couch. Wanting to wake him up and get him to come to bed, she went down to the living room where she found him still awake and blankly staring at the television. She sat down next to him and asked, "Why don't you come up to bed?"

"I can't… I have got something I must talk to you about."

"What is that, dear?"

"I've done something terrible, and I must tell you about it. I tried to keep it from you in hopes you would never find out," he said.

"What could you have done that is so terrible?" Maria asked.

"You remember about three and a half years ago when we were preparing the furniture to give to Elena for her new apartment?

"Yes, why?"

"When I was down in the cellar and cleaning it out, I told you about your uncle's trunk and his belongings left in it. What I didn't tell you is what else I found lying in the trunk. At the bottom of his trunk in an old sack, I found a linen cloth. I took the cloth out of the trunk and up to the backyard where I stretched it out. What I found was, what I first believed was a replica of *La Sacra Sindone*. I read through your uncle's diary trying to discover why he would have a replica of the Shroud. Instead, what I found frightened me. I kept this information from you so as not to frighten you. It seems during World War II, your uncle Sandro had been part of a conspiracy to create a forgery of the original Sacred Shroud. The King feared the Nazis would steal the original and take it to Germany as a spoil of war. A replica was made and switched with the original. The authentic shroud was kept hidden in secret place known only to the King and your uncle.

Chapter 22

After the King's death, your uncle states he was hired to help archive the King's belongings at the *Palazzo Reale* in Torino. There he found the original still tucked away in the back of the King's closet. He decided to steal it. Maybe it was bitterness and resentment towards the royal family that made him steal it, or maybe he intended to sell it someday. Unfortunately, for him, he died a few weeks after taking it and was never able to do anything with it. I never told you about it because I didn't know what to do with it either. I thought about giving it back to the church where it was before, but then I thought of selling it. Making a large amount of money began to obsess me to the point where I began to search for someone who would help me. And that's what happened. I sold it."

"Why didn't you tell me?" Maria asked.

"I wanted to protect you, and besides I didn't want you to tell me not to sell it, which I knew you would have," replied Bruno.

"Of course, I would have insisted you not sell it."

"Well, I did sell it. You remember a few months after Elena's wedding. I came home all excited with a *Tutto Lotto* ticket and claimed we won €400,000. Well, that €400,000 actually was the payoff for selling *La Sindone*."

"What about the lottery?" she asked.

"I never did win the lottery. I also never knew who got the Shroud. I have no way to get it back and making amends for what I have done," Bruno explained

"Is there anything we can do?" his wife asked while staring at him with her eyes filled with tears.

"No, there isn't. My only prayer is you forgive me; and the

Lord sees how sorry I am."

"Oh, Bruno," Maria sighed with tears beginning to fill her eyes.

"There is something else I need to tell you, *cara.*" Bruno added with his hands on hers and his eyes holding her gaze.

"What is it dear?"

"I've made a decision... I'm not going through chemo or radiation treatments anymore."

"Are you sure?" Maria said now beginning to cry.

"I've decided to allow nature to take its course. Why should I put myself, you and our family through the suffering," Bruno said.

"Bruno, I don't want to lose you," she sobbed as she held him close, her arms wrapped around his shoulders.

"My mind is made up. Please allow me to cherish the remaining time we have together."

Taking his hand gently, Bruno followed his wife up to bed. They never spoke of the matter again. They were both resigned to, and accepting of, the outcome of Bruno's choice.

Bruno worked for a telecommunications company as a bookkeeper. Perhaps because he worked around techies, he became fascinated with computers and loved learning about how they worked. He set up a small workbench in his cellar, where he would try to fix PC's. Sometimes the problems were hardware, so he would switch out components, but a lot of times he repaired corrupted software programs. He became known in his neighborhood as the "go-to-guy" with regards to home computers. This was before everything was done over the Internet, a time when you still bought software at a computer store, and it needed to be installed. He had the software for removing pretty much any computer virus.

One morning when Maria got up to go to work, she noticed Bruno never came to bed. Bruno's insomnia seemed to increase over time. Whether it was physical, due to his advancing disease or whether it was psychological, realizing he didn't have much time left, he found working on computers during the night became a way to pass those quiet hours. After she got dressed, Maria went out to the backyard, opened up the bulkhead door and yelled down to her husband in an aggravated manner, "Bruno, you need to get some rest. Go to bed!"

Bruno replied, "As soon as I finish downloading the software onto the Tosti's computer."

Still aggravated, she yelled, "Forget about that and get to bed—now!" She slammed the bulkhead door and stormed off to work.

When she got home that evening, she noticed the house was quiet. She also noticed the lights were still on. At first she thought Bruno had gone up to bed and forgotten to shut the lights. Walking gently up the stairs to see how he was doing, she noticed he had never been to bed. Realizing he still must be in the basement, she found herself even more upset with him, knowing he wasn't getting the rest he needed.

Going around to the backyard and opening up the bulkhead door, she yelled down to him, "Bruno, are you still down there?" There was no reply. She made her way down the short stairway into the cellar and noticed him lying on the floor in front of his bench. Shouting, "Oh my God!" She ran over to him. Bending over she noticed he was still alive but unconscious. She ran up into the house and called 112, Italy's emergency number. When the EMTs arrived, they went into the cellar to get Bruno. Maria had put a blanket over him and a pillow under his head. Several hours later, Bruno passed away never regaining consciousness. At the hospital with a few relatives, all Maria could think about was he had lain helpless on the floor probably for several hours. She regretted how her last words to him were angry ones.

A few weeks after Bruno's death, Maria decided to clean out her husband's computer repair work area. Buried under some of his computer manuals and magazines, she discovered the journal that had been her Uncle Sandro's. She decided even though she could not find who had taken the Shroud, she would at least let the Archbishop of Torino know what her husband had been involved in. She confided her secret to her closest girlfriend, Nella. Nella offered to accompany Maria to the Curia. So the two of them made the trip to see the Archbishop. Because he was unavailable, they were invited to meet with his secretary, Monsignor Pietro Scagnelli. They were escorted up to the Monsignor's office where they were cordially welcomed. Once they sat down, he offered them something to drink.

Signora Russo handed over her uncle's diary. She began telling Monsignor Scagnelli the story about how her husband discovered her uncle's trunk a few years back. She explained how upon the death of her uncle, his landlord gave her parents the trunk with very little explanation. She also explained that before the discovery of the journal, her family never knew about her uncle's career. Signora Russo told how, whenever her uncle came home on holiday, he never spoke about his work. In the end, the Monsignor found the story difficult to believe. He thanked the women for their kind visit and said he would study the journal make some investigations and be back to them as soon as possible.

For the next week Monsignor Scagnelli and a couple of his colleagues studied the journal to see if it was authentic. They had the handwriting studied by experts. They also discovered Alessandro Grassi truly was the private and personal aide of the King, during the period stated in the journal. Realizing the journal was authentic; they now came to believe the entries written in it were accurate and true.

To say the least, this caused a great stir in the Curia of Torino. There were a lot of conversations as to how they should handle this revelation, particularly how long they should attempt to keep it a secret from the public and the news media. They clearly realized it was only a matter of time before the story leaked out. They also knew they couldn't lie about it. They decided they needed to first prayerfully seek the Lord's guidance and wisdom. That was when Monsignor Pietro Scagnelli contacted his sister, Sister Grazia.

Chapter 23

While lying on the bed in my hotel room, I found it hard to sleep. I was still feeling the effects of jet lag and was still thinking about the events and conversation at the convent earlier that day. I also thought about how Dan was an accomplished private investigator before he retired. His time in the CIA certainly had given him extensive training. Soon I began to think, "What if he and I tried to find the Shroud? What if, after Ramiseto, we came back to Torino?"

"There's no way they would ever allow us in on their investigation," I thought to myself weighing the Pros and Cons.

"But, would it hurt to ask?" "Dan might not want to. Then again it might get his juices going." "I've got to get back home. But we could be helpful." After going over the possibilities of what might happen, I decided to call the convent. I wanted to speak with Sister Grazia to see if we could get in to visit with her brother before I headed for Milan in the morning.

I called the convent, "Pronto, Sisters of the Immaculate Heart of Mary Convent."

"Good evening, Sister. This is Marty Daniels, the one who installed your stained-glass earlier today."

"Oh yes, they are so beautiful."

"Well, thank you," I answered.

"How may I help you, Maestro Daniels?"

"May I speak with Sister Grazia?"

"Let me see if she is here in the convent."

It took about a minute, but then I heard the phone being picked up. "*Pronto, Sorella Grazia.*"

"Sister Grazia, I'm not sure if you saw me at the convent earlier today, but I am Martin Daniels, the craftsman from America who installed your stained-glass windows."

"Yes. Maestro Daniels, they are very beautiful. We are enjoying them very much. I'm sorry I didn't get to meet you. How may I help you?"

"The reason I'm calling is because I overheard your conversation with the Mother Superior just after lunch. I heard about why your brother the Monsignor called you."

"I am sorry. I hadn't realized we had guests. I was just so upset," she replied.

"You don't need to apologize. I want to help, and I think I may be able to," I said.

"You, help? How could you?" she asked.

"I can explain my reason why I think I can be of help to your brother. For now suffice it to say I have a friend visiting me here in Italy, who is a successful investigator from America. Is there a possibility you and Sister Bonny would take me to meet your brother, the Monsignor, at his office tomorrow morning?"

"I am willing to call and ask him if he would be available to meet with us, but I must ask Sister Bonny first," she said.

"Yes, I would like you to do that and call me back here on my cell phone."

"If she gives me permission, I will contact my brother and will ask Signor Gianni to drive us over there," she said.

"Please insist Signor Gianni first clean out his car. I don't want to have to hold his shovels again while driving through the streets of Torino," I said jokingly.

"Yes, we will make sure he cleans it out first," she replied with an obvious chuckle in her voice.

"Please, don't worry what time you call me."

"We will call you back. Buona sera," she said.

"Buona sera," I replied and hung up.

I decided to shower and get ready to go out and spend the evening with Massimo and Dani. It wasn't clear to me if Loretta would be joining us, but I hoped she would. Around

6:30 Massimo called saying he was on his way, and they would be by in about ten minutes.

I told him, "I'll be standing out in front of the hotel, so just drive up and give toot the horn. I'll jump in."

The evening was quite warm for mid May. Traffic in front of my hotel was fairly congested with evening commuters still trying to make their way home. I thought Massimo might have been optimistic thinking he'd get here by 6:45.

Several minutes later, I heard him beep and pull up in front of me. That evening we dined at his home with Dani and their thirteen year old daughter Alessia. Their apartment was on the eighth floor of a ten story apartment build in a section of the city where there was a forest of apartment buildings.

Alessia was all excited about the thought of getting teen magazines from America in English. She showed me a few of the ones she had. They looked just like ours and had English names like, 'Pop Star', 'Big Bop' and 'Teen Beat'. I noticed how many phrases contained English words too, but the articles were in Italian. She was trying to tell us about her latest infatuation. He was some member of a boy-band. I assured her I would make sure there were plenty of pictures of him and at least one interview of him telling his deepest secrets and love tips.

I noticed the table was only set for four, so I realized Loretta wouldn't be joining us for dinner. She did show up later for coffee.

It was not until after dinner I got a call back from Sister Bonny.

"We have spoken with Sister Grazia's brother," Sister Bonny said. "He was reluctant at first to let us come by to see him but later called back to say he decided to at least hear what you have to say."

"So you will be by to pick me up tomorrow morning?" I asked.

"Yes, we will. I'll call you in the morning."

"Very well. I look forward to meeting him."

In those few minutes, I couldn't help but reflect on how things were taking a new course. I thought I would be coming to Italy for a short week; a couple of days in Torino, a few more days up in Ramiseto visiting relatives, and my last couple of days visiting friends in Milan. Instead, something I had never dreamed possible has become the focus of my attention—*The Shroud of Turin.*

       *   *   *

At 8:45 Friday morning my cell phone rang. It was Sister Bonny.

"Maestro Daniels," she said, "Sister Grazia, Signor Gianni and I will pick you up in about a half hour."

"That will be great," I told her. "I'll be waiting on the sidewalk, so you won't have to park the car."

After checking out of the hotel, I went into the breakfast room for a quick bite to eat before heading out. As they pulled up, I noticed Sister Bonny was sitting in the front seat. Once they stopped, she opened the car door and climbed into the back seat with Sister Grazia.

"No, no!" I exclaimed. "Let me get into the back seat."

When I realized she wasn't willing to hear any of it, I finally acquiesced. Driving with Signor Gianni was always an adventure. He was doing his typical weaving in and out of traffic, and without using strong profanity, he let everybody know how much he didn't like the other drivers. He would comment how they either pulled out in front of him, cut him off, or did not drive fast enough for him. I thought to myself, "By the way he is driving; he must think we have four times the contingents of guardian angels on duty to protect our car." Our appointment was set for 10:00 that morning. We were early. Sister Bonny asked if I had had my morning coffee yet. I told her I grabbed a quick cappuccino and brioche in the breakfast room at the hotel, but I would not refuse another.

"I'm always happy to have a cappuccino," I said.

We went into a café-bar just outside the main entrance to the Curia. Once we were seated and enjoying our cappuccini, I wanted to make small talk so I said, "I'm reminded of the few times my wife has come with me to Italy. For her, if she doesn't have at least three cappuccini before 10:30, she is not satisfied.

It's almost comical," I continued. "Inevitably, when we travel to Italy, we stay with both sides of the family. She has her relatives about forty minutes north of Venice towards Trieste, where she was born. I have my relatives up in the Apennines above Reggio Emilia, which is where I'm going from here. Anyway, of course in the morning they always prepare our caffé and a brioche. Usually it is caffé-latte." About this time Signor Gianni grew fidgety and wanted to leave. He stood up from his seat and started pointing to his watch. Sister Bonny asked him to please allow me to finish. I continued, "As you can imagine, my wife thinks it would be very impolite to say, 'Can we have another?' So what she does is make the excuse that she wants to go for a walk around the village and enjoy the fresh morning air. However, she has only one thing in mind. She wants me to take her to the nearest café and have me get us another cappuccino or two," Sister Bonny laughed and said, "I too love Italy's coffee."

Chapter 24

The *Curia Arcivescovile di Torino* is on a narrow street. The building itself was plain stucco and very unimpressive considering where we were, at the headquarters of one of the most important Archdiocese in Italy. Walking into the Curia, we proceeded directly to the reception desk. The attendant gave us a friendly greeting, and made small talk with Sister Grazia, whom she knew. She told us Sister Grazia's brother had informed her to expect us and to send us right up to his office. As we arrived at his office, I noticed the name plate just outside the door: *Segretario dell'Arcivescovo di Torino Mons. Pietro Scagnelli.*

Our small entourage of four walked into the Monsignor's office, where we exchanged pleasantries. He appeared to be a mild-mannered man in his early forties. Like Sister Grazia, by his mannerisms, one could tell he had been raised in a refined family. I later found out that their ancestors were connected to the royal family that had ruled Ferrara, Italy back in the Middle Ages when Italy was broken up into city states. Presently their family owned a vineyard that produced a very expensive wine, and their father was an industrialist who owned a factory that made biscotti and pantone which was exported around the world.

Monsignor Scagnelli invited us all to sit down and offered us refreshments. Once we were served, he asked if we might first pray before we discussed our reason for meeting. Bowing his head, he made the sign of the cross and led us in "The Lord's Prayer." He then asked the Lord to bless the meeting and grant us wisdom and direction. I was struck by the humility of the man given the stature of his office. As we raised our heads, Monsignor Scagnelli said, "It is a pleasure to meet you, Maestro Daniels."

"Thank you, Monsignor. I'm very pleased to meet you."

"My dear sister informs me you have created four beautiful stained-glass windows and just installed them into their chapel at the convent."

"Yes, it was an honor to design and create the stained-glass for the sisters," I said.

"The American family that is paying for the restoration has been very generous to the nuns," the Monsignor added.

After a pause in which he looked up at a crucifix on his wall, the Monsignor said, "My sister has also told me you are interested in trying to help us find the Sacred Shroud."

"Yes, I think I might be able to help," I said, looking him straight in the eye.

He looked back at me and it seemed like he was trying to decide if I was right.

"Monsignor, when I left the States to come here to Italy for this trip, I never dreamed I would be sitting in your office today."

"Yes, I can imagine," Monsignor Scagnelli replied, nodding his head in agreement.

The Monsignor went on to explain how the Sacred Shroud had been owned by the House of Savoy, who ruled Italy until the end of the war. It had been in their family for hundreds of years. They originally came from France and kept the Shroud in a chapel in Chambrey, France. It was moved to Torino when St. Charles Borromeo, who was Archbishop of Milan during the middle of the 16th century, made a pilgrimage walking barefoot to the Holy Shroud. The barefoot trek was because during this time the "Black Plague" had spread throughout Milan. He promised the Lord he would make a pilgrimage to the Shroud if He, the Lord, would stop the plague, which at the time ravaged Milan, killing thousands throughout the city.

Although St. Borromeo was encouraged to flee the city because of the dreaded disease, he stayed and demanded his priests stay too, ministering Communion and the Last Rites to the sick. When the plague ended, in 1578, he believed the Lord heard their intercessions. To keep his vow to the Lord, he planned to walk from Milan to the chapel in France, as he had promised. The chapel in Chambrey, which is in the northeast part of France, was several hundred kilometers away and meant climbing over the Alps barefoot. It is said the royal family decided to move the Sacred Shroud closer to Torino so he would not have to walk so far. A more likely reason is they wanted it moved to Torino where the Savoy family was now living.

After listening to the story I said, "That's fascinating to think he would make such a sacrifice. Torino is about one hundred and fifty kilometers from Milan, so it was still quite a pilgrimage."

"Yes it was," the Monsignor agreed. Leaning slightly towards me he said, "My sister tells me you have a friend who is a successful investigator from America."

So I explained, "I believe my friend and I may be able to help. Shortly after leaving here this morning, I'm heading to Milan to meet up with a friend whose name is Dan Carlson. This friend of mine began his career working for the President in the White House. He went on to work for the CIA and eventually as a private investigator. I believe, because of his experience and training, he is uniquely equipped to investigate what has happened to the Shroud."

"Do you really believe you can help?" queried the Monsignor.

"I don't know how much we can help," I said, "But I'm willing to ask my friend."

Nodding and pondering the idea, the Monsignor said nothing.

"I'm hoping you will give us a week or so to see what we might come up with," I said. "Also, we may have an advantage because we're not Italian."

Still leaning back in his chair, pensively rubbing his chin and noticeably looking up at his crucifix on the wall he said, "You know, secrecy is a very difficult thing to maintain with a situation such as this. It is hard to find people you can trust. I'm very glad for your offer, and I can see an immediate advantage."

Sister Grazia, thinking she needed to help me said, "He made us such beautiful stained glass windows."

"I'm sure he did... You never know who will leak the story to a journalist, especially with regards to the Church," the Monsignor added.

"I never thought of that, but it is something to consider," I replied.

"Knowing we would be meeting, I first intended to discourage you from interfering. After all who are you? What makes me believe you could help with such an important task? I allowed this meeting mainly to please my sister."

"I certainly understand your reluctance," I said.

"Please wait a few minutes while I have my secretary make photocopies of Grassi's journal and personal papers, and also a copy of the report of our meeting with Signora Russo and our findings thus far."

After returning to his seat, he said, "We will continue with our investigations and I trust your inquiries will not hinder ours. Who knows perhaps you might find something out that will help us." I smiled in agreement and felt a leap of excitement inside.

As we waited for the photocopies, we chatted, mostly small talk. Monsignor Scagnelli wanted to know about my family. I told him about my wife back home, my children and grandchildren. I pulled out a photograph from my wallet and showed them a group shot of all of us on vacation on Cape Cod. He seemed quite pleased to see the size of my family and remarked what a blessing my family is in this day and age. He also wanted to know from Sister Bonny what was going on at the convent and some of the latest news. She didn't have a whole lot to say but informed him that the renovations were going well even if progressing slowly. After his secretary returned, Monsignor Scagnelli handed me a folder which had to be more than an inch thick. He said as he gave it to me, "Please be very discreet about this. I believe your friend knows how to keep secrets, and I trust you do too."

Chapter **25**

Once we left the Curia, Signor Gianni asked if he could first take the nuns back to the convent before bringing me to the train station. I agreed, in spite of the fact it meant driving through the city with him. I mainly agreed because I had time to kill anyway, and I enjoyed his colorful and animated company.

After dropping off the nuns at the convent, we headed first to the hotel to get my carry-on and the last crate. Next, we headed for Porta Nuova station. This time, Signor Gianni parked his car in a parking lot, probably because he wanted to spend some more time with me. We went directly over to the ticket counter, where I purchased my ticket. He asked if I'd like to get something at the bar and chat while I waited for my train. We made our way over to a café-bar at the end of the tracks. I decided I wanted an *arangiata,* which is an orange soda with pulp. While sitting at one of the tables in the bar my new friend asked me where the other stained glass window was going. I told him my grandmother's family came from an Apennine village above Reggio Emilia called Ramiseto. Just down the road from there is an even smaller village called Camporella. When signor Gianni heard the village's name he began to chuckle and asked, "Do you know what a camporella is in the Milanese slang?"

"What do you mean? It's the name of the village where this window is going."

"It also means to ahhh, to make love *nel campo al*

fresco." While telling me this he began to slide his left hand back and forth under his right hand in a sawing motion, a common vulgar gesture that has only one meaning. I had to laugh watching him with his facial expressions. I then thought to myself, "That's the last place Luiza would ever do it, out in the open, in a field."

Shortly after we finished our chat, it was time to say goodbye and get on the train. Even though our friendship had been short, I was surprised by his teary and sincere goodbye. I could tell he was sad I was leaving. He kissed me on both cheeks, all the while telling me he looked forward to the next time we would meet. I told him it probably would not be that long. I was sure I'd be back in Torino soon, hopefully with my wife. Mounting the train, I waved goodbye to my newly-found friend.

At 11:50 that morning the train pulled out of the station and we headed for Milan. The trip would take about two hours, and I would arrive about an hour before Dan's plane landed at Bergamo Airport. Settling in, I studied the landscape, which is one of my favorite pastimes when traveling on a train through Italy.

The Piedmont region is a particularly scenic region because it is the foothills to the Alps. The train traveled through the Po River Valley, a flat terrain perfect for agriculture which was apparent all along the way. There were poplar groves planted in perfectly even rows. Arborio rice patties, which when flooded, reflected the distant mountains and blue sky. The red poppies speckled the green hay fields for miles and miles. Beyond the flat cultivated land were meticulously terraced foothills where some of the best wines in Italy are produced. The majestic Alps rose up beyond the foothills. I sat on the port side of the train and on this clear day it gave me a magnificent view of the snow covered Alps.

As I gazed out my window, I reflected on the recent events: installing the stained glass windows in the convent, overhearing Sister Grazia's conversation, and then our meeting with her brother, Monsignor Scagnelli. I was feeling quite excited. It was a little too early to call Luiza and let her know about all that had transpired, and I could not wait to tell her. I was sure she would be excited too.

About half way into our trip, we pulled into the small city of Vercelli. My window faced the station, so I was able to watch passengers moving in and out of the station. There was a guy waiting on the platform with a small bunch of flowers in his hand. He was looking up and down obviously looking for someone. I assumed it would be his wife or lover. When he noticed her and walked over to her, I noticed they were for an elderly woman, I guessed his mother. Shortly after pulling out of the station, I went to the end of the car to where the exit doors were located to call Luiza. I didn't know if she would be awake, but I trusted she would have her cell phone near the bed. The phone rang four times before she answered, and immediately I realized she was still groggy by the way she said, "Hello."

Trying to be funny, I said, "Were you afraid it was a tele-marketer?"

"I'm not in the mood for jokes… I was in the bathroom."

"Sorry about that. I'll try not to call so early"

"I wish you would," she said sounding like she was scolding but really only kidding in her still sleepy voice.

"Luiza, I can't wait to tell you the exciting news."

"What would be so important you have to call me this early? Couldn't it wait a couple more hours?"

"No, it couldn't. I'm too excited. You remember I told you about what I heard Sister Grazia say to Sister Bonny and how they just had found out the real Shroud of Turin is missing?"

"Yes, did you find out you were wrong about Sister Grazia?" Luiza asked.

"No, no, it really was stolen. In fact, this morning we went over to the Archbishop's office and spoke to her brother, Monsignor Sgagnelli," I said excitedly. "Last night after I spoke to you, I called Sister Grazia. I had this *amazing* idea. Since Dan , who is an experienced investigator, is on his way to meet me, why not see if the two of us could find out what might have happened to the Shroud?"

While waiting for Luiza's response I stared out the train door's window. We were passing a large vineyard that had its rows perpendicular to the train tracks and as we passed, the patterns it formed fascinated and amused me.

After a seemingly long silence I heard Luiza say, "Oh my God... did I just hear you say what I think you said?"

"What do you mean?" I asked, surprised by her tone.

"Did I just hear you say you intend to get Dan to help find the Shroud?"

"Yes, why?' I asked with confusion.

"Are you crazy?" she squealed.

"Why do you say that?"

"Just who do you think you are? Magnum PI?" she asked, now wide awake.

"Why? I thought you would be excited for me. I couldn't wait to tell you," I said defensively.

"Excited for you?" she said, raising her voice, making it a question. "Why would you think that? Aside from the fact you could get yourself into serious trouble, you have to be home. There's work waiting for you in the studio...Marty, are you out of your mind?"

"Please sweetheart. Don't get upset with me. I would really like to try to help," I said pleading with her. "You wait and see. I'm sure Dan has a few tricks up his sleeves."

After another pause Luiza mocked, "Yeah, Dan may have tricks up his sleeve, but you have a few bats in your belfry."

Realizing she would not be convinced, I said, "I am going to have to go now. I'll be in touch... I miss you."

"Yeah, right...And now I'm supposed to go back to sleep thinking of you and Dan running around Italy playing Batman and Robin...saving the world from evil villains?"

"Luiza, please don't be upset with me," I pleaded.

"Alright, see you later, Boy Wonder," was her goodbye.

After I returned to my seat, I thought to myself, "Why is it a wife's gift, or better yet divine calling--to always rain on her husband's parade and try to ruin his bright ideas?"

Chapter 26

Settling in to gaze out the window again, I could not get my mind off meeting Dan. I thought it probably would be best for us to rent a car, since I was no longer heading up to the relatives alone. I didn't want to put a burden on them.

Dan Carlson came into my life because our wives had been friends. They met at a gym, where they exercised a few times a week. It was a gym for women only. I think it might have been called "Swerves" but we jokingly would say, "It's where the Battle of the Bulge is fought". Because my wife enjoyed Darla's company, the four of us would occasionally get together. The several times we had been with them socially, usually for dinner and cards, Dan had been always very congenial, full of stories and jokes. One of the stories he told us was how he went to Ripon College in Wisconsin and that Harrison Ford was his classmate. Bragging, he would add how he would beat him at cribbage.

However, the truth was you never learned anything revealing about his private life. He had that way of deflecting the spot light off himself if you tried to get too close. Another thing he liked to do (especially when he had a little too much wine) was take on the role of investigator. He would ask probing questions, trying to dig into your private affairs, prying for some juicy tidbits. Often times I would be aggravated with myself the next morning because I had fallen into his trap and pretty much told him anything he asked. When I reflected on the previous evening's events, I understood how women feel, who give into the guy they met the night before. I had no one to blame but myself. I called it – "the mourning of regret."

And then there was Darla, caring, compassionate and sincere. She wanted to know about you, but not like her husband. Her reason for asking questions about you was because she genuinely cared. In fact, I never quite understood their relationship. First there was their age difference. Dan was considerably older than Darla. How they met, I'm not really sure, but she certainly did love him. Dan Carlson was in his mid-sixties. He was an active and vigorous guy. Darla was also fit and trim. Not the most attractive woman, but then her warm personality made her pleasant to be around.

When he graduated from college, he went into the Army, where after a series of aptitude tests, an opportunity to learn Russian was given to him. Because of his gift for languages and a secretive personality, the Military saw he had potential. They sent him to study Russian at the Presidio in Monterey, California. Later he was assigned to the White House communications staff, where for eight hours a day he would sit and wait for the Russians to call. After his tour of duty with the military and the White House, he put his military training to use and became a gun for hire after seeing a small ad in the back of "Soldier of Fortune" magazine. His time as a mercenary was never discussed. I always assumed he was involved with something illegal. Wanting to marry Darla, he had to accept a more normal life. He used his clever ability and training to open a private investigation office in Worcester, Massachusetts, working along with Ted Casey, his partner.

Ted and Dan had a close friendship. Perhaps Ted was Dan's only true friend. Dan would tell stories that included Ted's role. Like situations they would find themselves in while on a "Domestic" (the term Dan used to describe checking on a spouse), or investigating corporate espionage. His favorite stories involved being hired to check out a company's security. At times, they would be hired to break into a secured building and prove they had gotten inside of it. What they usually would do when they had broken in was take photos as proof they had gotten inside. They would also hide little blue sticky dots in various places. Then they would give a list to the client of where to find the dots. Dan really liked to tell the story about the time he and his partner were hired to check out the security at a Fortune 500 Company. They got themselves past the security guards, made their way into the president's office and planted the blue stickers in several places. To add insult to injury, Ted decided to steal the president's computer off his desk. Dan told us the security guard unknowingly held the door for him while he exited the building.

*   *   *

Pulling into Novara, I thought it best to call Renato. Renato and Luigi Bronzoni are brothers and are two of my second cousins. As young men they studied electrical engineering and together they formed a successful company that manufactures custom electric motors. Over the years I've become close to them. Because of their generosity towards me when I've visited the area my mother's family originated from, I stay with one of them. I called Renato at work to give him a heads up. The office phone rang a few times before I heard a woman's voice say, *"Pronto, Bronzoni Motori Electrici."*

"Angela?" I asked. Angela is the office manager and Luigi's daughter.

"Yes, ciao Marty. Where are you?" Angela asked.

"I am on the train from Torino to Milan. I should be arriving in less than an hour."

"So, will we see you later today?"

"Yes, you will. May I please speak to Renato?"

"Don Luca came by asking if we had heard from you," Angela informed me.

"Let him know I made it, and I have his window."

"Okay, I will. I'll switch you to Renato now."

After waiting about a minute, Renato picked up.

"Allora, come andiamo?" he asked, wanting to know how things were going.

"Ciao, Renato, I'm on the train for Milan. I will be arriving there in less than an hour, so I should be seeing you this evening."

"Do you know about what time you should be arriving in Reggio?" Renato asked.

"No, I don't know, but you won't need to get me at the station. I have decided to rent a car. I will drive directly to Ramiseto. Also, I will have a friend from the US with me. I will be meeting him in Milan, and he wants to come with me to meet my relatives."

"Who is this friend?" Renato asked.

"His name is Dan Carlson. He's a friend from home. He happened to be traveling here in Europe and decided to come and meet me. You will like him, although he doesn't speak Italian," I said.

"I will have Anna prepare a room for him," Renato replied.

"No, no, you don't have to worry about him. He would prefer to stay at Iole's Hotel. In fact would you call Iole's and let them know?" I asked.

"Sure. Call me later so I'll know if you will be here for dinner," Renato requested.

"Yes, of course. I look forward to seeing you all," I said. With that, I ended the call and sat back in my seat and thought about arriving in Milan.

Chapter *27*

Since I had to wait for Dan, I thought I'd try to see if Mariano might be around and perhaps he could meet me at the station. Mariano Cavenago is an old friend who dates back to the time when I worked at the stained glass studio in Milan. He's the one who taught me how to cut glass and assemble windows when I apprenticed there. He also taught me how to swear in Italian—like *perla, catzo* or *stronzo*. I could swear in the Milanese dialect before I could put a proper sentence together. When I first started working there I spoke very little Italian, so I would say I primarily learned Italian from Mariano, whose work bench was next to mine for almost four years. Of course I taught him to swear in English too.

This time I decided not to be as polite as before by getting out of my seat to stand near the exit doors and make the call since no one else went out to a more private spot. I called Mariano and told him I'd like to see him today rather than Monday, if he was available. He said he happened to be in the city and would love to see me. He let me know he'd be waiting for me at the end of the track.

One good remnant of Mussolini's reign was he organized the train system in Italy and it is fairly punctual still. When we arrived I made my way to the end of the track where Mariano was waiting. We both were excited to see each other and gave each other "manly" kisses on both cheeks and didn't feign it like women do. After our greetings, I told Mariano I had a couple of hours before a friend would arrive here from Bergamo Airport. I explained who Dan was and how I came to be meeting up with him. Mariano was interested and said, "I want to meet him. In fact why don't we go pick him up at the airport?"

"Could we? How far is it?"

"It's just off the Autostrada-A4 for Venice about a half hour from here," he said.

"I also need to rent a car. Will you help me?" I asked.

"Of course. There are a number of rental companies right down at the front of the train station," Mariano reminded me.

So that's what we did. After taking care of the rental, we headed off for the airport. While on route, I texted Dan to call me ASAP.

As usual, the traffic in Milan was heavy and aggressive. Italians have their own style of driving. I see it as a dance. If you know how to dance together things can flow pretty well, but if you don't, it can create a bottleneck and can be scary. Just as we were about to arrive at the airport Dan called to say he got my text.

"I'm waiting for them to pull up to the gate. I only have a carry-on." Dan said.

I told him to exit the terminal and wait for me on the sidewalk. As it turned out we got there before Dan, so Mariano dropped me off outside the arrival door and said, "I'll wait in my car and if necessary drive around the airport and hopefully catch you here, back at this spot."

Entering the terminal, I looked up at the monitors for arrivals from Amsterdam. Dan's plane landed a several minutes before so I began to make my way over to where I expected him to come out. Bergamo's airport is not large, but it is a busy one. People were rushing about everywhere, except those confused travelers looking for their check-in counter or the exit. After a few minutes I saw Dan. I yelled and waved to get his attention. He was grateful he didn't have to wait for me. I told him that a friend was outside waiting for us. We made our way out to the sidewalk. However, Mariano was forced to do a go-around, but got back to us within a couple of minutes. Once Mariano pulled over to the curb he popped his trunk before he came to a full stop. We threw Dan's carry-on into the trunk and jumped in. I gave Dan the shotgun seat and climbed into the back.

Mariano stuck out his right hand to Dan and said in English but with a very heavy accent, "How do you do. I am pleased to meet you."

Dan with surprise in his voice said, "Well, I'm doing fine. Oh, so you speak English. That's great!" Mariano quickly replied while waving his hand back and forth, "No, no. I no speak English." We laughed and after the introductions, Dan explained his disastrous meeting with Darla's family. He was glad that he could visit Italy and get his mind off that encounter. Mariano asked if there was anything in particular Dan might like to see while in Milan. Mariano suggested going into the center where Il Duomo, La Galleria, and alla Scalla Opera House were located.

Without skipping a beat Dan said, "Oh yes, I would like to see where they hung Mussolini and his girlfriend." I could tell by Dan's quick response he had been thinking about it before now.

"*Allora, andiamo a Piazza Loreto,*" was Mariano's only replied, which affirm he would go see Piazza Loreto.

Even though on a city map Piazza Loreto didn't look that far from the airport, it still took us more than an hour to get there. On the way, Mariano explained why they brought Mussolini and his compadres to Piazza Loreto. It was because that was where the Partisans had been executed. In fact, in Piazza Loreto there is a monument to the Partisans, but no acknowledgment of Mussolini.

In typical Milanese fashion, Mariano found a spot to park up on the sidewalk. In Milan, because of the narrow streets and general traffic congestion, it's permitted to even park up onto the sidewalks. As we walked over to Vialle Andrea Doria, Mariano pointed out where the Esso gas station used to be. That was where they hung the already dead bodies of Mussolini, Clara Petacci, and several of Mussolini's cohorts upside down in April 1945. Being a World War II history buff, Dan was thrilled to see this place from the past that he had read about.

After we visited Piazza Loreto, Dan, Mariano, and I made our way over to Stazione Centrale where we picked up the rental car. Before we left Milan, Mariano wanted to sit down at a bar with outside tables and have an afternoon aperitif. He suggested we have a Campari and soda. Along with our aperitifs, the waiter brought out some potato chips to munch on. Dan wanted to chat about seeing Piazza Loreto and about how Hitler had rescued Mussolini from a mountaintop resort with a glider. He told us that apparently the German agents were able to get Mussolini into a glider and sail it off the mountain to safety.

He then told Mariano and me a joke he had recently heard which I tried to translate as best I could. The joke went more or less like this: "There was this pair of elderly twins who happened to be the oldest set of twins in the city and, being their birthday, the local newspaper wanted to do a story on them. So they sent a reporter and photographer over to their house. Unfortunately, the older sister was hard of hearing and so she would always ask her sister, 'What did they say?' and after she got the reply inevitably she would say, 'Oh, I see.' When the reporter and photographer arrived at the house, they politely introduced themselves, explained why they were there and asked if they might come in to interview them. Well, as usual the deaf sister asked, 'What did he say?' and her sister replied, 'They want to come in.' 'Oh, I see,' the deaf sister replied. Sitting down in the living room, the reporter said that they'd like to take a picture of them before they do the interview. He then went on to explain that the photographer must first take out his camera, and focus it. Well again the deaf sister asked, 'What did he say?' Her sister's only reply was, 'First he wants to focus.' The older sister with surprise in her voice asked, 'Why does he want to poke us?'" Because focus, *focale* and poke us, *colpirle* didn't translate well, it turned out to be one of those jokes that perhaps are better left untold. No matter how I tried, I was unable to translate the joke effectively to Mariano without a long explanation ruining the punch-line. Mariano's only reply afterwards was a quiet, "*Ora capisco*," letting us know he now understood. Dan and I found Mariano's confused reply funnier than the actual joke.

Chapter 28

It was about six before we hit the road for Ramiseto. I gave Renato a quick call to let him know, we probably would be rolling into Ramiseto around 8:30. He said they would have dinner waiting for us and he had already contacted the hotel and reserved a room for Dan. Because it was a Friday evening, a lot of people were leaving the city and heading for their weekend retreats. The traffic on the ramp to A1 Autostrada was heavy. Eventually, I slipped in my credit card to pay the toll, and we were on our way.

It had been a while since Dan and I had been together and we had some catching up to do. Before Darla's tragic death, we had seen each other occasionally. Dan went on to explain the hours he had sat at home alone brooding over what had happened. He expressed his bitterness, especially towards God for having stolen the best thing that ever had happened to him. In my response, I tried to explain that what had happened to Darla was not the Lord's fault. The fact is that there is evil in this world. Our enemy is God's enemy and he was out to destroy us, God's beloved creation. The very ones the Lord loves the most--mankind. I also tried to express that this evil entity always blames his doings on the Lord. It's a typical tactic of those who involve themselves in lies and deception. Dan understood about deceptive practices. The last thing I offered was, "This lie you believe to be true, has you running from the very one who desires to help you." I'm not sure Dan liked my point, because his reaction seemed to be less than positive. He expressed his belief that it's impossible to know what's beyond our five senses anyway. He basically went on to explain how he was trying to move on and get his life back on track. He had hoped this trip to Europe would have brought closure--whatever closure means. Not knowing how to reply, we basically drove in silence for a good stretch.

After awhile, I started telling him about what had happened in Torino while I was installing the stained-glass windows in the convent. I also told him my subsequent conversation with Monsignor Scagnelli at his office. Dan was pensively quiet and just nodded his head a few times. I told him about the folder Monsignor Scagnelli gave me.

"At some point I want to show it to you and review its contents. I'd like to know if you'd be interested in helping me search for the Shroud of Turin," I said.

"We'll see," was Dan's only reply.

For the past couple of years Dan Carlson had been a widower, after his wife Darla's horrific car accident. The reason for the accident was because Denis Ryan wanted to kill her because of her husband, Dan. Dan had been hired to see if the popular business owner named Denis Ryan was cheating on his wife. Dan did the usual surveillances, waited until Ryan would leave his office for lunch, follow him and record his activities. After work he'd follow him to see if he went directly home or to some rendezvous.

"It's amazing how easy it is to catch these arrogant executives, who think their above suspicion," Dan would say.

Once Ryan's wife got the report on her husband's extra marital activities, she divorced him. Dan's compelling evidence helped Ryan's wife get pretty much everything she demanded, which cost him his business. In a state of anger, despair, and revenge, Ryan decided to settle the score because he lost everything in the divorce. He devised a plan to get back at Dan. He wanted to ruin the life of the man he believed had ruined his –Dan Carlson.

Ryan became aware of Dan's devotion to his wife; first he observed how the two of them sat in the courtroom during his contentious divorce. Darla would often accompany Dan to court to help pass the tedious hours spent waiting for the case to unfold. Ryan stalked Darla for a couple of weeks and discovered she went to the gym three times a week. She would drive a stretch on Rt. 146, the highway that connects Worcester, MA to Providence, RI. It took her between Uxbridge and Northbridge to get to the gym. On this particular Monday morning, about 9:35, Darla was driving home southbound on146 towards Uxbridge. Ryan timed his travel so that as she was about to cross over the Mill St. Bridge, he rammed her Mazda convertible at about 90 miles an hour, pushing her first and then himself over the flimsy guardrail. Both vehicles landed on the street below which created an explosion, killing them both. Darla's wake at the local funeral home was closed casket and so was Dan's life thereafter.

Chapter 29

Finally, we arrived at the Reggio Emilia exit. We made our way through the city to the street that would eventually get us up into the mountains and finally to Ramiseto. Whenever I pass through Reggio Emilia, I have to travel down Vialle Umberto I, which takes me past the very spot where my mother spent her time in boarding school, while her parents were settling in America. I always think back to the stories my mom would tell us about those days and her friend Tamira Grappelli.

Seeing the signs for SS-63 (Strada Statale #63) and *Passo di Cerreto*, I knew we were on the right road. It took us about another half hour to get from Reggio to Castelnovo ne Monti, a small city in the middle of the Apennines. Passing through Castelnovo, I pointed out a unique rock formation to Dan. From a particular angle, it has a sheer cliff face that juts up perpendicular to the ground and is quite tall and steep. It's called *Pietra di Bismantova* and is actually mentioned in Dante's *Divine Comedy*.

I told Dan, "I have a dream that someday I'll have a house in Ramiseto that will have a view of Bismantova. I have already picked out my piece of property. I'll show it to you."

Again we drove a few minutes in silence trying to get glimpses of Bismantova. At a certain point I began to explain how Bismantova was instrumental in bringing me back to Christ.

Dan didn't react. I wasn't sure if he missed my comment or purposely ignored it. I thought he'd show more interest, since he did like to hear about personal stuff. He already knew about the car accident I had had which ended my time in Italy as a young man. He more or less had known the details of the accident. I told him how I was driving two friends back to their home, and we were fooling around a bit and trying to take the curves in the mountain roads as fast as we could. Unfortunately at one point I hugged the curve so close that the left front tire went into the dirt on the inside of the curve, somehow causing the car to flip up on its passenger side, slide across the road, and then smash into the stone wall on the steep side of the road. I was the only one hurt in the accident, and it required an ambulance to come up into the mountain pass to retrieve me. It took the ambulance about 40 minutes to finally get to my location, which at the time seemed like an eternity. They brought me to the emergency room in the small hospital here in Castelnovo ne Monti. Right outside my hospital window was Bismantova. Lying there in my hospital bed, I had time to reflect on how my fooling around nearly cost me and my companions our lives, and how the stone wall rather than a guardrail, most likely spared our lives. I thought of where I was spiritually at that time. I tried to explain to Dan how the accident changed the course of my life, but by his contentious comments, I realized he was in no mood for me to continue, so I dropped the subject.

It was actually close to nine by the time we finally pulled up to Renato's house. He and his wife, Anna, were excited to see us. We were welcomed in and quickly invited to sit down for dinner. They had waited for us, and I could see they wanted to eat. After we washed up, we sat down to a dish of tortellini al' ragù or Bolognese sauce. The second course was *manzo bollito con vedure*, which is basically a boiled meaty beef bone with vegetables. It was all very tasty, especially considering how hungry I was. After dinner we had a nice visit, and later I took Dan up to Iole's Hotel to check-in.

The next morning, after breakfast, I took the folder given to me by Monsignor Scagnelli and went up to visit Dan at the hotel. He was in the bar having cappuccino and brioche. I asked him if he wanted to review the file with me. Because it was all in Italian, it took me a while to translate. For an hour or more we worked our way through a lot of the documents. He found the file interesting and thought we might be able to make some headway, especially if we had an opportunity to speak with Signora Maria Russo, the widow of the man who sold the Shroud. Dan also noticed she claimed she had no idea what her husband's activities might have been. He thought that visiting her could point us in the right direction. However, for the time being, we needed to install my last stained-glass window at the church in Camporella. I explained to Dan how Gianni the caretaker at the convent had told me the word camporella means "Doing it in a field." in Italian slang. We laughed as I showed Dan the gesture he made. Never to be outdone, Dan's reply was, "Darla and I had a few camporellas on occasion."

I think we were on our third cappuccino when Signor Luigi Viappiani came into the bar. Viappiani was an elderly gentleman who had to be in his mid-80s, a retired Captain of Italy's Carabinieri. He had stopped by Renato's looking for us and was told that I was up at the hotel with a friend from America. Signor Viappiani was a self-taught artisan in wood, whose carvings truly are amazing. For example, several years ago when my wife and I brought the stained-glass windows to the parish church there in Ramiseto, he gave us a gift of a carved wooden bowl done in a basket weave pattern. The bowl was made out of one solid piece of walnut wood, an incredible piece of art which we still treasure today.

Viappiani had fabricated the wooden window frame for the church in Camporella, and he wanted to accompany us to help install the window. Since we didn't want to all be crammed into his tiny Italian car, we followed him and his little dog Tomi over to the church.

Chapter 30

When we arrived at Camporella, we found the church locked, and nobody around, so we tried to figure out a way to break into the church. The retired Carabinieri Captain had no problem with breaking and entering into a locked church, something I found amusing. When I mentioned it to Dan, he just rolled his eyes and grinned. Eventually, we found an elderly woman down the hill in the village who kept a set of keys to the church. Once in the church, we then realized we needed a ladder to get up to where the window was to be installed. It was directly above the front entrance of this small country church. The front doors were arched shaped and at the top mid-point was easily eight and a half feet tall. Then above that was probably another two feet of wall to the window above. Furthermore, the window ledge was approximately 18 inches deep. The church was made out of fieldstone and covered with unpainted stucco. We searched around the village for anyone who had a ladder, hoping it would be at least 12 feet tall. To our disappointment we couldn't find a single person with a ladder.

Standing just inside the church, staring up at the window wondering what to do, Dan came up with a solution. He noticed the confessional was just to the left of the entrance door. He suggested we get a couple of chairs, and climb up onto the top of the confessional. Then I could shimmy up his back, stand on his shoulders and climb into the window well. He felt confident he would get me high enough to be able to crouch into this small window well that was about 2 1/2 feet wide and no more than 4 feet tall. Being the adventurous type, it sounded like a good idea. After all, we didn't want to drive all the way back to Ramiseto to get a ladder because that would've taken about 30 minutes to make the round trip.

We both got up on top of the confessional and I started working my way up Dan's back who by this time was resting his arms and head against the wall. While trying to maneuver myself up into the window well, Dan had to reposition his feet to get a better stance. So he stepped with his left foot over onto the middle of the confessional, which turned out to be an 1/8th inch piece of veneer plywood. Being too thin to hold us, his foot broke through the roof of the confessional, and the two of us almost went tumbling down into it. Fortunately he was able to catch himself. Reflecting on what it must've looked like, I saw visions of Charlie Chaplin and his numerous self-inflicted disasters. Or better yet, "The Three Stooges." Only instead of Moe, Larry, and Curly, it was Luigi, Dan, and Marty. Without any further incidents, we were able to successfully get the stained-glass panels into the window and head back to Ramiseto.

That evening Dan and I were invited to Signor Viappiani's home for dinner. Dan was noticeably impressed with Viappiani's wood carvings as we took a tour through his wood shop and then up the flight of stairs into their home above. The evening was filled with delicious home cooked food, local wine, and lots of laughs. Of course, I had to be the interpreter for Dan. Viappiani and his wife, Adda, would tell a story or ask a question. Dan, wanting to be in on the conversation, would inevitably ask, "What did they say?" It was halfway through the evening when I turned to Dan and said, "I feel like a twin sister" in a voice like an elderly spinster. Dan didn't care for my comment.

The next day was Sunday and a special Mass was to be held at 11, followed by a luncheon at a local Trattoria. Camporella is a tiny village, which in the summer months swells to 3 to 4 times its population. This is not uncommon for the small villages peppered throughout the Apennine Mountains. Due to a lack of work opportunity, many young people have to leave their village and head for the cities where work can be found. During the summer months, when the cities are hot and uncomfortable, they make the trek to the mountains to escape the heat on Friday afternoon. Italy has a tradition going back to the Romans of taking the month of August off, known as *Ferragosto*. So during the month of August, these villages fill with friends, neighbors and relatives returning to their hometowns to escape the heat. It was mid-May when we were there, so the village was still relatively uninhabited.

Nevertheless, this particular Sunday Mass, included a dedication of the church's new stained glass window. The small village church was quite full. I was pleased Dan attended the Mass, and he actually seemed to somewhat enjoy it. After the service, we headed down the path to the village where there was a small bed and breakfast that had a Trattoria. As it turned out Don Luca, the pastor of the village invited anyone who wanted to come for lunch. There probably were about 30 people who joined us. Being the guests of honor, Dan and I sat at the head table with Don Luca, Don Giancarlo, another visiting priest, and a few of my relatives. The luncheon started at about 12:30. The meal began with platters of antipastos which were brought out one at a time. Then the first course came, which consisted of three different types of home-made pastas: tortellini, ravioli, and tagliatelli. Each prepared with a different sauce. These were also brought out one at a time for us to savor. Eventually, the main course appeared which was roast rabbit and rolled stuffed pork. The meats were served with small roasted potatoes delicately seasoned with fresh rosemary. Then, bowls of fruit and a variety of local cheeses emerged and lastly, a beautiful assortment of desserts. In Italy, no meal is complete without the region's own wine. This banquet was served with a different wine for each course. Suffice to say, we sat down at 12:30 and by the time we were getting ready to head home, the clock in the room was showing 6:15. Still today when Dan and I get together he reminds us of that day.

Chapter 31

The following morning it was time to head back to Torino. After breakfast at Renato and Anna's, I said my goodbyes and drove up to the hotel to pick up Dan. As I winded my way up the narrow, curvy road to Iole's Hotel, I couldn't help but smell the fresh mountain air. On this still cool morning, it was invigorating. You could already tell it would be a beautiful spring day by the wispy clouds being blown over the still snow covered top of *Monte Ventasso,* one of the highest peaks in the Apennine mountain range.

I found him in the hotel's café-bar trying to pay his bill and communicate with the elderly woman behind the cash register. He still had his credit card in his hand when I walked in. He thought the woman was telling him they don't take plastic. But what she was really telling him was the hotel bill had already been paid by Don Luca. Once Dan realized his bill was paid, he was even more confused. Why would Don Luca pay his bill? Dan hadn't realized it was Don Luca's way of thanking me for the new stained glass window. My only comment was, "They must have liked your jokes at the luncheon yesterday." Dan agreed that was probably why. It seemed to satisfy him, so we were off to head back to Torino.

*   *   *

I noticed the signs for the next *Autogrill*, an Italian rest stop. Since I was thirsty and had to use the men's room, I decided to pull in. While I coasted into a parking space, Dan, who had been snoozing, woke up and asked where we were.

"We're about sixty miles from Torino... I'm going to make a pit stop; how about you?" I asked.

"No, I'm ok."

"You want anything while I'm in there?"

"Yeah, get me a ginger ale or a Sprite, something like that," he replied.

After using the men's room, I grabbed a can of Sprite and for me a *mezza minerale frizzante*. As I approached the car, I found Dan leaning against the back hood. Feeling refreshed, he asked me if he could drive the rest of the way to Torino.

"Sure why not," I said. "I know you like to drive."

Once we pulled out of the *Autogrill* parking lot I told Dan about Loretta and how I'd like to see her later. I also discussed with Dan how much I should tell her, since it is confidential info. Being very secretive by nature, he thought we should say nothing and just tell her we came back to Torino because he wanted to visit the city, having heard about how interesting is. I told him I'm not good at lying and I don't think I could keep a straight face. I added that Loretta might be able to help us with the investigation. When Dan asked how, I was unable to give him a good answer, except to say I think she should know.

A few minutes later I picked up my cell phone and called Loretta at her office.

"*Pronto, buongiorno, Sancarlo Viaggi.*" I recognized her voice on the phone.

"*Ciao Loretta, sono Marty.*"

"*Ciao Marty, dove sei?*"

"*Siamo sull' autostrada A21 fuori Asti,*" I replied. My answer informed Loretta we were just outside of Asti.

"Why? I thought today you'd be in Milan getting ready to head home."

"Something has come up and I'm going to be a few more days here in Italy."

At that point I began to tell Loretta what happened from when I was installing the stained-glass at the convent to why we're on the highway for Torino. Her only replies were, "I see, mamma mia, that's unbelievable."

"Where can we meet you later?" I asked her.

"Meet me at my flat? I should be there by 6:00," she

said.

"Loretta, my friend Dan and I want to go to Roletto first. It's a small town outside of Pinerolo," I told her.

"Why would you want to go there?" she asked.

"I'll explain it all this evening, but for now can you tell me how to get there?"

"To get to Pinerolo you take the A55 exit off the Tangenziale Sud. There will be an exit sign. It is less than an hour southwest of the city," she replied.

"*Va bene, Ci vediamo sta sera,*" I said.

"*Ciao*"—"*ciao.*"

We were not much farther down the road when I leaned over to catch a glimpse of the speedometer – 155, almost 100mph. I realized that Dan not only liked to drive, but he liked to drive fast. When he noticed me leaning over, he turned to me with a grin and said, "No Staties."

Soon we exited the autostrada, headed for the toll plaza and onto the Tangenziale, which is what they call the highway that wraps around the city. Loretta was right. In about a half hour, we were in Pinerolo. We decided to stop and eat, since it was after one o'clock. We noticed a small restaurant shortly after entering the small city. The place was a small, working-class Trattoria and only had about 10 customers eating lunch. Finding a small table off in a corner, Dan and I sat down and were soon greeted by our waitress. Handing us a photocopy of their handwritten daily menu, all she said was "*Da bere signore?*" asking us what we wanted to drink. I suggested we get a half carafe of local red wine and a half bottle of mineral water-frizzante, which Dan agreed to, so I ordered, "*Una mezza rosso e una mezza frizante,*" letting her know we want half carafes of red wine and mineral water.

Ordering local wines in a trattoria or restaurant is simple and preferable. Almost always a trattoria and usually a restaurant have local wine sold in carafes. The wine comes from local producers and is drawn out of a *damigiana,* which is a glass jug about fifteen gallons and usually wrapped in an enclosed basket. The wine is always fresh, good and has no preservatives added. Although Americans think that Tuscany is the region where the best Italian wines are produce, many Italians will say the Piedmont region is truly the better region. I told Dan that I wouldn't dispute that opinion. The local wine we were served was called *Dolcetto d'Alba,* a dry red wine with lower acidity and fruity flavor. Dan was amazed how good it was and wanted to order another half carafe. I stopped him saying we can't sit here all afternoon.

Since we didn't want to spend too much time eating, we asked the waitress to bring us a plate of spaghetti *al pomodoro* and a plate of sliced salami. She had already placed a basket of rolls on our table.

After lunch, while paying the cashier, we asked her if she could direct us to Roletto. According to the information Monsignor Scagnelli had given us, Signora Russo lived on via Costa no.86. We got to the piazza in the center of town, which had a Catholic Church on one side and the town hall on the other. There on the side of a building was a street sign, a slab of white marble indicating via Costa. The Russo house had a galvanized gate that was open and a short driveway that led to the house. We pulled up into the driveway and walked up to the front door and rang the bell. Nobody answered. As we walked back down the driveway to the street, we noticed a woman coming towards us carrying some groceries. I approached her and asked if she knew Signora Russo and where I might find her. She told me she was one of the administrators who worked in the elementary school which was just back down the road towards the center of town. I thanked her. We decided to leave the car in the driveway.

When we arrived at the school, we asked a woman we met near the main entrance, where we might find Signora Russo. She pointed to a side room down the corridor. Signora Russo, a dark haired woman, neatly attired and attractive, was in the office talking to one of the young students. As soon as she was through, I introduced Dan and myself and asked if we might speak with her privately. Perhaps because she picked up on my accent and the fact that my companion didn't look very Italian, she asked, with a puzzled expression, "And how may I help you gentlemen?"

We followed her into a conference room which had a large table surrounded by several chairs. She sat at one end with her back to the window, and we decided to take the two chairs across from her. I asked her if our conversation would be kept private. She assured us she would do her best.

"Signora Russo," I started. "We have been asked by Monsignor Scagnelli to investigate the matter of the stolen Shroud and its disappearance." I explained who we were and how even though we were not Italian; we had been asked to investigate. I further explained to her how my friend Dan didn't speak any Italian, but was an accomplished private investigator. Her distraught look was obvious, realizing it was her husband and family who were responsible. She told us she had no idea what her husband might've done with the Shroud because he never disclosed his actions to her. He told her he believed it was gone forever and there was nothing they could do about it. She further expressed how she still was getting over her husband's death and had been missing him terribly, especially lately. We asked if she knew if her husband had any ties with the black market. She said she wasn't sure of that. I asked where he had worked at the time he found the Shroud.

She told us, "At that time, he was working in the office of a telecommunications company in Torino, and that he had only worked there for a few years. When he realized he was ill, he transferred his work much closer to home."

"Signora Russo, did your husband have any friends at his former place of employment?" I asked.

"Well, the only one I met was a man named Cristiano Bergeroni," she replied.

"Do you have any idea how we might find him?" I asked.

"I believe he still lives in Torino," she said.

She also told us that a couple times a month her husband went for a poker night with Bergeroni and a few other guys, whose names she didn't know. After a few more questions and conversation, we decided we gleaned about all we could. I left her my cell phone number and asked her to call me if she could think of anything else.

Chapter 32

After leaving Signora Russo, we decided to head back towards Torino. Dan suggested we try to find an Internet café and see if we could find the address of Bruno Russo's friend, Bergeroni. He told me he subscribed to several search engines and a couple of them were international.

"Actually, it's the first thing I do when I start an investigation," Dan said. "It's amazing what you can find out about people for a few bucks."

He pointed out you will not only get their name, age, address and phone number, but it also lists any legal notices such as restraining orders, foreclosures or judgments against them. Dan went on to explain how much the Internet watches your online use. Ostensibly the information is gathered so they can target you for advertisers. "Have you noticed how you get bombarded with those ads for middle-aged products such as Viagra, Depends, or skin creams? It's because they know how old you are and your socio-economic profile," he said and went on to explain how much they try to keep it under the radar.

"But you know something, with all the technology, sometimes the best way to find something is a little bit of shoe leather and patience," Dan said.

Once we got back to Pinerolo, we pulled into a gas station to fill up. Looking at the gasoline prices, which are sold by the liter, I found they are about what we pay per gallon back home. When you consider that a liter is about the size of a quart, you can see how expensive gas is in Italy. While the attendant was filling our car, we asked him if he knew of an Internet café in town. He said there was one at the Impermercato Shopping Center. After paying the attendant our €70 to fill the car, we headed to the shopping center to find an Internet café. Logging on Dan typed in the name, Cristiano Bergeroni. Sure enough, it gave us his home address, age, place of employment, and phone numbers. Although there was more than one Cristiano Bergeroni, only one worked at a telecommunications company. We also saw he was 58, the right age. We wrote down the information listed from the search and decided to try the phone. We figured he was probably still at work, but it was worth a try to contact him.

Fortunately for us, Signore Bergeroni was at home, having worked the night shift. I explained who we were and that we'd like to meet him. I told him we were a little more than a half hour outside of Torino, and we could be there by four o'clock. He said it would be a good time, and he looked forward to meeting us. Before saying goodbye, I asked him if he would give us directions to his home since I'm not familiar with the city. Dan thought it might be a good idea to grab a street map as well. Knowing we'd be getting back on the highway towards Torino, Dan suggested he drive and I navigate. Fortunately, Bergeroni lived in the southern end of Torino just outside Beinasco, so we didn't have a lot of city traffic to deal with.

Bergeroni lived in a high-rise apartment building that had to be 10-12 stories. Finding his name on the tenants list, we rang his doorbell. First he asked who we were and then buzzed us in. As we exited the elevator, we saw him waiting for us at his apartment door. We exchanged polite greetings. Signore Bergeroni seemed very happy to meet us. He welcomed us in and invited us to sit down in his living room. Once seated, he offered us something to drink. We politely declined saying, "We had no desire to take up too much of his time."

Bergeroni was a middle-aged gentleman with curly gray hair, high forehead, and full beard. He also seemed like a happy and lively individual, often chuckling and making short quips he found amusing but were impossible to translate for Dan. We asked Bergeroni if he would mind talking to us about his friendship with Bruno Russo. He told us they were not close friends but more work associates. He also told us they played cards together twice a month with another three men. He also said that none of them had been together since Bruno's death.

"He wasn't the best poker player, usually being the biggest loser of the evening. We even kidded him suggesting he was losing on purpose. It just isn't like it used to be since his death." Bergeroni lamented.

We asked him if he knew how Bruno came into so much money. He said that as far as he knew, he had won the lottery. So, for obvious reasons, he was always welcome at our poker games. We explained to Bergeroni that we were unable to tell him all the reasons why we believed Bruno Russo did not win the lottery but had instead sold something of great value. At that Bergeroni became very animated, "It was a sacred object or a religious artifact, wasn't it?" making it more a statement than question.

After translating his comment to Dan, I asked, "Why do you say that?"

"Because of a conversation we had around the card table probably a few years ago."

"Can you explain what you mean?" I asked.

"Yes. One night Bruno seemed to be in a strange mood. I can remember he was not his usual self. He was quiet and obviously had something on his mind," Bergeroni reflected.

"Did you ever find out what he was thinking about?" I asked.

"No, not exactly. All Bruno ever said was his family had a valuable sacred object in their possession. He thought it might be worth selling and didn't know how to go about it. Everyone else at the game seemed to have no idea how to help him except for Amato," Bergeroni said.

"Do you think Amato was ever able to help him?" I asked.

"Knowing Amato, I can only imagine he would try to get in on the deal."

"Why do you say that?"

"He was always into some shady deal or another," Bergeroni said. "Nothing was ever said. In fact, even though they denied it, I always thought they got together after the poker game."

"Can you tell me more about Amato?" I asked.

Bergeroni told us that he would play poker with them now and again but not regularly. "We knew he was involved with contraband cigarettes smuggled in from Switzerland. We all would periodically buy a carton from him, since they were about half the price of the cigarettes we buy here in Italy."

"I remember when I lived in Milan, I bought Marlboros from Switzerland," I said.

"And now to think of it, Amato seemed to come into some money about the same time as Bruno. Amato insisted it was an inheritance from a dead relative," Bergeroni remembered.

"Did you believe him?" I asked.

"We knew he was crooked, but we had no reason not to believe him," Bergeroni replied. We asked him if he knew how we might find Amato. He gave us a cell phone number and said, "He never answers his cell phone."

"You have to leave a message, and he may call you back." Then he told us of a bar where Amato sometimes hung out.

We gathered by the condition of the apartment Bergeroni probably was not married. Because Dan likes to pry, being in his investigator mode, he told me to ask Cristiano if he was married.

"I am divorced, and more than once. I'm currently dating a new girlfriend, whom I hope to marry next year."

He also went on to say he had no children and was happy that way. Wanting to get on the road, we asked Bergeroni to excuse us. He was pleased to meet us and sorry he was not able to communicate more directly with Dan. In an attempt to be gracious, as we were leaving, he said in English, "Thank you very much. Very nice to meet you. Goodbye."

Dan laughed and replied, "I enjoyed meeting you too."

Chapter 33

As we approached the car, I could see Dan was animated, so I asked him, "What are you thinking about?"

He said, "I know how we can contact Amato."

"What do you mean?"

"What I mean is, there's a good chance he'll never return our call, if we leave a voice message on his cell phone."

"Why do you say that? Why wouldn't he return our call?" I asked while I watched Dan unlock the door on the driver's side.

"Because as soon as he hears a foreign accent asking to meet him, he would be suspicious," Dan continued. "He obviously screens his calls to make it difficult for anyone tracking him down. The harder he makes it, the safer he is."

"What would you propose we do?" I asked.

"Bergeroni gave us the name of the bar where Amato likes to hang out. Hopefully he's there now, especially this time of day when people were getting out of work, and he can sell his cartons of Swiss cigarettes. We'll go to this bar and get ourselves a drink. We'll look around and see if we can guess which one is Amato. Before we go into the bar, we'll preprogram his number into your cell phone. Then without anybody seeing us we'll call that number and see if we hear it ring or see him look at his phone. We'll know that's Amato."

"Man, how do you come up with this stuff?" I asked, now with a grin on my face.

"You'd be amazed at the tricks you learn in this business," Dan said with an air of confidence.

"Yes, and I'm sure you keep those tricks up your

sleeves," I said half laughing to myself thinking of my comment to Luiza. Dan just looked at me.

*   *   *

We found the bar Bergeroni told us about. It was also a Tabbachi, a state regulated store, and definitely a working man's bar with a few tables and chairs just outside on the sidewalk. The cashier's counter was over to the far right. Several feet away from the front entrance and parallel to the front was the bar with the barista. Over to the far left a wide doorway led to a large room in the back that had a pool table, a couple of pinball machines, and a few more tables with chairs. One of the tables had four men sitting around drinking wine and playing cards. The type of cards they were using were traditional Italian cards that have only forty cards instead of fifty-two in the deck. We walked up to the bar. Wanting to appear to be natives, we decided to order two glasses of red wine. Dan pointed to one of the tables in the rear section of the bar that also had a good view of the men milling about in the front. After a few minutes of sitting and observing, I pulled out my cell phone, flipped it open, hit the send button, and we heard the preprogrammed number ring. One of the men sitting at the card table reached into his pocket and pulled out his cell phone. He looked at it and put it back in his pocket ignoring the call. We knew we had found Giovanni Amato.

We decided not to approach him right away but instead watched to see if he continued playing. To our good luck we only had to wait a few minutes before Amato decided he'd had enough of cards and wanted to step outside for a smoke. I decided to walk up to the cashier and purchase a half pack of cigarettes. I was glad they still sold half packs. Dan joined me at the exit door, and we stepped outside where Amato was sitting having a cigarette. No doubt he overheard Dan and me speaking in English but chose to ignore us. Turning to him, I asked in Italian, "May I speak with you for a minute." Without a word, he just looked over towards us and nodded his head.

"Are you Giovanni Amato?" I asked.

By his surprised look, we knew the answer before he

even said anything.

"Who's asking?" was his short reply.

"We are not the police or any other Italian agency. We're just a couple of Americans," I quickly replied.

"Well, why do you want to speak to me?" he asked while flicking his ash on the ground.

"We're private investigators and would like to speak with you briefly," I said. When I heard myself saying "We're private investigators," I got excited thinking that I just joined a select group.

"Why would any private investigators want to speak with me? I have nothing to do with America," he said insistently.

"We just happen to be Americans, but we want to talk to you about Bruno Russo and how you may have helped him," I said.

I could see mentioning Bruno Russo's name caused even more of a reaction from him. I noticed him beginning to shift around in his seat and flicking his ash now several times.

"What about him?" he asked.

"We know you played poker with him before he died."

"Yes, I heard he is dead. A nice guy but a bad poker player," Amato said.

"We also know you helped him sell The Holy Shroud of Turin."

With this, we could see Amato begin to panic, so I quickly added, "As I told you before, we're not the police and nobody is going to arrest you. We have been asked by the Secretary to the Archbishop to help recover the Shroud. They have no intention of prosecuting anyone; they only want it back."

I went on to tell him that I believe there might be a reward given to anyone who helps with the recovery.

Amato began to relax and even smile thinking how there might be money in it for him. He went on to say he was not positive who had the Shroud now.

"I believe a wealthy industrialist from Milan bought it," he said. "I'm not positive who he is, but I think he's involved with the occult practice called Stregheria." He then went on to explain, "The reason I believe this is people involved with this occult practice gather at a club I sometimes go to." We then asked if he would mind telling us the name of the club and where it is.

He said, "You can only get in if you're a member, or a guest with a member." He told us that the club was called *il Giardino della Fantasia Club.*

"If you can, speak to the owner, Sonia," Amato said.

We thanked him for his time and assured him we would help him collect a reward if we could. With the information we needed, we left and decided it was probably time to meet up with Loretta. On our way we decided to check into *il Principi di Piemonte Hotel,* where I had stayed a few days earlier.

Chapter 34

Just as we turned onto Loretta's street, I noticed a car pulling out of a parking spot.

"Quick, that car is pulling out. Grab it!" I shouted excitedly. This stroke of luck saved us half an hour of wandering around the neighborhood, looking for a parking place. Dan pulled up alongside the car in front of the empty spot and backed in, parallel parking to perfection.

"I've always wished I could do that," I lamented.

"I'll teach you my trick sometime. You'd be surprised how easy it is."

Getting out of the car, we noticed a small bar a few doors down.

"Are you ready for an aperitif?" I inquired.

"An aperitif sounds good," Dan replied.

We entered the bar, and I walked over to the cashier and ordered two Campari with white wine and ice, *"Due Campari spritzer -- on the rocks."* The cashier/barista told me it would be 5€, then suggested we sit down at a table where she'd bring it over to us. The bar looked like a family business, and perhaps she was one of the daughters. Just outside the door on the sidewalk, there were three tables with two chairs on each side, as is so often the tradition in Italy. We exited the bar and grabbed a table just to the left of the door. I could see by Dan's expression he was fascinated with Torino.

"You like the city?" I asked.

"It certainly is bustling," he replied.

Then I said, "Sometimes I think, if I were a single man again, I would like to live in the city."

"I'd like a small apartment in the city, and a house in the country, perhaps on a lake," Dan replied.

At this point, the cashier, barista and now waitress brought us our aperitifs with a small napkin-lined basket of potato chips and a small bowl of assorted olives. She was a cute waitress with thick blonde hair, cut just above her shoulders, and parted in the middle. She wore a tight fitting, low cut jersey, well-fitted blue jeans, and a small white apron folded in half across the front of her waist. While leaning forward to place our drinks and snacks on the table, she said, "Prego signore."

Dan said, "Grazie very much."

After she left, he leaned over to me and with a smirk said, "My thanks wasn't just for the quick polite service."

Italians love to sit "*al fresco*", in the open air, whether for a morning cappuccino before work or with an espresso after lunch at the local bar, or in the evening with an aperitif in the main square before dinner. I remember in past trips to Italy with Luiza, we would love go down to the local piazza, especially in the center of the city, find a café-bar, and enjoy mingling with the locals out for an evening stroll and aperitif. It's a great tradition and one that I'm convinced will extend your life.

Dan pointed up to the small narrow balconies along the buildings and the tall French style bi-fold windows, some with stained-glass panels on the inside being used as privacy blinds. We discussed the architecture, the ornamental elements, and how some of the stucco plaster over the buildings is etched to create a 3-D effect as though you were looking at a quarried stone building. After we finished our drinks and all the chips and olives, we headed over to Loretta's building. Again Dan looked all around, listening to the sounds of the city and this time with a look making me wonder if he changed into P-eye mode or former Army officer, attached to the President's security detail. Dan confirmed my suspicions when out of the blue he said, "The worst thing about windows is they may appear harmless, but they are black holes. A sniper doesn't just stick the barrel of his rifle out the window as they do in the movies. He sets up way back in the room using some type of stand to support his weapon. He shoots out of the darkness."

About this time, I saw Tram 15 cross the intersection of Corso Palestro on via Cernaia. It crossed two blocks down the road. Shortly after it passed, I noticed Loretta walking around the corner, having just gotten off that tram. While I watched her approach us, I thought to myself, "She is such an elegant woman, considering all she had been through." Loretta was engaged for a number of years only to find her hopes dashed when her fiancée left her for another woman. Her way of walking is graceful without swaying her hips side-to-side, as so many younger women do. She's a slender woman with slender legs made more so by her high heels. She was wearing her Sancarlo Viaggi uniform, which was a royal blue blazer and skirt with a light blue blouse. Around her neck was a multi-colored fular, (silk tie or scarf) tucked into her blouse, which had the top two buttons undone. Their logo was embroidered onto the left pocket of the blazer.

As she walked, she smiled because she noticed us waiting for her on the sidewalk. As she got closer, I noticed her hair pulled back in a ponytail or bun, not the usual way she wore it, which was to allow it to rest on her shoulders. Perhaps this too was part of the uniform. I also saw that her black pocketbook had a long shoulder strap over her left shoulder, but instead of allowing the pocketbook to dangle loosely behind her, as usually carried, she was holding it closely in front of her with her left hand supporting it from the bottom. I think this was a protective measure, used by women who live in the city.

While still several yards from us and walking briskly, she held out her hand to me. I grabbed her right hand and pulled her close to kiss her right cheek and then her left cheek in the traditional European fashion. After we had kissed, she reached over to Dan, grabbed his hand and began to shake it while I said, "This is Dan Carlson."

Loretta said, "I am glad to meet you, Dan." Her reply was in English with her beautiful Italian accent.

"I am pleased to meet you, too."

Then, Loretta pointed to the doorway and said, "Why don't we go up to my flat?"

We both said while nodding, "Sure!"

Once through the two sets of front doors, we were in the foyer of the apartment building. We followed Loretta over to the elevator; she pressed the up arrow, and we looked above the elevator door to see how many floors we had to wait. Once the elevator arrived, the doors opened, and an elderly woman stepped out and greeted us with a, "*Buona sera.*" We nodded, smiled and responded, "*Buona sera.*" Then we stepped into the elevator and Loretta pressed the button next to the number four.

Chapter 35

The elevator was small and cramped, built for only three to four people at a time. Loretta pushed the fourth floor button; the doors closed, and we began to feel the pull of the elevator as we ascended. Dan had his back against the back mirror; I was perpendicular to Dan with my back against the side wall, and Loretta was facing the closed doors. Then Dan commented, "I'd hate to get trapped in one of these things."

I asked Loretta, "Does this elevator ever stall or worse yet fall to the basement?"

Loretta replied, *Non scherzare*, knowing I liked to kid around.

Then Dan asked, "What did she say?"

Loretta quickly replied, "Your friend is crazy."

I looked at Dan and shrugged; we both grinned. A number of seconds later, I noticed Dan leaning forward a bit towards Loretta with his eyes closed. I could see he was enjoying the lingering fragrance of her perfume. It was at this point we felt the jolt of the elevator arriving at the 4th floor. The doors opened, and we followed Loretta down the hall. She inserted the key and turned the deadbolt several times counterclockwise, clicking with each turn. She inserted a second key just below the door knob, which opened the door. Then we entered in her apartment.

Loretta pointed to her couch and said, "Please sit down …Excuse me while I'm changing my clothes. I will prepare something to eat."

Dan, rather than sitting on the couch, decided to walk over to the French style windows. They were several feet tall and went almost to the floor. He opened the right side door with a twist of the handle and stepped out onto the narrow balcony. From five stories up you could begin to see over the tops of some of the buildings, which gave a pleasant view of the city.

Dan, in his "presidential-protector" voice, said, "This would be a nightmare to try to protect the President."

Yelling from the bathroom, Loretta informed us, "There's a bottle of white wine in the frigo, take some if you want."

I yelled back, *Va bene, grazie.* Her kitchen was quite tiny, galley style. On the left side was a sink with a couple of square feet of counter space. Above the sink and counter were a few cabinet doors where she stored dishes, spices, and condiments. Against the opposite wall was a fairly small refrigerator, perhaps five feet tall and at best two feet wide. It was tucked in against the corner wall. Between the fridge and left side cabinets was a narrow window looking out onto Corso Palestro. To the right of the refrigerator and closer to the doorway was another small counter space and then the stove, typical apartment size. The stove had four small burners and an oven that could barely fit a small turkey. I found a couple of water glasses in the dish rack above the sink. I have only seen these types of dish racks in Italy. They are hidden behind a pair of opposing doors and situated directly over the sink, so the water on the just washed dish can drop back into the sink.

"Very ingenious," I mumbled to myself. I grabbed two water glasses, put them on the counter, and reached into the fridge for the bottle of wine. After I wiggled out the cork, I filled the glasses, and then joined Dan on the balcony. Realizing we were in Italy together, with this beautiful view of the city, we clinked our glasses and both knew we were experiencing an unforgettable moment.

I don't think we were out there five minutes enjoying the skyline and looking at the architecture when my cell phone rang. The caller ID showed me it was my wife calling from home. Trying to be funny, I answered the phone, "*Pronto, chi è?*"

Her reply was only, "It's me."

"Hey, honey. So glad you called."

"I was wondering when you would call me back. I haven't heard from you in a couple of days," Luiza said.

"I'm sorry, my mind has been elsewhere and time is flying," I replied.

"You're supposed to be returning home tomorrow. Are you going to make the flight?" Luiza asked, and by her tone I gathered she was in no mood to joke around.

"Dan's here. We're in Torino at Loretta's. She's cooking us dinner." I was trying to avoid the question.

I then stepped back into the apartment so that I wasn't talking into Dan's ear on the narrow balcony.

"I asked, are you going be on the plane coming home tomorrow," raising her voice, a little more determined.

"Please, sweetheart, don't be upset. I'll be home as soon as I can, which hopefully should only be a few more days," I pleaded.

"Marty, you have work in the studio that's being ignored."

"It'll all get done," I assured her. "If you want me to make a few phone calls and explain my situation, I will."

"You better not; I wouldn't want anybody thinking you're gallivanting around Italy playing Sherlock Holmes and Watson," she said.

"Gallivanting! Is that what you think we're doing? We're on a serious investigation. Don't you understand what's at stake here?" I insisted.

"Serious investigation?" Luiza replied, raising her voice, making it a question.

"Yes, serious investigation. If Dan and I can help retrieve the Shroud, I think we will have done a great thing," I countered.

"That's the crazy thing about it. You actually believe you might succeed. You think you'll find out who has it and perhaps even get it away from them," Luiza said in her most dogmatic way.

I noticed that Loretta's bedroom door was left ajar. My

curiosity caused me to mosey over and peek in. Even though she may have expected to come home to an empty house, her bed was made and her room was tidy. It made me think about how Luiza never goes downstairs from our bedroom in the morning without making our bed and making sure the room is neat.

"No, I'm not saying they'll just hand it over to us, but I am hopeful that we'll at least find out who has it and, perhaps at that point, they can negotiate with the Church to get it back," I speculated.

"Yeah, like they're just going to say, I'll sell it to you for a few hundred Euros," she retorted sarcastically.

"Well, I guess we'll just cross that bridge when we get to it," I said.

"Sure you will…And when you do, you might find that it's 'A Bridge Too Far,'" Luiza countered.

"If you were in the mood to listen, I'd tell you the progress we've made, but since you're not, I'll have to tell you later," I said.

On more than one occasion, I've come out of the bathroom, expecting to crawl back into bed for another snooze only to find the bed was already made.

"Please don't stay in Italy too much longer. I want you home. I miss you," she said softly.

By this point I had wandered over to the couch and sat down. I noticed Dan had stepped back into the apartment.

"I miss you too, but I believe this is something I need to be doing. I don't believe it'll be much longer," I said. "I will have to talk to Loretta about changing my ticket. Hopefully her agency might be able to pull a few strings and get me home without it costing too much extra," I added.

"You think they can?" Luiza asked.

"I haven't mentioned it to her yet, but I hope to this evening."

"Don't wait three days to call. Let me know how things are going, perhaps this time tomorrow," she said.

"I'll try." Then I quietly said, "When I get home, I think

I'll have you call me Maestro."

"Why, because you do a good job taking out the trash?" she asked.

"No-no," I said coyly, "you know what I mean…"

"You're so fresh! I'm not going to do that," Luiza replied with a startle in her voice. Then harshly, but obviously kidding, she said, "Goodbye."

"Goodbye, sweetheart," I said softly, and we ended our call.

Chapter 36

It was about this time that Loretta came out of the bathroom wearing her *Wells for Kenya Project* sweatshirt and a pair of blue jeans.

"Ah, I see you're wearing the sweatshirt Luiza and I gave you on our last trip."

"Yes, I like to wear it like this in the house. It's more comfortable," Loretta replied. "Because I see Dan for the first time, I should dress up, but I am too tired after a long day of work," she said while heading into the kitchen.

"Oh no, please," Dan added, "don't fuss for me."

Turning towards me Dan asked, "*Wells for Kenya Project?* Isn't that the water wells organization you are involved with?"

"Marty, how is the things is going?" Loretta asked from the kitchen. Dan leaned over to quietly say, "I love that Italian-English way of speaking."

"Well, it's plugging along," I said. "Fundraising is not easy, nor is it fun."

I took a sip from my glass of wine, as I reflected on the way things sometimes develop. Drilling water wells in Africa is an ongoing need, but it doesn't always hit home like finding a cure for cancer or any other disease that can strike a loved one.

"For tonight I would to prepare, *Spaghetti alla Puttanesca*," Loretta said. "And *Bistecca Tonnato* (which is beefsteak with tuna and mayonnaise) --Va bene?" she said as she put the pot of water on the stove for the pasta.

"Very, *va bene*," Dan said with a smile on his face.

"Loretta, everything you cook is very good," I added. "I remember how much I loved your mother's cooking, and I know she taught you her secrets," I said, now sticking my head into the kitchen to see what she was doing.

"Yes, I really liked to help her in the kitchen," Loretta said.

As Loretta worked in the kitchen, I couldn't help but notice Dan watching her very closely.

"Loretta, is it true what they say about *Spaghetti alla Puttanesca?*" I asked.

"What do you mean?"

"My friend Mariano says, the women in Naples would go out and walk the streets to pick up a little extra cash while their husbands were out fishing. They were supposed to have dinner ready when their husbands got home, so they needed to have something made very quickly."

"It's really an interesting story, but I think it's not true," was Loretta's opinion.

"Why, what does Puttanesca mean?" Dan asked.

"The word *puttana* means prostitute," I said.
By the smirk on Dan's face, I could only imagine what he was thinking.

In a soft voice, so that Loretta couldn't hear me, I said, "Loretta is not that kind of girl. So don't get any ideas."

"What ideas?" Dan asked putting his hands out in a gesture to feign innocence.

"You know what I mean," I said.

Because I wanted to stay close to the kitchen entrance, so that we could talk without raising our voices, I grabbed one of the four chairs around the dining room table and moved it to just inside the tiny kitchen doorway. Dan also decided to move one of the chairs a little bit closer. I think he wanted to get a better look at Loretta working in the kitchen more than talk. Personally, I always found Luiza working in the kitchen or when we're together working in the yard a real turn on.

"How was your day? Did you find out anything new?" Loretta asked as she prepared the home-made mayonnaise by drizzling olive oil over two beaten eggs.

"Yes, I believe we did," I replied.

"Tell her what we found out," Dan said.

"We spoke with the widow of the man who sold the Shroud. She pointed us towards a friend of her husband who played poker with him. We talked to this friend, and he pointed us to this shady character, named Giovanni Amato. Amato told us that the person they sold the Shroud to he had met at a club called *il Giardino della Fantasia Club*," I said.

"Amato also said that the only way into this club is if you're a member, or as a guest of a member. He didn't really explain what type of club it is, but I can only imagine," I added.

"Why, what does the club's name mean?" Dan asked.

"It means 'The Garden of the Fantasy,'" Loretta offered.

"Oh, I see," Dan replied, with a snicker in his voice imagining what went on there.

"What do you think you'll do next?" Loretta asked as she dropped a handful of spaghetti into the boiling pot.

"I would like to try to get into this club," Dan said.

"I bet you would," I retorted.

"No, no, not for that, but to find out who they sold the Shroud to," Dan defended. He then added, "Amato also said that the club is a hangout for people involved with some strange occult practice. What did he call it?"

"*Stregheria*," I said.

"The word comes from *stregha*, which means witch in Italian," Loretta said to Dan while refilling our wine glasses.

"In fact we have a girl in our office who says she's a witch and she is part of *Stregheria*…It's interesting how here in Torino a lot of people are involved with all these occult and Satanic groups. Torino is known to be a center for these kinds of activities," Loretta added.

"That's right! I remember now; you mentioned her the night we went out to *Il Padellino*," I said. She then handed me the cheese grater and a chunk of Grana from the fridge; motioning for me to grate the cheese.

"Do you think there's any chance that she might be a member of this club?" Dan asked, still focused on the previous revelation.

"We could try to ask her," Loretta said.

I pushed the chunk of Grana back and forth over the cheese grater and reflected a little more. Dan continued to strain his neck to get a better view of Loretta cooking at the stove.

It looked as though we might be making some progress here, so Dan pressed Loretta a little further on the matter. "Do you know how to get in touch with her?" he asked.

"Well, I don't have her cell phone number, but I do know somebody who probably will," Loretta said. "I can call after dinner and see if we can speak to her."

He then asked, "Loretta, how would you feel if we invited this woman over to speak with us this evening?"

"Having her here in my apartment is not the most pleasant thought. But if she can help, I'm certainly willing," Loretta said, now handing me three shallow bowls for the pasta and three plates for the steak and salad. The tiny apartment was filled with incredible aromas from the meal to be served. I could not wait to eat.

Chapter 37

Setting the table brought me back to Segrate, when I lived with the Grappellis. Although it was usually Massimo's chore to set the dinner table, now and again I would help out. It was a fond memory for me, especially putting out the cloth napkins with napkin rings. I had wanted Luiza to have cloth napkins with rings to remind me of my time with the Grappellis, but she always insisted paper was easier.

"If the Shroud was bought by a member of this group, do you think they want to use it in their rituals?" Loretta asked.

"I have heard somewhere that they try to get their hands on anything sacred," I said.

"Why would they want it anyway?" Dan asked, "I would have thought they would prefer to stay away from anything religious."

"Perhaps they think they get some power from defiling or desecrating it…Kind of like sticking their finger in the Lord's eye." I added.

"I'll be upset if they already destroyed it or violated it in some way," Loretta lamented.

"I hope that won't be the case," I said.

For several more minutes we chatted about Dan's reason for coming to Europe and how he came to be in Italy with me. Loretta could not believe someone could be so evil as to murder his wife that way.

"Yes, just the mention of the name, Denis Ryan, makes me cringe," Dan said while lowering his voice and stiffening his jaw.

"*Pronto a mangiare*," Loretta announced while ladling

the sauce onto the large bowl of spaghetti. We moved our chairs back to the table and she served us healthy portions. Then she took out an unlabeled bottle of red wine out of the cabinet. Getting the corkscrew from the utensil drawer, Loretta handed it to Dan to open the bottle. Dan, noticing the bottle had no label, asked, "Is this homemade wine?"

"Not exactly," Loretta said. "I take a damigiana once every couple of months from a vineyard near Asti. This is Barbera."

I could see Dan enjoyed speaking to Loretta. He asked, "Do you go to the vineyard to get the wine?"

"No, usually I call them and ask them to drop one off the next time they come through the city. Once in a while I'll visit the vineyard if I'm driving in the area," Loretta said.

Getting the damigiana from the vineyard reminded me of the time the Grappellis had taken me out of the city to pick one up for their home. It was a day I still remember fondly.

"I wish we could have fresh wine in bulk. It seems it would be much healthier," Dan commented. He also mentioned the carafe of wine we had earlier that day.

"Before I cook the beefsteak, I'll try to get in touch with Paola and ask her to come over," Loretta said.

"I remember you saying that she always dresses very sexy at work," I said.

"Oh yeah? Tell me more," Dan said, raising his voice with enthusiasm.

"A flirt?" I offered.

"Yes, she is a flirt," Loretta replied.

"Great, let's get her over here and flirt a little," suggested Dan. "Is she hot?" I could see that Dan was enjoying the wine. He had no problem refilling his glass.

"Loretta did you know that Dan worked in the White House for the President and after that for the CIA?" I asked.

"Vero?!" said Loretta.

"Yes, I was a Russian translator for the hotline," Dan said while swirling his finger around the lip of his wine glass.

"Can you tell us some secret?" Loretta asked.

"The hotline isn't a telephone. It is actually a teletype. At least it was when I was there back under the last two years of Johnson and first two years of Nixon."

"I just always assumed it was a telephone where the president could pick it up, push a button and say hello, Premier Brezhnev," I said.

"Kind of like the bat-phone?" Dan asked, raising one eyebrow.

"I guess so," I said.

"Any other interesting tidbits about being in the White House, you could tell us about?" Loretta asked.

"Tell her about your first day in the White House. You've told Luiza and me that story a few times," I said.

"Oh, please tell me what happened," Loretta insisted.

"Well, my first day on the job was also the first day a serious message was transmitted over the hotline teletype from the Russians. I thought this thing happened every day. But I found out this was the first time," Dan said.

"As you told it to us, Wasn't it the beginning of the Six-day Israeli War in June of '67?"

"Yes, it was when the USS Liberty was attacked by the Israeli Air Force," Dan replied.

"I thought the US and Israel were allies. Why would the Israeli Air Force attack a US ship?" Loretta asked.

"Because they knew we were spying on them. The USS Liberty was a spy ship and they were afraid we would tell the Russians what the Israelis were doing to defend themselves from the invading Arabs," Dan said.

"That's exciting!" said Loretta. "Did you like working in the White House?"

"No, not really. In fact, it was quite boring," he replied.

While watching Dan tell his stories to Loretta, I remembered how Darla would interrupt Dan and say that no one wants to hear your stories. I always thought she was protecting him, which I found interesting, since Dan never really let you know him too personally.

"Another story you liked to tell Luiza and me was how you're mentioned in a Tom Clancy novel. Tell Loretta about that," I said.

"Well, in Clancy's novel *Sum of All Fear,s* he mentions the hotline and how we would do our half-hour checks to make sure the hotline was functioning properly. We would send the Russians a message, and they would reply or vice-versa. At first we would just send 'Quick brown fox etc'. I knew from my Russian studies they love poetry so I decide one day to send a Russian poem instead. We would send Alexander Pushkin or Emily Dickinson poetry back and forth. I was the first one to use poetry to check the hotline, just as a joke at first. Then Clancy mentioned the poetry in his novel. It showed me he had done his research and had contacts deep in the White House," Dan explained.

Then, Loretta broke into the conversation, "Who wants more spaghetti? We must finish it or it will be thrown out."

"Thrown out!" I exclaimed. "That's tomorrow's lunch after I zap it in the microwave."

"Oh no, in Italy we never eat spaghetti the next day. It's not fresh or still al dente," Loretta insisted.

We chatted about home, work at my the studio, and some of the tours Sancarlo Viaggi was planning. I suggested Loretta bring a group to visit a couple of Outlet Malls in the States and make sure they were near enough to Boston so that she could visit us. She said another tour agent, Elenora Tanelli, who's Signor Luca Tanelli's, sister, took a group to New York City on a shopping spree. Luca Tanelli is the agency's CEO, and according to Loretta he's quite the ladies man, who because of his position travels quite a bit and likes to bring a companion along, usually his latest girlfriend.

Chapter 38

Loretta excused herself from the table to call Paola and to cook the second course. She scrolled through her contact list and came to a name she hoped might have Paola's number.

"Here he is, Leonardo" Loretta said.

Hitting send at Leonardo's name, Loretta waited for him to answer.

What we heard from our end of the conversation was, "*Ciao, Leonardo sono Loretta dal' Agenzia*. . .Yes, we miss you too . . . It was unfair how they let you go . . . Sure, perhaps we could meet sometime . . . Listen, Leonardo, I am calling to find out if you have Paola 's cell phone number . . . 348 . . . what did you say the rest of the numbers were? . . . Thanks for your help."

Then Loretta said while tapping in her number, "Ok, let me see if Paola is available to come over."

"Ciao, Paola, it is Loretta . . . Yes, from the office . . . Yes, I never have called you after work . . . Paola, I have two friends from America here, and they would like to meet you. Would you be able to come by my apartment this evening to meet up with them? . . . It is because they are curious about your involvement in Stregharia . . . My address is Corso Palestro, no.9 . . . Great we look forward to seeing you." After Loretta ended the call she said, "I hope you two know what you're doing."

We had just finished having some fruit and cheese when we heard the door buzzer. As soon as Paola pushed Loretta's buzzer, the video camera showed her on the small video screen next to the front door. Loretta hit the door opener after saying,

"*Avanti.*"

While we waited for Paola to make her way up to the apartment, Loretta cleared the table, put the dishes in the sink, and Dan poured us another glass of wine. When the doorbell rang, Loretta answered the door, "*Ciao Paola, sono contento che potevi venire,*" letting her know how please that she could come by.

Paola stepped inside and glanced around at Dan and me and in English said, "I wanted to meet your American friends, so I just had to come over."

"I want to present to you my friends Marty and Dan," Loretta said.

"Marty," Paola said making it a statement. "Isn't this the one you have spoken about at the office? The American who lived with your family many years ago?"

"Yes, he is," Loretta replied.

"Who's this new friend of yours?" Paola asked in a more curious way.

"This is Marty's friend, Dan," Loretta replied.

"I see you speak very good English," Dan said to Paola.

"Yes, I not only speak English but, I also speak German and Russian."

When Dan heard Paola also spoke Russian, he immediately replied, "*Tak vi govorite po Russki?*" Asking if she spoke Russian.

"*Da,ya govoriu?*" Paola asked Dan in Russian if he spoke too.

"*Da, Da,*" was Dan's only reply with a big smile on his face.

"Loretta, you never told me how Marty is distinguished," Paola said while extending her hand to shake mine.

I could see Paola took care of herself. She had a muscular and trim figure, dressed smartly, and wore only a slight wisp of perfume. She was not all painted up with makeup, as I expected her to be--no wide red lips or raccoon eyes.

"Yes, I have to say he became very distinguished,"

Loretta replied.

She also wasn't dressed in a sexy outfit, as I had imagined she might be. She had on a small tight denim jacket, which she removed as she entered Loretta's flat. She also had a short sleeved printed blouse, black trim slacks, and a sheer red scarf around her neck.

We made our way over to the couch and arm chair. Paola sat on the couch, Dan joined her, and I grabbed the arm chair. Loretta drew a chair from the table, which she turned towards the living room area.

After a bit more bantering, out of the clear blue Paola turned towards Loretta and me and asked, "Did you two ever done... you know?"

I had just taken a sip from my wine glass when I gasped, nearly choked as I said, "Wow! You certainly know how to be direct." She smiled and continued her quizzical gaze in Loretta's and my direction.

"Who, Marty?" exclaimed Loretta. "Why! I know him since I was eleven. He's like a big brother for me."

"She's like my little sister," I added.

Loretta could see I felt particularly offended at Paola's insinuation. Looking for a way to change the subject Loretta asked, "Who wants some coffee?" We all said we would like some.

"Tell me, Marty, does that hot temper hold true in the bed?" Paola asked grinning coyly.

"My, you *are* direct," Dan said.

"Loretta told us you like to be provocative, and now I see what she meant," I added.

"I think so. I like to see men's reactions... Tell me, do you go with other women?" Paola asked me in a somewhat seductive way.

"Only when my wife lets me," I replied.

"Does she ever?" Paola asked.

"Not with other women, if that's what you're asking. I never asked her if I could." Then I added, "I think that's why we've been married thirty years."

"You must be bored. Nowadays it is not common,"

Paola taunted.

"After thirty years, I still enjoy chasing her around the kitchen," I insisted.

"That's what everybody say, but I don't believe it," Paola replied in a dismissive manner.

I think it was about this time Loretta really regretted inviting Paola.

Out of the corner of my eye, I could see Dan was taking it all in. He was intensely studying our reactions. I began to wonder what he might make of this. The rubbing of his chin made me think he wished he had a beard and looked more like Sigmund Freud.

"Paola, Dan and Marty want to ask you about a private club, *il Giardino della Fantasia Club*," Loretta interjected.

"How do you know about *il Giardino*?" Paola asked.

"What kind of a club is it?" Dan asked while staring at Paola.

"Well, it's basically a club in which couples can meet other couples…If you know what I mean?" Paola said looking at Dan with a slight smile.

"Then you are familiar with it," Dan said. "Are you a member?"

"Yes I am. I like to go there sometimes."

"We met a Giovanni Amato, and he told us it is a place where believers in Stregheria like to meet," Dan said.

"Amato? He is so rude." Paola responded.

"So, you know him? Why do you say that about him?" Dan was now in his investigator mode.

"I only know him from the club," she replied. "He comes in sometimes, always has some illegal goods, and likes to take advantage of women," Paola added.

"What do you mean, take advantage of women?" Dan asked.

Chapter 39

"Stregheria is a religion. Part of our faith is that through sex, we don't have just sexual union, but we also have spiritual union. These unions increase our power to express our love. Instead, this Amato just want to have sex for his pleasure. Like I said he's a rude man," Paola said.

"*Pronto caffè,*" Loretta announced, walking back from the kitchen with a small tray that held four small sets of cups and saucers, a sugar bowl and the traditional octagonal espresso coffee pot, called a *Moka.*

While taking a demi-tasse from Loretta, Paola asked. "Why do you want to have anything to do with Amato?"

"Because we're pretty sure he sold something to someone he met there," Dan responded.

"Amato also said we should speak to the owner, whom I think he called Sonia," I said.

"Yes, Sonia is the boss," Paola said. "And you are hoping I will help you get into the club, so you can figure out who may have bought something there?" Paola stated in an incredulous tone.

"Well yes, we were hoping you'd be willing to help us," Dan said.

"I didn't have the intention of going there tonight, but if you two are ready for fun, andiamo."

"I'm not going there. Can't you just hear my wife Luiza's reaction?" I said a bit emphatically.

Dan had a look on his face like he was considering it. Loretta, who was not excited about the conversation so far, decided to add, "You're not actually considering going are you?

Do you think you can wander around with a note pad like some investigator and go up to somebody and say, 'Excuse me but do you know who has the Holy Shroud of Turin'?"

"*La Sindone*! Are you try to find out who could have the *La Sindone*?" Paola asked struggling a little with her English. "Are you saying if someone have stolen it?"

I gave a look at Loretta like, "Why did you say that!"

Dan instead calmly said, "We weren't so sure we should let you know what we were looking for because of the ramifications of other people knowing. But now that you know what we're looking for, we can only hope you'll keep it private."

After thinking about it Paola then said, "If anybody is going to know who Amato may have seen, it will be the boss of the club, Sonia Troia."

"Then, could you help us speak to Sonia?" Dan asked Paola.

"She is going to be too busy at the club tonight, but if you want to go tomorrow evening before the opening, she may meet us," Paola said. "I'll ask her tomorrow and will see if she's able to meet us."

"Would you please not tip her off as to why we want to see her?" Dan asked.

"I'll try. Why does it matter?"

"Because we want to use the element of surprise to judge her reaction," Dan said.

"Dan, for you I'll do everything," Paola said teasingly

I could see Loretta wasn't amused. I started to wonder if Loretta was attracted to Dan. Over dinner she certainly enjoyed his stories and laughed at all his jokes even if they weren't funny like the one he told while she cleared the table.

"What is the Pope really saying when he does the sign of the cross from his Papal balcony?" Dan had asked her.

"Why, he is blessing the crowd," Loretta answered.

"No, not really, he is actually saying 'alla you'a people ina the backa and youa ina the fronta. Get offa mya piazza,'" Dan said while trying to sound Italian.

Well you would have thought the funniest comedian

just told his funniest joke by the way Loretta laughed. Now to see how she is reacting Paola's comments made me wonder.

"Please Paola, just call Sonia and ask if your two American friends could come by. If you need to tell her why, tell her we're interested in possibly opening a similar club back home and we're looking for ideas," Dan said.

"Hopefully she won't ask why and will just agree to meet us," I said.

"I could say maybe you want to become members and you want to look around before it opens. Who knows, it might not be a lie. Especially for you, Dan," Paola said while reaching her hand up to touch the side of his face and caressing it gently.

I caught a glimpse of Loretta, and her body language was not relaxed. I think she had just about enough.

"Who wants to try some nocino?" Loretta asked purposely interrupting.

"Nocino? What's nocino?" Dan asked.

"It's a digestivo made from green walnuts," Loretta said.

"Green walnuts? Doesn't sound that good."

"It actually is and does seem to help," I quipped.

"Help? How do you mean?" Dan asked.

"That's why it is called a diii-gesss-tiii-voo," Paola said stretching out the word.

Loretta, always the gracious host, got four small cut crystal stem glasses from a hutch in the corner of her living room and put them on the table. Reaching into at the bottom of the hutch for the bottle of nocino, she poured each of us some of the dark colored liqueur.

Taking his first sip Dan exclaimed, "Wow, it's strong. A few more of these and I won't care if my bowels do move."

"It's made from pure alcohol. The green walnuts are cut up and soaked in the alcohol for over a month," I explained.

About this time, Paola wanted to know more about Dan. She asked him some personal questions and about his career. She was quite impressed when he spoke about his White House days and his CIA assignments. Loretta politely endured the conversation often looking at the floor and seeming to zone out.

I was starting to get tired myself and wanted to get back to the hotel to call Luiza.

After a while I said, "I need to get my beauty sleep, or else I'll look not so distinguished in the morning."

"It isn't that late. I'm having a great time," Dan said.

"Loretta has had a very busy day at work and now has looked after us all night. They have to work in the morning. So let's get out of their way," I insisted.

Within minutes we were kissing goodbye and heading for the elevator.

As soon as the door closed and we were descending, Paola asked Dan, "If you want to visit the city by night, we could first go to a local bar and chat some more."

"Sounds like fun. We can speak a little Russian," Dan added.

"Look, you two can do whatever you want, as long as I can have the car to get back to the hotel," I said.

Chapter 40

It was almost midnight by the time I made it back to our room. I was not in the mood for Italian TV, nor was I ready to go to asleep. I flopped down on the bed and flipped open my phone to call Luiza. I wanted to chat with her awhile.

"Hey! I thought I wouldn't hear from you until tomorrow," she said answering the phone.

"I just got back to our room and wanted to say hi."

"Did you decide to come home tomorrow?" she asked.

"No, we're still on the hunt."

"You're sure it's a hunt and not just a wild goose chase?"

"No, we're making progress, and tomorrow we're going to meet with someone who might know who has the Shroud," I said.

"Well, I hope it works out. By the way, did you ask Loretta about fixing your ticket?"

"Oh no! I didn't. I completely forgot about it," I said, aggravated with myself.

"Will you see her tomorrow?" Luiza asked

"Yes, uh... after work."

"You can ask her then," Luiza said.

Flipping through the channels, I stopped for a minute to watch what I assumed was a fortuneteller speaking to a female caller and asking questions, the fortuneteller told her new love was just around the corner.

"What are you doing now?" I asked.

"I'm watching Jackson and Austin. Laura had to go out and do some errands...We were just coloring in a coloring book."

"Are they being good?" I asked.

"Yes, they are the sweetest boys," she replied.

"You know? I love being a grandparent," I mused. "Tell the boys I miss them, and I'm bringing them a surprise."

"Have you gotten them something?" Luiza asked.

"No, I haven't gotten it yet. I was hoping you'd grab something at Wal-Mart."

"What kind of surprise is that?"

"Hey, Luiza, did I ever tell you what happened the other day when I first arrived at the train station here in Torino?"

"No, I don't think so... You did tell me you've fallen in love with a Nigerian nun and now want to be called Maestro," she said.

"Are you gonna call me Maestro?"

"No!"

"When I got off the train, I dragged my crates off to the side and began to look for a porter."

"Oookay? By the way, are you and your new love going to live in Italy? I was just wondering where?" Luiza joked.

"Well we could, but only if I could get her to get out of that habit," I said.

"Very funny, ha ha," Luiza quipped.

"Come on let me tell you what happened," I insisted.

"Ok, what happened?"

"Anyway, I saw this porter, who happened to be a female and had to be more than a train car away from me. I yelled at the top of my lungs, '*Facchino, Ho bisogno un facchino,*'" I said chuckling at my humor.

"So what? I don't get it"

"Ho bisogno—I need?...a facchino... *ch* has a hard *C* sound and *ino* means little," Then raising my voice knowing Luiza wasn't getting it, I said, "In the train station I yelled at the top of my lungs, 'I need a quickie!'.Get it?"

"Man you have a strange mind," was all she said.

"Come on, that's pretty good. Yelling to everybody in a train station 'I need a quickie!'"

"You think you're soooo hilarious," Luiza mocked.

While still chuckling I said, "You never laugh at my jokes."

"Because you're not funny and it's usually vulgar. Have you ever noticed you're the only one who laughs at your humor?"

Flipping again through the channels, I stopped on an Italian comedy. It seemed to take place in a small hotel. Half-dressed men and women were hiding in closets and under beds, while a rotund, unattractive woman with a frying pan was looking for her husband. I thought, "Of all the move genres, these have to be one of the dumbest. But it's amazing how many there are."

"Hey, Dan's out on a date," I said lowering my voice as though I was sharing a juicy secret.

"What do you mean, out on a date," she asked.

"We met this woman, Paola, who works at Loretta's agency. She may be able to help us. We asked her to come by Loretta's and discuss her involvement in a private club. So anyway, Dan wasn't ready to hit the cot so she invited him out to see the city by night."

"Is she attractive or what?" Luiza asked.

"Why is that so important to women? What does it matter?" I asked.

"You know, Marty, you can be so full of it. I know the second you saw her, you were checking her out."

"Actually, it's kind of funny what happened. At Loretta's apartment they have this video system. When someone rings the doorbell, a TV monitor turns on so you can see who's there. When Dan and I noticed Loretta going over to the monitor to buzz her in, we almost tripped over each other trying to get a glimpse of her."

"Well what's she like?" Luiza asked.

"Yes, I would have to say she is attractive and very Italian looking, with a trim, muscular figure. She also has a lot of dark hair that is parted in the middle and is curly, kind of kinky...Oh, speaking of kinky. That's why we invited her over. She claims to be a witch or at least she's involved with some kind of modern day witchcraft. Like most occult practices sex is involved."

"That's all I need to hear," Luiza interjected.

"Don't worry.' I didn't get the vibe from her. In fact, she aggravated me a bit."

Luiza paused for a moment, as if considering what to say next. After several seconds she said, "What do you mean by vibe?"

"She's a bit pushy and direct. She likes to get a rise out of men... Oh sorry, no pun intended," I chuckled. "She goads them by asking provocative questions, and I didn't like it."

"What about Dan?" Luiza asked.

"Paola speaks Russian, so Dan jumped all over that."

"Does she speak English too?"

"Yes, and quite good English. German also I think she said. So between the Italian, English and Russian, we had a regular UN meeting going."

Now I was watching the news. There must have been a bank robbery that ended badly. The get-away car was smashed into a wall with another car involved. I didn't understand who was killed. They showed a tarp draped over one of the cars and a lot of Carabinieri milling around.

"Oh, before I forget. I want to tell you about the dish Loretta made for us. She made this sauce she spread over a thin piece of steak. The sauce was made of home-made mayonnaise, which she made by beating a couple of egg yolks then drizzling in olive oil and a squirt of lemon. She added tuna, capers, and a little salt and pepper. You know how I love capers. She cooked the steak in a frying pan."

"It sounds interesting. Doesn't putting mayonnaise with tuna over steak sound weird though?"

"Yes, but it was really tasty and easy to make. The steak was a bit thin so she quickly seared it leaving it nice and rare. Dan asked her to throw it back in the pan for a little longer."

"Did she?"

"Yes, she did. She scraped off the mayonnaise, cooked it so it was well done, and then put the sauce back over it. Loretta was very apologetic about not cooking it more. I told Dan that Italians enjoy the tender flavor of a steak *'al sangue'* more than shoe leather. They assume most people feel the same way."

"What did Dan say to that?"

"I don't think he cared for my comment, and I shouldn't have teased him. Perhaps I felt he should have just quietly enjoyed the steak," I mused. "Anyway, tomorrow we're going to some crazy club."

"What do you mean?" Luiza asked.

"Well, we know it's frequented by members of this cult. It's a private club, members only. Amato goes there apparently to meet women and work his deals."

"Hmm, members only, huh, I'm not sure I want you going there." Luiza said.

"I think it is what you think it is," I offered. "This evening when Paola was asking me if I fool around, I told her I still like chasing you around the kitchen. When I get home, can I chase you around the kitchen?"

"The key is, when you get home. That could have been tomorrow night."

"Oh man, why do I get myself into these things," I lamented.

"Hey, you made that decision not me," Luiza scolded.

"I better end this conversation before I have to take a cold shower. I must keep my thoughts pure," I said.

"Pure? When did you ever want to be pure?" Luiza chided. Then with her face away from the phone and in a loud voice I heard her yell, "Hey! Boys stop that...The boys are arguing. I've got to go," Luiza said quickly.

"Always the grandkids before me," I lamented.

"Stop that! I miss you--come home soon," Luiza said.

"I miss you too sweetheart, Bye."

"Hey, Marty,"

"What"

"Yelling I need a quickie in the middle of a train station *is* pretty funny. I can't wait to tell Randa and Ernie."

"I knew you'd like it."

After I ended the call, I continued to click through the television stations, thinking of Luiza and Paola's comments about marriage. I thought about times when things were difficult, how Luiza and I stayed together for no other reason than-- the kids. Although it seems hard to believe, I remember how bitter and rejected I had felt towards Luiza for years. How we finally realized how wrong we were to be harboring so much anger towards each other. We broke through to the other side and fell in love all over again. I thought about Don Henley's song, *The Heart of the Matter*--"I think it's about forgiveness."

I continued to flip through the channels and stumbled on "The Late Show with David Letterman." I decided I needed to hear some English, so I ended up nodding off to David and his Top Ten list.

It was well after 2:00 AM when Dan finally stumbled into the room. Although he tried to be quiet, he woke me up. I think he was fairly drunk. "So how did it go?" I mumbled.

"I'll tell you about it in the morning," was his gurgled reply.

Chapter 41

Dan rolled out of bed about nine the next morning and made his way into the bathroom. I wasn't in any rush to get up, so I lay there reading. Several minutes later he came out the bathroom moaning and holding his head. Then, he wandered around the room dressing and combing his hair.

"What are you reading?" he asked.

"My daily, devotional Bible."

"You read that thing every morning?"

"No, not every morning, but I do try to spend several minutes in the morning reading and praying."

"Anyway, what's on the agenda today?" Dan asked.

"Frankly, we're on our own until Paola gets out of work and can take us to meet the club owner, Sonia Troia."

"What do you think you want to do?" I asked.

"The only thing I can think about is getting a cup of coffee."

"There's a breakfast room downstairs," I said.

"Are you ready to get up and get dressed?" Dan asked.

"I'll be ready in two minutes. If you want, go call the elevator."

We headed down to the lobby and into the "Breakfast Room". Dan was pleased to see it was not just a "Continental Breakfast". It included everything from hard-boiled eggs to sausages and pastries to fresh fruit. I commented about the wide selection. His only remark was "Where's the coffee?"

As we stood in the doorway looking around, a waiter approached us. He invited us to find a seat, and offered us a cappuccino. We found a table off in a corner where Dan made sure no one could walk behind him. I have seen this paranoia before from an Aussie cousin of mine. Because this cousin is retired, he's able to visit us now and again in the States. When we are together and out at a public place, I try to get him to sit with his back to the crowd. He only says, "No way mate, I'm not exposing my back." He also doesn't like to sit in a booth. He says it makes him feel trapped.

Not being too hungry I grabbed a yogurt, some fresh fruit, and a few slices of cooked ham. Dan got himself a bagel with marmalade, a couple of hard boiled eggs, and some Bel Paese cheese wedges.

"So, you ready to tell me about last night or do you need your second cappuccino?" I asked, once we settled into our breakfast.

"Man, I almost had a dream come true last night," Dan said, with a smile from the corner of his mouth, and while looking down at his plate.

"What do you mean?"

"Well, let's just say I could have had it all. In the end, the spirit was willing, but the flesh was weak," Dan lamented.

"Well, what happened?" I asked curiously.

"After we left you, she took me to this nightclub around the corner from Loretta's. The place was wild. There was loud disco music, flashing swirling lights, waitresses wearing tiny skirts, fish net stockings and black choker collars. I have a thing for fishnet stockings and chokers, especially chokers." I could see Dan drifting off thinking about the waitresses.

"Well, go on," I insisted, moving my hand in a small circular motion to encourage more information.

"There were dark cozy corners everywhere. No one was dancing. They just huddled close trying to talk over the loud music. We got pretty close just trying to talk. She had to speak into my ear, which turned me on, and I had to speak into hers."

"Oh man," I said leaning in.

Dan continued, "She had a couple glasses of wine. I asked for a dry Martini but they served me a glass of Martini and Rossi dry vermouth. I corrected it and had her get me a vodka Martini. I made sure they added the olive."

"How long did you stay there?" I asked.

"I'd say we were there a good hour. I couldn't believe the

bar tab. It's a good thing they don't expect the high percentage we usually give for tipping."

"It probably had a cover charge on it anyway, about 5%-10%," I added.

I could see the different people who came down to breakfast. They were basically working class. I wondered why we did not see more tourists and business execs; perhaps because it was the middle of the week.

Dan continued. "Then we left the club and went for a drive around the city."

"Where did she take you?"

"I'm not really sure. We drove around the city for a while. She'd point out the different landmarks."

"Well?"

"Her car is a small Italian make with a standard transmission. I never realized how sexy it is to watch a woman shifting, especially jamming the stick into gear."

"I'll have to get Luiza a standard next time," I said.

"When we were stopped at red lights she'd want to hold my hand or rub my knee. Then after a while she asked if I wanted to get a room here at the hotel and spend the night together."

"I guess you didn't since you staggered in about two this morning. I could see you were kind of drunk."

"I don't know if I was drunk, or just deadbeat tired," Dan said. "Anyway, as we approached the hotel, I had to tell Paola that it's been a few years since I've been with a woman. At my age and this late hour, I didn't think I'd be any good," Dan admitted with a look of resignation. He went on to say, "She told me there are pharmacies open all night. They have pharmacists on duty who take turns, so in cases of emergencies people can get their medicine. She wanted me to get something to help. She told me there should be a list of all night pharmacies at the front desk of the hotel."

"Did you?" I asked.

"When I told her I'd need a prescription. She told me no pharmacist in Italy would ever stand in the way of—*amore*. She assured me they would understand and no doubt have something. I just said let's call it a night, and I'll see you tomorrow. She was obviously disappointed, but said nothing," Dan motioned for the waiter and pointing to his cup indicated he wanted another cappuccino. He seemed more interested in his breakfast than his story. He started to look and sound better. There was hope for him and this day.

After we finished our breakfast, we asked the desk clerk about touring the city. She told us about a few places we might enjoy visiting. She suggested we visit the Mole Antonelliana and make sure we take the elevator to the top, where we'd get a spectacular look of the city. My only reply was, "Not me. You won't get me in that all glass elevator." She also suggested we consider taking the *Cremagliera railway* up to the *Basilica di Superga.* She lastly told us about Torino's Sightseeing tour buses like they have in New York City. She said it is called *City Sightseeing Torino* and explained we could catch it at Piazza Castello. We decided, since we had the day to kill, why not?

It was about the time we were getting to *Villa della Regina,* I noticed Dan had a pensive look on his face. Catching me looking at him, he asked, "You're not one of those holy Christian types."

"What do you mean by that?" I asked, unsure of what he meant.

"I mean you don't act like those holier-than-thou types, or like the ones you see on TV, always preaching *at* you, trying to get you saved or something," Dan tried to explain.

"I'm not sure what you're getting at."

"You're a regular guy. You don't put on religious airs. You're not spooky to be around," Dan said.

"Thank you-- I think," I replied.

"Yet, this morning when I got out of the bathroom, you were reading your Bible, kind of like reading any book. Also, you didn't seem to need to go through some type of ritual or incantation," Dan said.

"It's how I enjoy starting my day. In the morning, I wash myself, brush my teeth, eat breakfast, and have a devotional reading and pray for the day. It's my routine," I explained.

A few more minutes passed while we listened to the tour guide telling us about how the castle was built in the 1600's by some cardinal who was a prince and son of the Duke of Savoy. Then I said to Dan, "I think Jesus was a regular guy. I mean I don't think he put on religious airs."

"Why do you say that? What makes you think he was just a regular guy?" Dan asked.

"Perhaps calling him a regular guy isn't the best way to express it, but the hyper religious types didn't like him, but the people did. In fact, the religious ones criticized him for his eating and drinking too much. One of their criticisms of him was they accused him of being a drunk and a glutton. He must have liked to eat and drink with sinners. What I'm saying is, the people didn't feel judged or criticized when they were with him. There was something about him they liked. I believe they understood how he deeply cared about them," I said. "Perhaps that's why the religious types missed it. They were looking for a flashy tele-evangelist. Instead they got a homely son of a carpenter." After thinking a bit about what I had just said, I added, "I'm not sure if the Shroud really is the burial cloth of Christ, but I have to admit the face on it looks pretty homely."

Dan and I decided to leave the tour and find a small restaurant for lunch, since we could hop on and off the bus anytime for twenty-four hours. While sitting in the restaurant and waiting for our pasta Dan asked, "You think they used it yet?"

I looked at him with a look as if to ask, "What are you getting at?"

"You know, in one of their occult rituals?"

"Oh, I don't know," I said. "You'd have to think, that if they've had it in their possession for these past few years, it's a good probability."

"Does it bother you to think that some Satanists were performing their satanic ritual and using the Shroud as part of it?" Dan further asked.

"I'm still not sure the Shroud isn't some medieval hoax created by some clever alchemists. Or better yet, da Vinci himself as so many people believe," I said.

"Since I really don't believe in all that religious stuff, I don't even wonder if it's a hoax," Dan stated.

After eating in silence awhile, and soaking up the Italian atmosphere, which I enjoy so much, I said, "I think I'll give Loretta, a call and see what time we can come by the office. I'd like to see where she works and ask her about fixing my ticket. Hopefully the boss or manager won't mind us stopping by."

"Sounds like a plan. You have her number?" Dan asked.

Chapter 42

I called Loretta and asked if we could come by the agency. She said it should be fine but not before four that afternoon. She advised me she had just talked to Paola about getting together after our meeting with Sonia. Loretta said she hoped we would again have dinner at her apartment this evening.

After lunch, having time on our hands, we decide to get the Piazza Modena and take the cog railway up to the Basilica di Superga, which the desk clerk told us about. After about an hour and a half, we made our way back to Porta Nuova train station because Loretta's office was just around the corner. We walked into the marble-faced modern, office building, went up to the receptionist. I said, *"Buona sera,* we are here to see Loretta Grappelli."

The receptionist, who greeted us, picked up the phone and called Loretta, "Your friends are here, what should I tell them? . . . *Si, va bene, ciao."* Putting down the phone the receptionist told us, "She will be with you in a few minutes. She's busy at the moment."

She motioned towards a few chairs off to the side, suggesting we take a seat. When Paola heard we were waiting in the foyer, she came out from the offices walking briskly, smiling and saying, "Ciao, ciao. I'm so glad you came by." After greeting us, she encouraged us to sit and visit with her a few minutes. She asked if we enjoyed touring the city. I found Paola engaging, which made me realize why she was so good at her job. I was also intrigued to see how friendly she was to Dan without showing him special attention. I thought to myself, "She must have gotten over him already—win some, lose some." Dan on the other-hand was noticeably quiet and squirmy. I don't think he was particularly happy to see her.

I didn't notice Loretta coming until I heard, "*Ciao, Dan. Ciao, Marty.*" We immediately stood up and did the Italian two-cheek kissing routine with Loretta. I could not help but notice Loretta actually kissed Dan's cheeks. "What's going on here?" I thought.

"As you know already we did the bus tour around the city," I said.

"I'm amazed how wide your streets are," Dan commented.

"With all the porticoes, it makes Torino very interesting and quite a beautiful city," I added.

"All I've heard about Torino is that it's 'Italy's Detroit', which made me think I'd see coal driven factories, large depressed areas, 8 Mile Rd," Dan said, referring to Detroit's well known features.

"We've been trying to get the world to see Torino as it actually is," Loretta informed us. "It is a very international and beautiful city."

"Not only for its history, beauty and museums but it's a great place for Alpine skiing." she continued. "That's why we were so happy to successfully host the 2006 Winter Olympics. From that international exposure, it's our hope the English speaking world will continue calling our city Torino instead of Turin."

"Tell us what you saw today?" Paola asked.

"First we went to Piazza Castello and wandered around there for awhile. We visited the Royal Chapel and saw where they keep the Shroud," I said.

"Then we join a group touring Torino on a Hop on-Hop off bus. I've enjoyed getting to know the city," Dan added.

It was just as Dan was about to tell the girls more of what we did, one of Loretta's colleagues came in and decided to listen in and join us.

"Let me introduce Massimo, he's the head of sales and

also oversees retreats and conferences," Loretta said.

While Loretta was introducing him, Massimo was sticking out his hand and saying, "Very nice to meet you."

"Ah, nice to meet you too. So you speak English?" Dan asked.

"Yes, I do. In fact at times I am asked to also translate literature from English into Italian when it's necessary." Massimo said.

"Where else have you gone?" Loretta asked Dan and me.

"Well, we heard about the tram that goes up to the Basilica di Superga. The girl at the hotel said we should take the railway up to the Basilica." I said.

"We also discovered it was the site of a plane crash," Dan added.

"Yes it was. The football team known as "Grande Torino" were all killed in a plane crash back in May 1949. Not only were they killed but the couches and several famous newspaper reporters too," Massimo said. He went on to explain, they were five times the champions of Italy and still today are considered Italy best football team ever. It was a tragedy that we still speak about today. They were returning from Portugal after a friendly match.

"It sounds like the Buddy Holly, Richie Valens plane crash," Dan offered.

"I don't think you can compare one of the greatest football teams perishing and shocking our country to a few who died in a small plane crash," Massimo insisted quite passionately.

"No, what I was comparing it to is that both crashes are still spoken about today, after all these years. There was even a popular song written about it." Dan tried to explain.

It was obvious Massimo was a passionate football fan.

Loretta believing she needed to interrupt before Massimo retorted said, "Would you like to see our offices?"

Dan and Massimo looked at each other and began to laugh and shake hands. Massimo asked, "So you are finding Torino a beautiful city, true?"

"Sure, in fact, I need to ask you to see if you can fix my

ticket," I said.

"I'm not sure if I can do anything for you. It may need help from Signor Luca Tanelli, and he's not in his office now because he is in India to sign a contract with a resort there," she explained. "Shall we go?" Loretta asked, while standing up and motioning with her hand towards the doorway to the inner offices.

Apparently, Sancarlo Viaggi is quite an operation with satellite offices in Milan and Rome. I had always assumed it was one of those storefront travel agencies where you go in and book a flight with one of the staff behind the desks, the kind that were popular before the Internet. They were always decorated with posters of exotic places all over the walls and with stacks of brochures and magazines in racks. Sancarlo Viaggi, however, does a lot of other types of travel work. In addition to booking vacation packages, they organize corporate meetings, retreats, and group tours with hostesses, which is what Loretta does. As a hostess, she is assigned to accompany groups to exotic places usually to seminars or retreats. Her tasks are numerous ensuring the trips run smoothly through addressing any issues the travelers may encounter whilst away.

Visiting the belly of the beast, the part never seen to the normal traveler, we discovered it was a very busy place, with agents in cubicles wearing headphones talking to clients, personnel and accounting departments. They even had a couple of employees whose job it was to travel to places they wanted to market and to evaluate the suitability for their potential client base. "Where do I sign up for that job?" I thought to myself.

After the tour of the agency's inner workings, we went to the break room for an espresso and biscotti. Paola joined us, said she'd be free in half an hour and that Sonia was expecting us. Because we left our rental back at the hotel's parking garage, Paola drove us to the club. Dan was right; it was a small Italian car.

Chapter 43

Sancarlo Viaggi was around the corner from Porta Nuova train station, near the center of Torino, and *Il Giardino della Fantasia Club* was off in the northwest outskirts, tucked away in a somewhat residential area known as La Valletta. The traffic was quite heavy at that time of the day when most people were heading home. It took us almost an hour to get to the club. There were no neon signs announcing the club, and you wouldn't have known where it was located if you hadn't been there before.

After parking the car, we walked up to a large arched doorway, the kind that when both doors are open, a van or panel truck can drive through into the inner courtyard. On the right side door was a smaller security doorway used for personal access. When we were buzzed in, the door popped opened. We walked under the portico and into the courtyard, which was a good size, surrounded by four buildings which were no more than three stories tall. We noticed the club's entrance over to the far left side. We made our way over to the entrance and saw, just to the right of the glass and aluminum door, a small plaque that read "*Il Giardino della Fantasia Club*" with "Private, Members Only" in English just below. "How chic," Dan commented running his index finger under the words.

Just inside the doorway was a small foyer with a sliding glass window to the left, which was closed and the curtain drawn, behind the glass. I surmised that was where patrons showed their membership cards. As we were walking through the door, Sonia Troia was also arriving. She smiled warmly and greeted Paola.

Their embrace was more than warm and lasted longer than might be considered usual. Rather than the traditional kiss on both cheeks, they kissed on the lips. After their embrace Paola turned toward us and said, *"Miei nuovi amici."*

"So these are your new friends you were telling me about," Sonia said.

Sonia seemed excited to meet us. Her greetings were warm and enthusiastic but no long embraces. She was not heavy, but busty and well rounded. Her dress was loose fitting and resembled a kimono with large flowers printed on it. Sonia was either a well preserved seventy-year old or a burnt out fifty-year old. I guessed her to be around fifty-five years of age. She invited us to follow her into the club. As we walked through the pair of interior doors, she waved her hand around and said, *"Mio terreno di gioco."* I thought to myself, "I've never seen a playground like this." As we passed through the different play areas, Sonia explained how the club functioned. Our imaginations were going wild. I looked at Dan wide-eyed, while he acted nonchalant as though he encountered this every day.

We made our way to the back of the club and down a small hallway to Sonia's office. The office was cramped with stuff. It had a desk in the far right corner covered with papers, magazines, and junk. In front of the desk along the left wall was a couch and just to the right inside the door was a pair of padded metal chairs. Sonia sat at her desk and invited us to sit on the couch. Paola and Dan sat on the couch. I grabbed one of the metal chairs. The thought of what might have transpired on that couch made me cringe. Once we were seated and the small talk was over, Sonia asked, "How may I help you? Is it true you are considering opening a club like this in the United States?"

Paola shrugged and said in English, "She asked me why you wanted to meet her."

I said, "No, that's not exactly why we were interested in meeting you. We asked Paola not to reveal the real reason, because we wanted the chance to speak with you directly."

"Why would two Americans want to speak to me?"

Sonia asked.

"Because we are hoping you might be able to help us," I replied.

"Well, I will if I can, but I'm not sure how," Sonia said somewhat quizzically.

"I am hoping we can trust you to keep this quiet. This is quite a delicate matter and needs to be kept between us," I further said.

"Believe me, if you knew who came into this club and what goes on here, I could expose many. So you can be sure I know how to be discreet," Sonia assured us.

"Thanks for your reassurance," I said.

"We have discovered members of an occult group meet here," I said.

"Yes, you must be talking about those who believe in Stregheria. I, too, am a follower," Sonia said, almost with pride. Smiling, she said, "We believe in love. We desire to love as often as we can. We believe in expressing our love and not holding back. Do you think me wrong for that?"

"I am not here to judge, but I would like to ask you about Giovanni Amato. Is he a member of your private club?"

"Amato?" she repeated, like it was a question. "Yes, I know him. He's a pig. He's not full of love. He is just full of vulgarity," Sonia spat out. "What do you want to know about him? Are the international police looking for him because of his smuggling?" Sonia asked.

While Sonia was speaking about Amato, I noticed on the shelves behind her were boxes about the size of cigarette cartons, labeled, Preservativi- Pamitex Classico, misura normale, some labeled, Xtra-Largo, Comfort. I also noticed she had about three times more boxes of the Xtra-Largo than boxes of the normal size. I mused to myself, "I'll bet no guy buys the normal size. They only get the XL and pin it on if they had to." After chuckling to myself, I heard Paola say, "No, these Americans are looking for the Shroud of Turin."

"Ah, the Shroud, you believe I can help you." Sonia said with a pensive tone.

"We are not the police. We are just two Americans who

have met the widow of the man who found and sold the Shroud. She is the one who pointed us to Amato. He tells us it was secretly sold through contacts who are members of your club. We are hoping you may have heard something and are willing to help us," I explained.

"What will you do if you find the Shroud?" Sonia asked.

"Sincerely?" I paused. "We want to restore it to its rightful owner--The Catholic Church."

"Give it to those horrible men! Those sexually frustrated old men," she hissed. "I don't know if I want to help you do that."

After quietly thinking about it for minute or so Sonia said, "The truth is we got cheated out of getting the cloth."

"Cheated?" Paola asked. "By whom? How?"

Chapter 44

"That bastard politician from Milano, Domenico Mitcelli," Sonia said, obviously infuriated at the very mention of his name.

"How were you cheated?" I asked.

"Well, a few years ago, Amato came into the club saying he knew how to get his hands on a very important sacred artifact. He was always scheming and trying to work some deal, so we didn't believe him at first. He asked me if we could have a private meeting in my office. I agreed and the two of us came in here. He took one look at my couch and with a crude smirk on his face, proposed we have a quick one."

I could see from the look on her face that even the thought of the encounter with Amato disgusted her, and any relationship between the two of them was strictly business.

"Anyway, after making him leave me alone, I told him the information he had better be important or he'd be thrown out and never allowed back."

Paola was translating for Dan and doing an excellent job, almost word for word.

Sonia continued, "He had a satchel with him and after he sat down, he pulled out this brown leather bound book. He explained it was the private diary of an aide to King Victor Emmanuel III, dating back to when he was King. He started showing me these passages, how a certain man named Grassi worked for the King. Some of his duties had included scheduling public events, overseeing staff and privately advising the King. He showed me in this diary how the King feared the Nazis would steal the Shroud, so he had this aide create a forgery of it. He then turned to the back of the diary and showed how Grassi had gotten his hands on the real Sacred Shroud. It had never been put back in the Royal Chapel after the war. The counterfeit one was still in the Chapel, and no one knew it," Sonia explained.

"Did you believe the diary to be authentic?" Dan asked and then motioned Paola to translate for him.

"I wasn't sure. I hoped it was, but it was Amato showing it to me. He could very well be involved with some scam," Sonia said.

"How did you come to believe it was genuine?" Dan further questioned. Again Dan asked Paola to translate.

"I finally believed it because of a friend who had worked in the Palace. This old friend of my parents was a caretaker there. I asked him if he knew the name of the King's personal aide. He said he remembered a bitter old man, who had been an aide to the King. Although he wasn't positive, he thought his name was Grassi. As soon as I heard him say Grassi, I knew the diary may be authentic," Sonia said. "Then, Amato had me meet Bruno Russo. Russo was a timid man who wasn't sure if he wanted to sell the Shroud. Amato seemed to be pushing him to sell it. Once I met Russo, I knew he wasn't an actor, and it wasn't a scam," she explained. "I have seen and met many men coming and going from this club. He had a sincere, simple, honest look about him, someone to believe."

"At first Amato said they wanted €1,000,000 for the article. I said no one would pay that kind of money for it. He suggested we find donors and put our money together. We were able finally to get them down to €500,000, a more reasonable price, but none of us had that kind of money."

Still distracted and curious, I continued to look at the shelves behind Sonia. She had all kinds of sex toys and miscellaneous related paraphernalia. I decided I was getting more of an education than I wanted.

"How did Mitcelli get his hands on it?" I asked.

"Was it Mitcelli who put up the cash?" Dan asked.

"Yes. He was here one night. He had seldom come to the club, because he lives in Milano. Now and again his business brought him to Torino. On those occasions he would bring a girlfriend to the club. On this particular night, he apparently paired up with Valeria, a regular here. She's also a member of Stregheria," Sonia said.

"Yes, I know her," Paola interjected.

"Well, for whatever reason, she told Mitcelli about Amato trying to sell the Shroud to us. Mitcelli wanted to know more, so Valeria brought him over to me and said he wanted to help us. The three of us met later that evening after everyone was gone, and we discussed the matter. He was very wary of being found out, so he insisted no one else know he was willing to help. He also indicated he was interested in joining us in *Stregharia*, which made me believe he was sincere," Sonia said shrugging her shoulders and raising her two hands. She then continued, "Anyway, the next time Amato came in, I told him I had someone who could pay for the Shroud but wanted to remain anonymous. We decided a secret meeting should be worked out where we would exchange the money for the Shroud."

"This is so exciting," Paola said.

"How was the exchange worked out?" Dan asked again through Paola.

"We agreed to meet in an abandoned parking lot not far from here. There were not many buildings near it, and it was fairly isolated. The back section away from the street was darker and more hidden by the surrounding trees. The plan was, at 2:00 AM after the club closed for the night, to have Amato park at one end of the lot near a dumpster. Mitcelli and I would park at the other end. I was to first make sure all the money was in Mitcelli's briefcase. After a flick of the headlights, he was to meet me in the middle of the lot with the Shroud. I would meet him there with the money. No problem, we're all friends right?" she said raising her voice to make it a question.

"I looked over the money to make sure it was all there, then Mitcelli's bodyguard flashed the lights. I met Amato in the middle of the lot, as planned, to make the exchange. I walked back to the car where Mitcelli was parked. As I got near the car, Amato was already driving away, and the bodyguard got out of the passenger's side. I knew immediately something was up. When the three of us drove to the lot, Mitcelli and I were in the back seat while the bodyguard drove. Apparently, as I was making the trade, Mitcelli slipped into the driver's seat and his bodyguard slid over into the passenger side. As soon as I got near the car, the bodyguard jumped out, rushed over to me, and quickly snatched the cloth from me. All he said was 'It's not too far a walk from here.' He gave me a slight push away from the car, jumped into the passenger's seat and off they went, leaving me stranded. I cursed them all the way home."

"What happened then?" I asked.

"I felt like a fool for trusting that pig. I didn't want anyone to know what an idiot I was, so I've kept it quiet. I told Valeria it never panned out. I have been concerned if Amato told anyone, I might be arrested. But he doesn't want to be implicated or barred from the club, so he keeps his mouth shut."

"Have you ever heard or seen Mitcelli since?" Dan asked.

"No, he wouldn't dare show his face here again," Sonia said. She added, "I recently heard he's planning to run for Mayor of Milan. I'm thinking of dropping a line to the newspapers."

"Is that why you're willing to let us know what you know?" Dan asked.

"Yes. As much as I hate the Catholic Church, and I'm happy they got screwed out of their precious relic, I hate that pig more. I hope those Bishops put a curse on him so his penis withers up and falls off just before he dies and burns in hell," Sonia said with venom in her voice.

We talked some more and allowed Sonia to vent her hatred for Mitcelli. She hoped she wouldn't be incriminated, and we would be successful. She also told us if we wanted to come back later tonight, she would make sure we had a memorable time. I said I'd have to call my wife to see what she thought about it. Sonia laughed and said, "Next time your wife comes with you to Torino, let me know." Not wanting to offend her, I said, "We'll see about it."

Chapter 45

After our meeting with Sonia, Paola, Dan and I made our way back through the club heading for the exit. A couple of housekeepers or maintenance people had arrived to clean and prepare the place for the evening. I secretly wondered if they sterilized the place.

As we made our way out onto the street and were about to get into Paola's car, out of the blue, Dan said, "There's a parallel universe, there really is a parallel universe."

Not getting what he meant, my mind immediately went to some Sci-fi scenario or a Steven Hawkins discovery. Paola, on the other hand, rather than guess what Dan meant asked, "What do you mean?"

"I mean there's a whole other reality that comes out at night. They are barbers, bankers, and businessmen by day and at night they're sexual perverts wearing masks and costumes, thinking they're some super hero," Dan explained.

By Paola's expression, I could see she took offense at his comment.

"Do you think they see themselves as sexual perverts?" I asked.

"We are not perverts," Paola insisted. "It is how we express our love for each other. We play together and have fun like adult children."

"Like I said, it's a parallel world right here among us," Dan said shaking his head.

I thought to myself what different views we had of love. I thought about what the Apostle Paul said about love, how it is patient, kind, not envious, nor boastful, etc. I said nothing not wanting to aggravate Paola further. I also thought to myself, Dan's comment was probably the end of any prospects of romance with Paola.

On the way to Loretta's, Paola informed us she would not be joining us for dinner. By her tone it was obvious she had been offended by Dan's criticism and would rather leave us at the curb. As we approached Loretta's building, I said in Italian to Paola, "I have enjoyed meeting you. I am very sorry you were hurt by my friend's comment. Is there anything I could say that would help you change your mind?" Her only reply to me was, "Perhaps another time. *Sono stanca sta sera.*" she said, indicating she was tired.

Dan watched us, and made no comment except to ask, "What'd she say?"

"She's tired."

"Oh," was his only reply.

After we got out of the car, I reached in through the passenger's window to shake Paola's hand and say good bye. She then said with a half-smile on her face, "Next time you're in Torino, please bring your wife and leave him home."

"*Va bene d'accordo,*" I replied, agreeing to her request

She added, "I can see why your younger sister likes you so much. She has spoken about you and your family at the office. It is perhaps the main reason I was glad to be invited over last night. In fact, I remember her concern for your son. Is he ok?" "You mean our son Pete's bout with Hodgkin's Lymphoma a few years earlier? Yes, it is now three years and nothing has re-occurred. In fact his wife just had a boy, Jordan Peter."

"I remember Loretta was very concerned for him at the time," Paola said.

"So were we. Anyway, now we have another beautiful grandson." With that I shook Paola's hand again, smiled and stepped away from her car as she drove off.

"I wonder what Loretta is planning for dinner," Dan said nonchalantly, disregarding my conversation with Paola.

We rang Loretta's doorbell, heard, "*Avanti*" and then the buzz of the door. Once in the elevator, I started thinking about

Paola's belief system. It seems so often we equate sex with love. As the elevator opened, I asked Dan, "Do you have any idea as to what we should do next?"

"Yes, enjoy Loretta's cooking and relax," he said.

We made our way to her apartment. The door was already ajar inviting us in.

"If you want to wash your hands, the bathroom is over there," Loretta called from the kitchen.

Dan went first. When I came out of the bathroom, Dan handed me a glass of chilled white wine. I also noticed he had already moved a chair close to the kitchen doorway, intending to watch Loretta cook. I chose to sit on the couch, at least for the time being.

"How did it go?" Loretta asked from the kitchen

"It went well," Dan answered. After a pensive pause, he added, "Now that we know who bought the Shroud, we will have to figure out a way get to it."

"So did you find out who has stolen the Shroud?" Loretta asked with an obvious excitement in her voice.

"Yes, a Milanese politician named Domenico Mitcelli," I said raising my voice from the living room.

"Marty, why don't you bring a chair next to me?" Loretta called from the kitchen. She asked Dan, "So, tell me what happened."

"This club is a strange place," Dan said.

He went on to describe the layout of the club. He told her details of the place, such as what it looked like, and what his impression of the establishment was. After getting to the end of his description Dan concluded, "Well let's just say it's a whole other world."

"Tell her what Sonia told us," I said to Dan.

"She said Amato did try to sell the Shroud at the club. First he hoped to get €1,000,000, but when no one came forward to buy it, he dropped it to €500,000. Then apparently this Milanese businessman said he would be willing to finance it for this group of witchcraft believers with whom Paola and Sonia are involved. Anyway, apparently at the time they met to make the pay off, Mitcelli and his bodyguard grabbed the

Shroud, shoved Troia out of the way and took off leaving her alone in some abandoned parking lot. She said all the way home she cursed him, wishing his penis would fall off."

"Did she really say that?" Loretta asked.

"Yes she did," I said, now standing near Dan who was sitting in the doorway to the kitchen.

"Loretta, you know what Sonia Troia called Mitcelli?" I asked.

"No, What?"

"A pig, she called him a pig for what he did."

"So, what's the point?" Dan asked.

Chapter 46

"Well, Sonia's last name, "Troia" actually means sow, female pig. It gets better, when you realize that *son* in Italian means 'I am.' Every time she says her name she's saying 'I am a female pig.' But it doesn't finish there. In Italian "sow" is also a vulgar term for whore. Every time she says her full name, Sonia Troia, she's saying, 'I'm a whore'" All three of us had a pretty good chuckle over that one.

"*Allora, cosa prepari sta sera?*" I asked, interested to know what Loretta had made for our dinner this evening.

"First I am preparing risotto Milanese ,and then, I went to the Salumeria to buy some Prosciutto crudo." Dan looked at me, and we burst out laughing thinking how prosciutto comes from a sow's rear-end.

We enjoyed our time together that evening. I was thinking of the last time I had had such good risotto *alla Milanese* was when I had lived with the Grappellis in Segrate many years before.

Loretta told us about her upcoming tour when she would be taking a group of corporate executives to a resort in the Azores. She explained some of her duties when she takes these corporate executives on exotic retreats designed to build unity and common purpose. When Dan heard about her responsibilities, he wanted to tell us all about one of the jobs he and Ted were hired to do.

"Let me tell you about the time we were hired to bug and record the activities of the twelve executives of this manufacturing plant from the south. Their retreat weekend was in April over *Patriots Day* weekend. It was also the weekend of the Boston Marathon. It seems the President of this company had some relative who fought in the Revolutionary War and wanted to trace his heritage while in the area. Anyway, we were told when they would be coming and what hotel and rooms were reserved for them. So, the night before they checked into this swanky Boston hotel, we occupied all their reserved rooms. We bugged the hell out of the rooms. They couldn't even pee without us recording it."

"Isn't this illegal?" I asked with concern.

"Sure, it's as *illegal* as it gets."

"But you did it anyway?" Loretta asked.

"The money was great. If you only knew what we got paid," Dan said without any regret in his tone. Loretta and I looked at each other not knowing how to react.

"You want to hear the story or not?" Dan asked a bit defensively.

"Oh, of course," I said.

"Anyway, this top boss wanted to collect dirt on his executives, so he could keep them in line with the dirt he gathered."

"*Mamma mia!*" Loretta offered while putting her hand on her right cheek.

"Did he get any?" I asked.

"He sure did. One of his execs brought one of the waiters from the hotel restaurant back to his room for a tryst."

"You mean another guy?" I asked.

"Yes, and he's married."

"A few of the others found themselves companionship, apparently with the help of the concierge at the hotel. Then there were these two executives for the company, who decided to sleep together. They too were both married."

"Another couple of men?" Loretta asked.

"No, I think she was head of accounting and he was head of quality control or something like that. Apparently not their first time either."

"Kinda puts a new twist on combining departments," I quipped.

"No, it is more like mergers and acquisitions," Loretta

offered. We all had a good laugh at Loretta's comment.

"Dan, did Luiza ask you to come and keep an eye on me?" I asked only half joking.

"No, but you better be good," Dan offered.

"I know she can be possessive of her man," I said shaking my head and acting like I was adjusting my tie in pride.

"I better be good on this trip and any others in the future," Loretta resolved.

"Have you ever?" Dan asked with that look on his face that I've seen before.

"Loretta, watch out. Dan has switched into his inquisitor mode," I said.

"No, I haven't. I'm always so busy. I'm constantly running around making sure it all gets done. I'm too exhausted to think about anything else," Loretta explained.

The savory odor of the risotto was making me hungry. Loretta leaned towards us straining to hear Dan. I asked her if I could help stir the risotto, which she gladly obliged. While she ladled in a little more chicken broth, Dan continued with his stories.

He went on and told us about some of his adventures, or should I say misadventures, in the White House, some funny, others more serious.

"Marty, I know I never told you and Luiza this thing that happened during the first year of the Nixon Administration. Frankly after all these years, I've never told anyone."

"*Madonna mia*, it's very Top Secret," Loretta said with a serious stare on her face.

"Are you going to tell us now?" I asked.

"It's been almost forty years, and I can't believe it'll ever get back to the ears of the Pentagon or the Department of Defense," Dan said with some hesitation.

"Well?" I asked moving my hand in a circular motion.

I could see that Dan wasn't comfortable, and I could also sense it was more than just trying to impress Loretta.

Chapter *47*

"What happened was that the US military almost nuked Kiev by accident."

"What do you mean, 'nuked Kiev' and what do you mean almost by accident?" I asked Dan.

"Well, in order to keep our forces in readiness, periodically there are exercises that simulate the US being under a nuclear attack. On this particular exercise the B-52's were scrambled and heading for their targets. Well, when they're flying towards their targets there are these periodic checks to see if they should turn around or continue towards they destination. Anyway, this one bomber loaded with H-bombs didn't get the 'return to base' signal, but instead was to continue to the target. They thought it wasn't just an exercise but the real thing. At a certain point the pilots and crew shoot out these metal shards to confuse the radars and become undetectable. At that point the President and his Joint Chiefs of Staff knew they were going for their target. We couldn't see them, and we didn't know exactly where they were. Also, they were never detected by the Russians either."

"You're telling me that we were about to bomb a city in the Soviet Union, and they didn't know it?"

"There was a computer glitch that actually sent a bomber loaded with nuclear bombs, similar to what happened in the movie 'Failsafe'." Dan explained. He then claimed he couldn't give us more details, but said we were very close to bombing a major city in the Soviet Union and the Russians would have been caught off guard. Dan even said there were generals on the Joint Chiefs of Staff who encouraged Nixon to go ahead and allow them to hit their target, since we had the first strike, and they were obviously unaware of what was coming. Dan insisted to Nixon's credit he refused to listen to them. Apparently they scrambled fighter jets over the North Sea that flew a one-way mission trying to intercept the bomber.

"What happened to the fighter jets and pilots?" I asked.

"They were lost somewhere over the North Sea."

He finished the story by telling us they convinced the pilots to turn back by getting their wives to share intimate secrets about themselves that only they could have known. After the pilots returned, they were court marshaled for not obeying orders.

"You mean we came *that* close to a nuclear war?" I asked.

Dan nodded, to silently indicate a yes. Perhaps Loretta didn't want to comprehend the ramifications. She just asked, "Now that you know about this Milanese guy, what's next?"

"We'll have to head for Milan tomorrow morning," Dan replied.

"Loretta, you remember the Bonzi family from Segrate? They had a large family. I've remained friends with Franco. He's now the police commissioner for Segrate. I'm hoping he can shed some light on this Mitcelli," I said. "Before I left the States, I told him that I'd try to see him when I got to Italy, so calling him tomorrow would be good."

"We can check my search engines too," Dan added.

"To see what there is on him?" I asked.

Ignoring my question, Dan only asked if there was any nocino before we got on our way. He was making himself right at home in Loretta's apartment, I thought.

The next morning Dan and I got up and did our various routines. We had a leisurely breakfast in the breakfast roon and allowed the morning traffic to die down. We checked out of the hotel about 10, stuffed our bags into the compact rental and hit the road for Milan. It now was apparent that Dan was the default driver. He kept the keys and no longer asked if he should drive, which actually was fine with me. I seldom enjoy driving, especially long distances. In fact, back home Luiza often drives. Once on the Highway, I decided to call Franco and Mariano to let them know we were on our way to Milan.

"*Comando, Polizia di Segrate*," answered the Segrate Police controller "This call is being recorded," he informed us when answering the phone.

"I would like to speak with Commissioner Bonzi please."

"*Chi parla?*" he asked. In an attempt at humor I replied, "Lieutenant Colombo." There was no reply, just a grunt and then the buzz of a phone ringing. Another Italian who didn't like my attempt at humor, I surmised.

"Bonzi," was all Franco said when he answered the phone. Franco and I had been friends since my early days in Italy. We lost contact for a number of years but reestablished our friendship in 1990, when I returned to Italy for the first time.

"*Ciao, Franco, sono Marty.*" I said announcing myself.

"Ciao Marty, where are you?"

"On the Autostrada A4 from Torino," I said.

"I thought you had already gone back home."

"Not yet. Something has come up."

"I was hoping to see you, but never heard from you again," Franco said.

"When I called you before leaving home, I thought I'd have seen see you before now too, but something unbelievable has come up."

"Is that why you're still here?" Franco asked.

"I'd really rather not explain over the phone." I replied. "Can we come by the station when we get to Milan?"

"Of course, we can have lunch together. Will you be in Milano by 12:30?" Franco asked.

"Yes we should be. Is there a restaurant nearby where we can speak privately?" I asked.

"We can always close the door to my office, if you want to be sure our conversation is private," Franco offered.

"And then go to lunch?" I asked.

"I can be free for an hour at lunch time, unless something urgent comes up," Franco assured me.

"By the way, I'm not alone. I have an American friend with me. He's a former private investigator who is now retired."

"*OK, ci vediamo più tardi, ciao,*" Franco said confirming our seeing each other later and ended the call.

Before calling Mariano, I tried to relax and resist my fears; at least as much as I could. Unfortunately, Dan was daring to break the sound barrier with our rented car. The car's speedometer was heading north of 180 kph (110 mph).

"How fast do you intend to go?" I asked, thinking how this would get us fined if caught travelling at over 110 mph back home.

"It's amazing how fast and smooth these little Italian cars are," was his only reply. "Why, I'm not making you nervous am I?" he then asked half smirking.

"You broke my comfort barrier back around 150, and now you've broken the white knuckle barrier," I said.

"I didn't realize you don't like speed. You didn't say anything the other day," he said while he began to slow it down to 145 and just cruise.

"*Pronto, Studio Prisma,*" Mariano answered his phone.

"*Ciao, Mariano.*"

"*Ciao, Marty dove sei*?" he asked.

"We're about 50 kilometers from Milano."

It was about the time we were getting near to Novara that I called Mariano.

"Will I see you and your friend today?" he asked.

"We're heading to Segrate to meet up with an old friend for lunch. After that I was hoping we could see you," I replied.

"I'm here at my studio until five. Can you come by before then?"

"Sure, as soon as we're done with lunch," I replied.

"Very well, I'll see you a little later," I said.

"*Ciao.*"—"*Ciao.*"

After saying good bye, I turned to Dan, "Mariano wants us to come by his studio and visit. He is northwest of Milan, about a half hour drive from where Bonzi is."

Dan said nothing but nodded and smiled.

Chapter 48

After a period of silence, Dan asked out of nowhere, "Didn't they prove the Shroud is fake using Carbon-14 dating?"

"Yes, they did. Carbon-14 tests were done back in '88. The results showed that the cloth dated to the 13th or 14th century," I replied. "That's because they were testing a piece of cloth from the forgery. Apparently, the forgers used an old tarp that may have already been centuries old," I speculated.

Again, we drove along for a while in silence. I could tell Dan was mulling over something. I just didn't know what. Then out of the blue again Dan said, "I'm not sure Jesus ever came out of the grave." He paused and then added, "I think his followers stole his body and lied about the resurrection."

I replied, "Well, the Bible tells us that the Jewish religious leaders, who plotted to have Jesus crucified, asked Pilot to place a Roman soldiers to watch the tomb, just in case they tried to steal the body. They told Pilot, 'That deceiver claimed he would rise from the dead after three days.'"

This time Dan listened rather than try to change the subject. I went on to say, "The Bible further records how the Roman guards who were ordered to guard his tomb were later bribed by the Jewish leaders to tell that very story. As a way to explain the empty tomb, the guards said that Jesus' disciples stole His body while they slept."

After further consideration of this scenario, Dan blurted out, "That's nuts. Anyone who knows anything about the military, and especially the Roman military, knows if that happened those guards would have paid with their lives. They wouldn't have had the chance to claim anything. Besides there were perhaps as many as 10 to 20 soldiers charged with the task. They would never have slept at the same time when assigned a watch. They would have switched every couple of hours."

My next point was, "Another thing to consider is that pretty much all 12 original apostles were martyred, or better yet, brutally murdered, one way or another for saying the man the Romans and Jewish leaders crucified had risen and was alive." Then I added, "I can understand religious fanatics dying for an ideal or belief but for a known lie? I mean,
they would have known it was a hoax to claim Jesus rose from the dead, if in fact they did steal his body."

"I know a bit about liars," Leif commented. "They always lie right up to the point of no return. Then it's amazing how they can tell the truth. Also, I know a bit about group lies. All you need is to get one to break and spill the beans, and then it's over. It's impossible to get everyone to stick together and to be willing to die... I doubt it!"

Several minutes later he said, "I'm actually glad Darla's relatives made me feel unwelcome."

"What do you mean by that?" I asked.

"Well, I felt guilty for what happened to my wife. I regretted I got that loser Ryan pissed off with me."

"Why would you think it's your fault? Ryan is the only one responsible for what he did," I said.

"In a funny way, I finally feel free. Darla was a good wife. She loved me dearly. I feel in my heart she's with her Jesus," Dan said. Then added, "I think this is what they call closure."

"But why are you happy they were angry with you?" I asked.

"Because now I'm free of them and won't have to host them if they come to the US, as they were hoping. And besides, I got to come to Italy,"

"I'm glad you came too." I replied, knowing I now meant it.

After a pause for a few more minutes Dan then said, "Ever since Darla's death, I've been depressed. Today may be the first day I feel happy and even peaceful."

"Hopefully you've turned a corner and better days are ahead," I said thinking this adventure may have helped Dan move on.

With only the help of a few road sign translations, Dan got us to the police station in Segrate. They had a few spots for short term parking; we grabbed one and made our way through the heavily secured doors into the station and up to the desk clerk. The clerk asked us what our business was. "We are here to see Commissioner Bonzi," I replied.

The clerk's only response was, "Ah, Tenente Columbo," as he picked up the phone to buzz Franco. I would have said "Si" if he had had a smile on his face, but I decided to look at the ground and check out the floor tiles. Several long seconds later the clerk said, "Those two Americans are here, should I send them up?" "*Si, si d'accordo,*" we heard in reply. As soon as the the front desk officer hung up he said to us, "At the end of the hall to the right is a stairway; the Commissioner will meet you at the top of the stairs." Then he buzzed us in through the next set of double doors. These very thick glass security doors only allowed one person at a time. First, you stepped inside a tiny, all glass chamber, and then the next door opens to give entrance. You better not suffer from claustrophobia.

At the top of the stairway Franco waited for us. "*Ciao, Marty!*" Franco said with his hand out and a big laughing smile. I ran up the last few steps and, with a warm embrace, said, "*Ciao Franco.*"

"May I present my friend Dan Carlson," I said while grabbing Dan's shoulder.

"Dan, this is Franco, the only guy I smoked pot with in Italy."

As we made our way into Bonzi's office, Dan mumbled out the corner of his mouth, "If this place is bugged, you just got your friend in trouble."

"That was more than 30 years ago," I said. "I would think there's a statute-of-limitations."

We sat in a couple of leather padded chairs in front of Franco's desk. As he was sitting down behind his desk Franco asked, "So why are you still here, and why the secrecy?"

"The reason is because we're on an investigation. It's a long story, but in a nut shell we're trying to find out who has the real Shroud of Turin," I replied.

"What do you mean, who has it?" Franco asked raising an eyebrow.

"Ok. As you know, I went to Torino to install some stained-glass in a convent chapel, and from there we went on to visit my relatives in the mountains above Reggio Emilia. Well, as fate would have it, when I was at the convent I overheard something one of the nuns told the Mother Superior. This Sister Grazia told the Mother Superior that her brother, who is the secretary to the Archbishop of Torino, had just discovered that the real Shroud was stolen and the one in the 'Royal Chapel' is a fake. They also found out that a duplicate was created back during World War II."

"What! They are just finding out about it now?" Franco asked somewhat incredulously.

Chapter 49

On one of Franco's office walls, there were a few windows. His desk was positioned so that he could easily look out the windows that faced the piazza in front of the station. I thought to myself it made a great location to either day dream or to just keep an eye on the comings and goings of the station.

"Well, yes, according to Sister Grazia's brother, it was stored in a trunk for more than 50 years. Apparently the King had a duplicate Shroud made because he feared the Nazis would steal it. Then shortly after the war, the royal family fled Italy. The King never made it back to Torino to switch it back. As I understand it, a former aide found it hidden in the King's closet and decided to keep it, only to die suddenly a few weeks later, thereby sealing the secret seemingly forever in his trunk."

"That is incredible. So what happened next?" Franco was very interested, but not sure he should believe the story.

"According to the Monsignor at the Curia, a few years ago this guy cleaning out his cellar found an old trunk," I said. "After reading the aide's journal, he realized that he had the authentic Shroud. Instead of returning it to the Church, he decided to sell it, figuring it to be worth a sizeable ransom."

"*Vero?*" Franco asked, unsure how true this all was.

I nodded my head, confirming the truth, and continued, "Anyway, shortly after he died, his wife went into the Archbishop's office and told the whole story to the Archbishop's secretary, a Monsignor Scagnelli."

Before I could continue, there was a knock on the commissioner's door. *"Scuzate,"* Franco answered the door and softly spoke with a police woman. They talked briefly and then he returned to his desk.

When he sat back down he said, "Excuse me... Please go on. This is amazing."

"Well," I said. "The Monsignor called his sister, who is a nun at the convent. She excitedly told the mother superior about his call, and I overheard their conversation. Then, by good fortune, Dan called me from Amsterdam, saying he wanted to come to Italy for a few days before heading back to the States. I thought, since Dan is an experienced investigator, why not try to see if we could discover who has the real Shroud?"

"Well, how is it going so far?" Franco asked.

"The truth is--quite well. We found out that this Milanese politician named Domenico Mitcelli bought the Shroud in Torino for €500,000. We think that he has it now."

"Mitcelli? I certainly can believe he would be someone who would like to get his hands on it," Franco speculated.

"Do you know anything about him?"

Franco went on to explain, "*Allora, sua famiglia sono molto ricche*", advising us he was from a wealthy family. "They own several companies, an oil refinery in Sardinia, and some manufacturing plants north of the city. He even owns Milan's football team, AC Milan. I think he could have bought it because he also owns a couple of TV stations. They mostly broadcast shows brought in from America and at least one soap opera from Argentina, but after midnight the TV shows are all x-rated and fortune tellers who read the fortunes of viewers who call in."

I wondered to myself, if he owned the station that had the fortune teller I saw when I was back in the hotel in Torino.

"How can we find out where he lives?" I asked.

"I understand he lives out in Brianza, which is a town just north of Milan."

"There's no way to get near him with his team of bodyguards" Franco said. "How would you even approach him?" Franco further speculated.

After a pause, Dan interjected, "How about lunch?" He seemed fidgety, perhaps because he couldn't get in on the conversation in Italian.

Franco understood his request and said, "Ah, yes, just give me a few minutes, and I'll meet you in front of the station." He then escorted us to the top of the stairs. We made our way back through the security doors and waited by the car. It was several minutes later when he finally came out of the station. He apologized for taking longer than expected. He then indicated there was a pizzeria around the corner we could easily walk to. I asked him if our car was ok parked where it was. He assured me that if they put a parking ticket on it, he'd take care of it. We laughed and walked on. While walking to the pizzeria Franco continued to warn me about how dangerous Mitcelli could be and suggested we let the Curia in Torino know what we had discovered.

Not having seen one another for a few years, lunch for Franco and I was a chance to catch up. However, I could see Dan was bored listening to us ramble in Italian. I tried to fill him in on what we were reminiscing about, but it was old times talk and Dan couldn't relate. Whilst I had a moment of concern for Dan, my desire to hear Franco's news meant we chatted and Dan had to patiently watch the world around us.

When our pizzas arrived Franco and I proceeded to cut up the pieces with a knife and fork the traditional Italian way. Dan on the other hand cut out a wedge about a sixth of his pizza, grabbed it with his hands and ate it 'al Americana.' I think he wanted to let everyone in the place know he was an American. His only comment was, "Pizza, beer and football—doesn't get any better." The pizzeria was full of Soccer memorabilia. The owner was obviously a passionate fan for "l'Inter" as the locals referred to The Internationals Football Club, one of Milan's professional soccer teams. After lunch, we walked back to our car and said our good-byes. Franco said, "Although I think you should let this crazy search go, let me know if there's anything you need. I'll see what I can do."

I assured him we would be extremely careful and discuss his advice later. After a warm embrace of friendship, we headed off to see Mariano. This time I suggested to Dan that I drive, since I knew the way. He reluctantly agreed.

Chapter 50

Mariano's studio is in a small town northwest of the city heading up towards Lecco, and in the middle of a residential neighborhood. It is basically in three garages behind a large apartment building; a most unassuming spot. Whenever I visit his studio I am always amazed at the quality of work they produce. Like mine back in the States, it is a relatively small studio, and only has two other craftsmen. When he needs an artist to paint a window, he calls on one of a few stained glass artists to do the painting on the glass.

We arrived at the studio around 2:30 that afternoon. Mariano was cutting glass for one of their projects, while the other two craftsmen were assembling panels with lead channeling, known as caming.

After greeting everyone, the three of us went into Mariano's office to chat. The first thing Mariano did was offer us an espresso, which we gladly accepted.

"Marty, I thought you were supposed to leave Monday, why are you still here?" Mariano asked.

"Well, last Friday when we met and then picked up Dan, I wasn't sure I should have told you about what I found out in Torino," I said.

"Why?" Mariano asked.

I looked over at Dan and asked what he thought. He only shrugged as if to say, "Why not?"

I went on to explain, "It'll probably be in the papers anyway, so it won't be a secret much longer." I proceeded to tell Mariano the story about the duplicate Shroud and all about how the real one was sold. "We believe the guy who has it is here in Milan," I concluded.

"So who is this man from Milan?" Mariano asked.

"The guy's name is Domenico Mitcelli," I said cautiously.

"Yes, I've heard of him. I've heard he likes the women." Mariano said.

"Well we believe he's the one who has it."

"Good luck. But I don't know how you're going to find him." Mariano offered.

We sat and chatted for a while about other things that have been happening with him and his studio. Mariano wanted to show us the project he was working on. He also wanted to discuss the possibility of visiting me in the near future. He reminded me how his wife is more afraid of him going to the US than to Tehran, Iran. Because of all of the violent American TV shows Italians watch, she thinks Americans run around shooting each other. Mariano's work has taken him to Tehran a few times when doing the new stained glass windows for a Catholic Church attached to the Italian Embassy there. To my mind a place where personal safety is more challenged than my own country.

"My wife, Patrizia, is looking forward to seeing you again and meeting your friend. She wants you to come for dinner this evening," Mariano said.

"We would love to," I said. "After we've checked into our hotel and have taken a shower... See you around seven?"

"So do you know where you're staying?" Mariano asked.

"Yes, there's this place where Luiza and I stayed on our last time here. We liked it a lot so I've booked us in there. It's called Eco-Hotel La Residenza."

It was just after five by the time we made it to our hotel. After checking in and going up to our room, I told Dan I wanted to lie down and rest. Dan decided he would prefer to head down to the park and would be back to take a shower before we left for Mariano's.

      *   *   *

Mariano has a beautiful apartment not far from Stazione Centrale. It has high ceilings, a large living room, that holds a baby grand piano covered with family photos. The two bedrooms and bathroom are closed off from the living room by a pocket door which has a stained glass window, slightly illuminated from the small cubical where the four doors met.

We sat on a large white leather sectional and chatted. Patrizia asked about the violence on the city streets in America. Dan basically agreed with her, that the streets of America are dangerous. I tried to let her know that it really isn't that way.

Mariano told his wife why we were still here in Italy and hadn't gone home yet. She thought that we were crazy to think we could get near Mitcelli. Dan didn't quite agree. He felt that if we could find out where he lived, there would be a way to break in and retrieve the Shroud.

"The truth is, I'm thinking I'm gonna call Monsignor Scagnelli and let him know what we've found out and leave it at that," I said to Dan.

"Really? You mean you don't want to pursue it any longer?" Dan asked in an incredulous manner.

"I'm missing Luiza and she wants me home anyway."

Once Mariano understood what we were discussing he added, "I think you're making the right decision."

"I'll call Loretta tomorrow and see about getting my ticket fixed. I'm sure Luiza will be happy to know I'm finally heading home," I said.

Patrizia agreed, but it was obvious that Dan was disappointed.

After a few minutes of silence from Dan, he mumbled under his breath, "I guess I can go back to Torino."

Off the eat-in kitchen, they have a balcony on the side of the apartment that faces the inner courtyard. It is large enough for a small table and chairs and a small gas grill. Patrizia set the table out on the balcony, which made for a very nice time. Their balcony is unusually large for a typical balcony and it is perhaps because their apartment is on the first floor. Looking over the wrought iron rail into the courtyard, I noticed several other smaller balconies, all seeming to have potted plants. Some flowering plants cascaded down over their railings and some were pots of flowers, herbs and tomatoes. Considering how plain the stucco façade of his building was, it was a pleasant surprise to see so much natural beauty in the middle of a busy city.

The evening was warm and fun for me, but I'm not so sure it was for Dan. Unfortunately for him, the more wine I drank the less I translated and towards the end of the evening my translations were little more than grunts and hand gestures, with Mariano's wife doing her best to use what little English she knew.

Chapter 51

The following morning we were unsure what to do with ourselves. Down around the corner from our hotel was a stop for the city's subway system, the *Metropolitana*, so after our leisurely breakfast, we decided to take the *Metropolitana* to the center of the city.

First we visited *il Duomo*, Milan's famous gothic cathedral. It is huge with hundreds of statues all over its white marble exterior.

"You know, it never ceases to amaze me how they built these places," Dan said looking around in amazement. "I mean, how did they do it?"

We took the elevator to the top, walked along the roof and up to the spire where we had a panoramic view of the city. Unfortunately for us it was a field-day for a group of junior high students who were all over the roof, crowding the small viewing area. From there we went into *La Galleria*, which has to be one of the first and oldest covered shopping malls. It was built around the time of Italy's unification in the mid-1800s. It is essentially a group of stores that run north-south and east-west intersecting in the middle. The floor is totally done in mosaic tile with heraldic symbols covering it.

Of particular interest to most visitors, in the very center of the galleria is a mosaic bull up on its hind legs with its *coglioni* dangling between its legs. The tradition is that for good luck you have to take your heel and spin around on the bull's *coglioni*.

After we took our turn to spin on the bull, we walked through the gallery out to *Piazza alla Scalla*. Here there is a famous statue of Leonardo DaVinci. I couldn't help staring at the statue's face wondering if I could see a resemblance to the face in the Shroud.

In front of the Piazza is the world renowned opera house, *Teatro alla Scalla*. However, what interested me the most was walking down the street just to the right side of the Opera house towards via Brera, which is where the art school I attended was located— *Accademia della Bella Arte di Brera*.

To my amazement little had changed over more than 30 years. The courtyard looked the same. The half-finished sculptures that line the corridors were still there.

Acting like we belonged there we walked to the back end of the school. I wanted to see if the espresso vending machine was still there. Back when I attended the night school, it was my tradition to get a 50 lire, or about 15 cents today, espresso before I took the "O" bus for home. It was still there, although a more modern version, so, in honor of a long ago tradition, we had an espresso.

It was about this time that my cell phone rang. Not recognizing the number I answered, "*Pronto? Chi é?*, I asked checking who it was.

"*Ciao Marty è Luca*. Mariano told me you're in Milan."

I had known Luca Pacca for many years. He worked as a freelance stained glass artist. Mariano used him to paint the kiln-fired enamels and stains to create the designs on the glass. He was one of the best artists I had ever known and a very likable person. Luca worked for the same studio where we had all worked many years ago but not when I was there. Now and again he and Mariano worked together on projects.

"*Dove sei?*" I asked, wondering where he was.

"I'm at Codena's studio, which is on via Piranese around the corner from where you used to work."

"We're about to have lunch. How about if we swing by after?" I asked Luca.

"Yes, I'll be here. In fact Mariano is coming by to pick up a couple of designs I've done for him."

"Great. I'll see you after lunch," I said while saying goodbye.

After lunch, I made Dan jump on the number 24 tram from Piazza San Babila to Vialle Corsica. I felt like I had never left this place, so comfortable was I moving around. At the end of Vialle Corsica was a large red brick church. In the basement of that church, the stained glass studio where I apprenticed was located. The entrance to the studio was around on the left of the building. Passing through the side doors, as a young apprentice, I would go down into the cellar or as they call it in Italy—the crypt. I lived in that crypt for more than a year. Basically my bedroom was a cleared out storage room, where the church normally stored donated furniture. I had learned to live in fairly primitive conditions as, except for the evening, when they held Mass at six, the place was never heated. Unfortunately, the old studio no longer existed and I was a little disappointed that I could not take Dan to meet my former employers.

We walked down the street beside the church, to via Piranese and then to where Luca was waiting for us. Because I hadn't seen Luca on my last trip, it was now a few years since we had seen one another. Mariano had already arrived and so we went in to see the studio and his latest project. When we got there Luca was at the large glass easel applying the shadowing on a window depicting the Assumption of The Blessed Virgin Mary with grisaille, which is special black enamel paint. It was an interesting window in that the baby cherubs surrounding her were ethnically diverse; some were Asian, some African, others Semitic, and a few Caucasian. These cherubs with wings surrounding the Blessed Mother were done in a very contemporary style.

As is customary, Luca invited us over to where the espresso machine was and offered us an espresso. Luca, acting as our barista made them.

While waiting to be served I heard Mariano ask, *"Senti, Luca sai perchè Marty è ancora quì?"* wondering if Luca knew why I was still in Italy.

"No, ma perchè?" Luca asked, clearly not knowing the reason for my delayed departure.

"Well, he and his friend are searching for who stole the 'Shroud of Turin,'" Mariano said.

"*Ma Va! Come mai?*" Luca exclaimed incredulously.

"Marty, tell Luca what you've told me." Mariano suggested.

"Well it really doesn't matter now, since we've decided to let it go, and just head home, but yes, when I was in Torino I found out that the Curia of Torino has just discovered that the Shroud, in the Royal Chapel is a fake and the real one is missing."

"So you are heading home?" Mariano asked.

"*Aspetta*, did you just say the real Shroud is missing." Luca insisted.

"Yes, apparently some *Pezzo Novanta* got it. His name is Domenico Mitcelli."I informed Luca, naming a well-known big shot.

Luca, who had just finished his coffee stopped in his tracks, "Did you say Domenico Mitcelli?"

"Yes, why?" I replied.

Chapter 52

"I know him. I painted the stained-glass windows for his new villa several months ago," Luca said.

After translating what Luca just said, Dan exclaimed, "That's unbelievable!"

"I was commissioned by their architect to design and execute several stained glass windows that were being installed during the renovation of their villa."

"You mean you know him?" I asked.

"Well, not him, more his wife. They bought this old country home that is part of a farm in Brianza, and they've been restoring it over the past year. You should see this place!" Luca said excitedly.

Luca went on to describe the windows he had made for them. He said that some of the stained-glass windows had these intricate vines with grape clusters growing on a trellis. Then there was three other windows depicting an ornate fountain with some birds flying around and some birds splashing in the fountain. Luca found the sketch of the fountain window on his desk and handed it to Dan. "There's even a large peacock in one of the windows. They were quite beautiful, if I must say so myself. We also made two more windows for him in the style of Mucha."[2]

Again Luca handed the drawings to Dan and me to see.

Luca then continued, "As you can see, there are two models facing each other. One is mounted to the left of the

---

[2] Alfons Mucha, was a Czech Art Nouveau painter and decorative artist, known best for his women used in his paintings

room and the other to the right, in what would be a second floor library. We used two girls from his variety show who were from Eastern Europe," Luca explained.

"Would there be any chance of going by to see this place?" Dan asked and then motioned to me with his hand, indicating he wanted me to translate.

"I think I could arrange it," Luca said. "I got to meet Mitcelli's new wife; she's more beautiful than the two models we used. I think she's Russian. She once told me they decided to buy this property because after Mitcelli's divorce from his first wife, he wanted to start anew."

"Do you think we could get over there this afternoon?" Dan pressed, wanting to see their place.

"Sure, I can finish up in a few minutes and we can head over," Luca said.

We sat and chatted for a while about other things that have been happening. Luca wanted to show us the project he was working on. He also wanted to discuss the possibility of visiting me in the States.

Once Luca finished up and was ready to go. Mariano decided he wanted to come along too. I suspected he just wanted to get a look at Mitcelli's wife. We drove over in Mariano's Volvo wagon since it was larger than our rental.

Brianza is north of Milan heading towards the Alps. It is still basically a farming community. However, over the years it has been increasingly taken over by manufacturing plants, which was perhaps why Mitcelli moved there. Once in Brianza we drove through the old village with its narrow streets and medieval central piazza and then out to the flat fields beyond. The terrain was very flat and off in the distance we could see the snowcapped Alps. Finally we turned onto a dead end street where at the back end of a cul d' sac was a pair of wrought iron gates. Mariano pulled up near the gates and Luca jumped out and walked over to the box on the left pillar. Pushing the buzzer, Luca explained who he was and that he was accompanied by a couple of Americans who had come to see the stained glass windows they had created. The person on the other end said Signora Mitcelli was not there, and we could not be allowed entrance. Luca repeated who he was and asked if he could speak with Signora Moro, the house keeper. There was a long pause, then finally the gates began to open, and we drove slowly down a long gravel road towards the villa.

The drive to the villa was an eye-opener. The road lay between hay fields and was tree lined with poplars on both sides. Several white Roman style statues were strategically placed along the path. We pulled up to the front of a three storied eighteenth century villa set at the rear end of a circular driveway. The front of the villa had a round portico supported by two columns. Above the portico was a wrought iron fence, forming a small veranda. From this veranda I envisaged a magnificent view towards the front portion of the property. Around to the side was a 4-car garage. We parked over near the garages next to a white van marked with "Decolore 2000— Faux Painting Contractor."

"I don't believe it actually says 'painting contractor' in English," I pointed out.

We were met at the front door by the groundskeeper and Signora Moro, the elderly housekeeper. They immediately recognized Luca from when he had been there installing the stained glass.

"*Buona sera, Maestro Luca,*" the housekeeper greeted Luca.

As he approached her, he said, "*Buona sera, Signora Moro.* Let me present my two American friends Marty Daniels and Dan Carlson; Cavanago," he said indicating Mariano, "Is another craftsman who collaborates with me sometimes." Because they recognized Luca, they were much more relaxed about allowing us in to roam around the house and ostensibly look at his art work.

Signora Moro escorted us into the large open kitchen and dining area towards the back of the villa. There we saw the spectacular stained glass windows that had vines and clusters of grapes mounted in the wall that faced the rear of the property. The kitchen was huge with an island in the middle that had to be six by ten feet with a counter top made of Carrara marble.

"This is where Signor Mitcelli likes to cook," she said

pointing to the built-in char-broiler. "Now and again, when the Mitcellis had guests, Signor Mitcelli will cook." She explained. Normally Signora Moro did the cooking for the family. The stove was installed into the wall with ceramic tiles around it and a tile exhaust hood above.

"This is not your typical kitchen," Dan commented.

As we made our way through the kitchen, Mariano pointed to a huge wine cooler, which was larger than a double door refrigerator and must have held dozens of bottles of wine. From the kitchen she escorted us to an outside ceramic tiled patio that had rattan lawn furniture. The cushions were out of sight, since they weren't expecting guests. Over to the side was a brick wall about 9 feet tall and 30 feet long. The wall screened the deck from prevailing westerly winds. The brick work was attractively done, with a gabled capping along the top and randomly peppered with colorful ceramic tiles. In the middle of this partition were Luca's three stained glass windows depicting nature scene. The design of the stained glass window included a large peacock with its tail lowered behind him, and other small birds flying around an ornate water fountain. The entire back yard was, to me, a beautiful piece of paradise.

"Man, I can't believe the way the house has been restored, decorated and landscaped," Dan exclaimed.

As Signora Moro took us up to the second floor, I noticed the painters were working in one of the bedrooms down the hall. At the top of the stairway was the door into a private library. When we entered this lavishly decorated room, we saw a bookshelf that covered the whole right wall. It was fully stocked with books except for the center area which featured a well-stocked bar. Along the left wall we noticed an entertainment center with a large movie screen and huge speakers to the left and right. Facing the screen were several leather arm chairs.

It was what was on the wall directly in front of us that made my eyes widen and caused Dan to quietly nudge me in the ribs.

Chapter 53

The back wall faced the rear of the villa and had Luca's two Mucha style windows. The windows were about 10 feet apart. The nearly bare breasted women faced each other. They were dressed in silky dresses that appeared to flow in a breeze exposing most of one breast. Between the windows were two cabinets with various trophies, plaques and awards on display. In the middle between the trophy cabinets was a marble table. On the table was a gold plated glass case with filigree. It reminded me of some of the decorated glassware you might see in a Venetian glass shop. The case was about 2/3rds covered with the filigree of gold-leaf and applied colors, but the clear areas showed what was inside. Looking closely you could see it held a folded tan cloth. I could see Mariano and Luca noticed it too, but said nothing. While appearing to casually stroll around the room, we made our way towards this back wall to inspect the stained glass windows.

Dan commented, "I wish I could have been there when Luca was drawing those two women."

Mariano agreed. While the three of us admired the stained glass windows, Dan carefully inspected the glass case that housed, what we believed could be the Shroud. He noticed in the back of the case were wires and tubes installed into the wall. We weren't sure why they were there. Once we left the library and were back in the hallway, we saw one of the painters putting away his equipment in a utility closet at the end of the hall.

After checking out a couple of bedrooms, we made our way downstairs where the housekeeper said, "La Signora

Mitcelli phoned to say she'd be home soon and hoped Maestro Luca and his friends might wait." Then she went out to the rear terraza and began to place fluffy pillows onto the patio chairs. The housekeeper encouraged us to come outside and sit. "*Prego,* please come outside and I'll prepare you an aperitif." We gladly decided to wait.

I don't think we were out on the terraza ten minutes before we heard Signora Mitcelli come into the kitchen. We overheard her as she spoke with her housekeeper saying, "Here are the steaks for this evening. They should be freshly butchered." Then she came out to the terraza and greeted us. She extended her hand and said, "Ciao, Luca, I am so glad you came by. I am most happy with the beautiful windows you created for us." She had an obvious foreign accent, but spoke Italian beautifully.

"Thank you Signora Mitcelli, I was pleased to have the opportunity," Luca said while shaking her hand.

Then as she took Mariano's hand he said, "My studio sometimes fabricates Maestro Luca's designs."

"Well, these must be your American friends?" Signora Mitcelli then asked.

"Yes, this is Marty Daniels and his friend Dan Carlson," Luca said.

"I'm pleased to meet you. What brings you to Italy-- vacation or business?"

"Partly to visit family and friends and partly to install new stained glass into a convent in Torino and a church in Emilia," I answered.

"You made stained glass that is here in Italy?" she asked raising her voice in feigned surprise.

Luca interjected, "Why yes, Marty has done several churches here in Italy. He studied in Milan and is now very well known in America. His work is all over the world." By her expression, she was quite impressed. I could see Dan rolling his eyes when he understood how I was introduced. He even waved his hand subtly in front of his face to indicate he could smell the stink from the BS that was flying. I had to hold back my laugh. Even though, what Luca said was exaggerated, I decided not to correct him—it sounded so good.

Eventually Luca said, "This is Marty's friend Dan Carlson."

Mariano then said, "Dan worked in the White House for the President of the United States."

"How interesting, what did you do at the White House?" she asked slowly in English.

When Signora Mitcelli found out that Dan had translated the Hotline for the President she asked, "*Tak vi govorite po Russki?*" wondering if Dan spoke Russian.

Dan's face split with a huge grin as he replied, "*Da, da,*"

Dan, thinking she was Italian, asked her in Russian, "How is it that you speak such beautiful Russian?"

"I am from Belarus—Minsk. I came here a number of years ago as a model and stayed."

"How did you meet Signor Mitcelli?" Dan asked her.

"First, I was one of his showgirls, and then I helped him with choreographing the girls in his shows. Shortly after he divorced his wife, he asked me out on a date. We were married about a year ago."

Since the conversation was in Russian and Dan wasn't translating, all we could do was stare at Signora Mitcelli. Mariano was in a wide-eyed trance with a mesmerized look on his face. I started thinking to myself, "Do women realize how much men lust over them? Do they enjoy it?" Anyway, after some more banter, Signora Mitcelli turned towards us and said, "This evening we are having few friends over, just for a fun evening. My husband likes to use his new barbeque. Why don't you come over? I know he would like to meet you all."

We all repeatedly nodded our heads yes while smiling. I thought we looked like four bobble head dolls with goofy grins. After a while, it was time to leave, we said our goodbye's promising to return by seven thirty that evening.

On the way back to Milan, Mariano and Luca discussed whether or not they should go to the party that evening. Luca was obviously uncomfortable about it and preferred to stay home. Luca can be very congenial but often times he doesn't enjoy socializing and finds it uncomfortable. Mariano on the other hand couldn't wait to see Signora Mitcelli again. We decided to meet back at Mariano's studio about seven.

When we got back to the hotel Dan asked me, "How do you say flashlight?"

I replied, "*Torcia or torcia electtrica.* Torch like the Brits say it. Why?"

"No reason, just wondering...Hey, I think I'm going for a walk. I'll see you back in the room later." Dan definitely had something on his mind, but I wasn't sure what he was thinking and chose to leave him be.

Chapter 54

Arriving at the gate to the villa, we announced ourselves. The gates slowly began to open, allowing us to drive through. As we approached the Villa, we saw a couple of cars already parked in the curved driveway. Something else I hadn't noticed earlier that day was a small bungalow off to the edge of the property. It had a couple of cars parked around the side. I wasn't sure if it was the caretaker's home or where Mitcelli warehoused his body guards. Franco had mentioned he had a few. Aside from that speculation, I didn't notice any visible high security.

We were greeted at the door by, Signora Moro, who was more dressed up than she had been earlier in the day. She told us that everyone was around the back on the terrace. We made our way through the house to the back where we met Domenico Mitcelli for the first time. Mitcelli was a middle-aged man, mostly bald, not very tall and with a bit of a paunch. He was, however, definitely the alpha male type: aggressive, loud and generally overbearing. He appeared unimpressed with our presence and when he extended his hand to greet us, I was consumed with a vision he had an expectation that we would kiss his ring or something equally regal acknowledging his esteemed position. When Dan and I didn't, he clearly decided to dismiss us. Mariano, on the other hand, was very jovial and expressed how pleased he was to meet Mitcelli.

When we arrived Signora Mitcelli was not on the terrace, but joined us after a few minutes. She came out of the house and with her hand extended walked directly over to Dan speaking in Russian. Dan replied and they bantered back and forth for a few moments. I could tell she enjoyed speaking to somebody in her native tongue. There were also a couple of middle aged execs there with their wives. After a few minutes, Signora Moro brought out a couple of trays holding several types of antipasto delicacies.

Like all dominant personalities, Mitcelli controlled the conversation with stories about his recent adventures both at work and at play. He talked about his soccer team, AC Milan, and what they were hoping for the next season. Dan on the other hand, was enjoying himself keeping Signora Mitcelli entertained. I had no idea what they were talking about, but they were clearly enjoying each other's company. I think for Dan, he was also enjoying a rare opportunity to speak Russian again. Apparently Mitcelli didn't care; he was having too much fun talking about himself. At a certain point, one of the wives sitting near me turned and said in English, "Why are you here in Italy business or pleasure?"

"Mostly to visit," I responded. "But it's funny you would say it that way," I added.

Then she got up and changed seats to get next to me and asked, "Why is that?"

"Because last week when I arrived in Italy, and was going through passport control, the officer, while stamping my passport, also asked me if I was coming to Italy for business or pleasure. My reply was 'It is a pleasure to do business in Italy.' He didn't find my comment very clever. All he did was give me a stern look and hand me back my passport."

"They are always so serious. They must hate their jobs," the woman giggled.

"Oh, yes I agree." Then I went on to say, "If you really want to know why I'm here, it's because I'm a stained glass artisan. In fact, I apprenticed here in Milan, more than 30 years ago. I recently installed four of our stained glass windows into a convent in Torino and another one in a small village above Reggio called Camporella."

"Did you say Camporella?" she asked chuckling again. "Do you know what the word camporella means?"

"Yes, I do." I said with a chuckle. But not wanting to

make Signor Gianni's hand gesture to another woman, I quickly moved on. "And now I'm here in Milan visiting a few old friends before returning home. How do you know Signor Mitcelli?" I asked her.

"He and my husband are negotiating the sale of my husband's business. He has a small manufacturing plant not far from here and Mitcelli believes it would help him increase the production at his plant, also not far from here," she said.

I noticed her husband didn't pay much attention to the fact that we were chatting. She seemed to be unusually interested in me, and I wasn't sure how to take it. I guessed she was in her late forties and very attractive, so why did she want talk to me? I decided she enjoyed speaking in English, which she might not have the opportunity to do at home.

"I see you have a wedding ring. Is your wife back home?" she asked.

"Yes, she is. We've been married 30 years. We have four children who also are married, and now we have several grandchildren," I replied.

"My, you don't look like a man who has been married that long. Nor do you look like a grandfather. Your wife must take good care of you."

"Why thank you. She does, and I'd like to think, I take good care of her too," I said not realizing the double entendre at the time.

"I'm sure you do," she said with a coy grin.

Then Mitcelli announced to us all, "This evening I am going to prepare for you a very special barbecue." He was going to put the steaks on the grill soon and asked how we would like them cooked. It was the way he phrased the question that made it more of a statement. He basically said he would be cooking them all *al sangue* unless anybody had any objections. I raised my hand a bit and said, "Excuse me Signor Mitcelli, but my friend Dan would prefer his steak well done, please."

I could tell by Mitcelli's expression he didn't care for the fact that he had to cook one of his steaks more than the others. Then he told us his wife had picked up the steaks at an

Equineria in Milan. Unsure I understood him correctly; I leaned over and asked my new friend in Italian, "Does that mean the steaks are horsemeat?"

"Why, yes it does, a specialty here in northern Italy," she replied.

I quickly decided I better not let Dan know what he was eating. Then I remembered one other time I was asked to try horsemeat. It was served raw, ground up and seasoned with garlic, scallions and olive oil. Although I'd had difficulty swallowing, because of the thought of eating horse meat, I was proud of myself for not insulting my host, who served it especially for me. It actually didn't taste that bad once I managed to suppress my gag reflex.

With plenty of wine, attractive women and watching Mariano and the other two guys fawning over Mitcelli, I ended up having a fairly decent evening. However, I was still nervous thinking about the Shroud and what Dan might be thinking.

One of the executives who spoke English fairly well was now talking to Dan. They had been sharing war stories during dinner. Dan was telling him about some of his investigations and how at times, he was asked to do corporate espionage.

After we finished dinner, we moved back out to the terrace. We were out there less than five minutes before Dan excused himself and asked where the bathroom was. Before he walked into the house he turned and gave me a funny look raising my suspicions to *Red Alert*.

Chapter 55

After he was gone for a few minutes I decided I wanted to check up on him. I excused myself and indicated I needed to use the bathroom. I noticed that the first floor bathroom door was closed and I could hear the water running in the sink. I knocked on the door and in a loud whisper asked, "Dan, are you in there?" There was no answer. I turned the knob and opened the door. He wasn't there but he had left the water running. I wondered, "Is this some spy trick, to make you think someone is in the bathroom?"

I figured he must be upstairs in the library, so I decided to see what he was up to. At the top of the stairs, I could see the library door ajar. Opening the door, I saw the room was dark. I found the light switch on the wall. No Dan! As I looked around the room, I noticed the glass case seemed out of place, disturbed somehow. Upon closer inspection, it was obvious. The cloth was gone! The lid was off and leaning against the left trophy case. Just as I reached the glass case the lights went out. Turning around immediately I saw a figure in the doorway and a flashlight shining in my eyes, blinding me. He impatiently whispered to me, "What the hell are you doing here?" It was Dan.

"Looking for you," I whispered.

"Well you found me, now help put this paint tarp into the case before anyone else wanders up here."

"Where did you get this?" I asked; more because I was, by now, sweating bullets and not because I wanted to know.

"Bedroom closet, where the painters left it. Now put the lid on and let's get outa here."

"Where's the Shroud?"

"I'll tell you later. Be quiet!"

The library door was still ajar and just as we were about to open it, and get back to the party, the lights in the hallway went on. Dan who was just in front of me pushed me back into the room and put his finger over his lips. Then he went to the back of the door and peeked out the crack just below the upper hinge.

"Shit, it's Mitcelli and one of the wives." Dan whispered barely audible.

We held our breath expecting Mitcelli and his new girlfriend to come into the library. Instead the two of them walked past the library door and into the bedroom at the end of the hall. As they passed the library door he was whispering into her ear and she was giggling like an infatuated school girl. The second the bedroom door was closed, we slipped quietly out of the library and back down stairs. Dan appeared pretty cool about this encounter. I, on the other hand, felt myself shaking until we found the security of the terrace. While we were stepping out onto the terrace, Dan held my arm and made like he had just told me a funny joke. It actually was the one about the twin sister only this time the punch line was, "First he must focus…The both of us!"

Sitting back down I politely smiled and noticed that no one seemed to notice or care we had been missing. My mind raced, wondering, "Were we gone only a couple of minutes or was it hours like it seemed." Dan on the other hand smiled, sat down and asked for his glass to be refilled. He sipped his wine and looked at me with a wink and coy smile. It made me realize he felt pretty proud of himself. I think he liked the adrenaline rush.

Perhaps it was only five minutes later when Mitcelli came back alone with a big grin on his face. Knowing how quick that encounter had been, I leaned over to towards Dan and said, "Now I know who the fastest gun in all Italy is."

Without missing a beat, Dan replied, "I heard that Marilyn Monroe once said about a lover, 'It was the happiest ten seconds I've ever known.'"

My new friend, the executive's wife who spoke English, overheard our banter and looked at us with a curious grin, not quite getting what was going on.

It was well after eleven. I thought it was time for the three of us to get going. The woman I had been sitting next to most of the evening, who at times seemed uncomfortably close, even touching my knee, seemed particularly disappointed about our decision to leave. I used the excuse that I would be flying back home in the morning and still needed to pack. Mitcelli didn't bother to say goodbye. He seemed rather happy we were finally leaving. His wife showed the three of us to the door, and in Russian said to Dan, "You helped me enjoy this evening very much. I'm sorry you have to go."

As we walked over to the car, Dan said, "Wait a sec." He ran around to the far left side of the house away from the garages, and returned with a black trash bag. He jumped into the back seat and said, "Quick, let's go."

As Mariano drove us away, Dan excitedly explained what he had done.

"After I snuck upstairs to the library, I checked out the wires and tubes coming out the back of the Shroud's display case. I realized it was probably some kind of atmospheric control system set up to protect the ancient linen." Trying to catch his breath he continued, "I saw what I thought might be alarm wires. I couldn't figure out if it was alarmed or not. I decided what the hell; the worst thing that could happen is he'd throw us out of the house. Mitcelli wasn't going to call the police and report us for trying to steal the Shroud of Turin. But as it turned out, there was no alarm. I was able to open the top of the case and remove it. I remembered the painters put their equipment and supplies in a bedroom closet, which made me wonder if there might be a cloth tarp. I looked in the closet where their painting equipment was and sure enough, there was a grubby cloth, full of paint splatters on one side, but on the back, it was relatively clean. I figured this would be close enough. Also, in the closet, there were heavy black trash bags, so I put the Shroud in a trash bag and dropped it out of a bedroom window around the side of the house."

"So that's what you did with it?" I asked.

"I didn't want you to know it landed in the bushes," Dan replied.

As Dan explained what he did, I could tell Mariano was not happy. Mariano explained how he never wanted to be part of this escapade. Eventually he calmed down and said, "Maybe it will help me get into Heaven."

Mariano then went on to say that he was kind of glad that we had left early because none of the women seemed to be interested in him anyway.

"What do you mean by that?" I asked.

"Don't you realize we were being sized up for later?" Mariano said.

Chapter 56

"Sized up for what?" I asked.

"You know, for when the bunga-bunga starts."

"What are you saying?" I asked incredulously.

Dan caught the word "bunga-bunga" so he asked, "What does that mean?"

All I said was, "Orgy."

"Apparently, Mitcelli and his wife invite couples over for sex. We just happened to get out of there in time," Mariano went on to say.

"You mean Mrs. Mitcelli wanted me? Can we turn back?" Dan asked; obviously joking.

Mariano then added, "I realized I was going to have to share one of the women or sit there and watch. As far as I'm concerned I'm glad we got out of there."

Dan felt he needed to encourage Mariano so he said, "No I think the old housekeeper was your date." Dan and I burst out laughing.

"I can just hear the conversation with Luiza now, 'So how was your evening? Did you have fun at the Mitcelli's?' 'Yes, it was a lot of fun until…'"

We made our way back to Mariano's studio and were chatting outside, standing around next to the cars. We probably were there about fifteen minutes, talking over the night's events and I couldn't stop laughing because I had just told Dan that the steak he ate was horse meat. After making like he was gagging, Dan said it wasn't the only time he ate something strange.

Mariano couldn't understand why Dan thought it was unpleasant. About this time, Mariano's cell phone rang and it was Mitcelli. Because Mariano usually keeps the speaker on when driving, we could hear what Mitcelli was saying. He was shouting at Mariano cursing him out and promising that he'd kill him. He basically said that after we left, he took his friends up to the library where they planned to continue their evening. He noticed that something was wrong with the glass case. He said when he opened it, he pulled out a filthy painting tarp, and he knew we had taken the Shroud. Then he asked Mariano, "Where are your American friends?"

As I listened to Mitcelli curse and swear, I became aggravated and perhaps just plain tired of his arrogance. So rather than wait for Mariano to answer, I said, "You are one of the biggest *stronzi* I've ever met. You're a true *perla*. I frankly don't care what you think. Mariano never knew what we were up to because he wouldn't have been willing to help us."

Then Mitcelli threatened us by saying, "I know who you are. I know you're heading back to Torino. You'll never get past us. You'll never make it there. I already have my men after you and they'll get you."

Then while Mitcelli was still listening, I said, "Mariano, I'm sorry I got you in the middle of this, but it was something we had to do. We better get going. I don't want to encounter Mitcelli's men."

With that, Dan and I jumped into our car and sped off. Unfortunately for us, Mariano's studio was down at the end of a long narrow driveway that went along the side of the large apartment building. Just as we turned out of the driveway onto the street, we saw a car speeding down the street towards us. Dan, realizing who they were, excitedly said, "That's got to be Mitcelli's goons. Let's get the hell out of here!"

Slamming the car into reverse, we sped backwards past a few houses. Dan grabbed the emergency brake and spun the car around with one of the slickest maneuvers I've ever been part of. We were now speeding in the opposite direction away from them. Fortunately, because of the late hour, very few cars were on the road.

We raced down a narrow street, and then through the center of the small town. We headed for the highway. Mitcelli's men weren't far behind. If it wasn't for Dan's skillful driving, I'm sure we would've been rear-ended or pushed off the road. We made it to the highway and were heading towards Milan. Because of the highly stressful situation, we were shouting back and forth, I was yelling at Dan about what I saw them doing, and Dan was yelling at me what he was doing.

It was about this time that I heard my cell phone ring. As I flipped it open and checked the caller ID, Dan shouted, "Who the hell could that be?"

"It's Luiza," I said excitedly.

"Does she have to call now? For crying out loud. What the hell could she want now?"

What Dan hadn't realized was that when I flipped open the phone Luiza heard what he said, so she asked with a raised voice, "What the hell do I want? What does he mean by that?"

Because of the adrenaline surging through me, I was shouting in the phone, "What do you want? Why are you calling me now?"

"I haven't heard from you in a few days," Luiza said even more agitated.

Dan continued to yell, "Say goodbye, say goodbye. For crying out loud you can't chat with your wife now."

"What's going on? Marty, I can tell something's happening," Luiza's voice was edged with fear.

"Nothing, I can't talk now."

"Marty, you better not be in any danger, because if you are I'll kill you, when you get home."

"We'll be fine, don't worry," I shouted.

"Tell me what's happening," she demanded.

"I gotta go."

"Marty if you two have gotten yourselves in trouble, I'll show you what trouble is when I get my hands on you! What's happening?" again Luiza demanded.

Knowing she was afraid and upset, I tried to calm her down, "Please sweetheart. I'll tell you all about it later."

It was about this time that one of Mitcelli's men shot at

us, but because of Dan's expert driving maneuvers, they were unable to hit the car or us. Perhaps forgetting the fact that Luiza was still on the phone Dan shouted, "Those bastards are shooting at us. They're trying to kill us." That's all Luiza needed to hear, with trembling in her voice I heard her say, "Oh dear Lord, please don't let anything happen to them."

"Luiza, I'll call you back. Don't worry we'll be alright," I stuck the phone in my pocket and looked and saw them almost on our bumper.

An instant later Dan said, "Hold on!" He then grabbed the emergency brake while hitting the footbrake, causing us to skid and making them speed past us on the driver's side. Then, just as they were speeding by, Dan turned the steering wheel sharply, whacking them right by the back part of their rear door and just in front of the rear wheel, all while he down shifted. Then he gunned it. This was all done in a seamless motion. He drove through them. The push from accelerating our car spun their car off the highway and into the ditch off the road. Dan continued to accelerate and increase the distance between us. When we were about a quarter mile ahead of them, we pulled over to see their wreck. By this time the two of them were climbing out of their over turned car. Steam was coming out of the punctured radiator and they didn't look too pleased.

Chapter 57

As we left them, we shouted with excitement. We even tried to high-five each other, but instead I whacked the ceiling of the car and hurt my wrist.

I said, "Man, I can't believe your driving skills."

"Not the first time I had to make a quick getaway," Dan replied smiling wide out of the side of his mouth and tried to make it sound like, 'It was all in a day's work.'

It took several minutes before we had calmed down enough to plan our next move.

Making our way back to the city we discussed if we should stay at our hotel or head back to Torino. Although we didn't think Mitcelli could find us, we weren't sure, so we decided to head towards Torino that evening rather than wait 'til morning.

We parked near the front entrance of our hotel planning to stay only long enough to run up to our room, grab our stuff and check out. As we were getting out of our car two very big muscular guys approached us from around the corner of the nearby street. They obviously had been waiting for us.

In a thick accent one of the guys asked, "Which one of you is the American spy?"

"What?" I replied.

"Which one of you worked in the White House?"

Dan and I looked at each other and I wasn't sure how to reply. Just as I looked back I saw the gun in the hand of the second thug.

"Oh, no," I said.

Dan coolly said, "Don't look scared and try to look

them straight in the eye."

"Don't look scared?" I whispered under my breath, making it a question.

"I'm shaking from fear," I whispered again.

"Signor Mitcelli wants it back," the first guy said while the second one waved his gun a little, perhaps to make sure we noticed it.

"Cosa voi?" I timidly asked the obvious leader of the two, trying to find out what they wanted.

"What you stole from him, the old cloth," he replied in Italian, perhaps having exhausted all the English he knew.

Dan repeated what he said before, "Try to keep eye contact."

"Give it to us...NOW," he insisted.

"Sure, but please put your gun away," I said.

"I don't think so. You made Signor Mitcelli very angry and he wants us to bring you to him."

"What's he saying?" Dan asked me.

"They want us to go with them to Mitcelli," I said.

"Don't let them get us in their car or we're finished," Dan whispered.

"Andiamo!" the one with the gun said waving it towards the side street.

While the four of us were standing towards the back of our rental, Dan with his hands out to the side a bit, and me with my hands raised to my ears, the two goons insisted we move towards their car. Then all of a sudden, two Carabinieri police cruisers sped around the corner with their lights flashing. They quickly stopped next to us. Immediately Mitcelli's men realizing what was happening began to run. Two of the four Carabinieri jumped out of their cars and began chasing after them. The other two came to see if we were ok. As we stood there on the sidewalk, Franco came around to corner. While I was making a gesture which asked, "Why are you here? Or what's going on?" he pulled up and got out of his car. He was still wearing his household sweats and furry slippers. Still confused as to what was going on, Franco explained, "Luiza called me all in a panic saying you were being chased in your car and being shot at. She told me where you were staying. I called the Carbinieri and ask them to check on you and make sure you were ok." As we were chatting outside the hotel the two Carabinieri who chased after Mitcelli's men returned empty handed. They gave up the chase and decided that they'd investigate who they were later, since they had already taken off in their car.

"So how did this all come about?" Franco asked.

I told Franco about our evening at Mitcelli's. He didn't think we had intended pursuing the matter of the Shroud any longer, so we explained how a friend from Milan got us into Mitcelli's house and how we discovered the Shroud under a glass case in his library. Franco suggested he take the Shroud and he'd make sure it got back to its rightful owners. When Dan realized what he was suggesting he said, "Oh, no. I know how these things work. I worked for the government, remember? Your buddy will take all the credit and we'll be forgotten."

"What does it matter?" I asked.

"It matters to me. We risked our lives to get this thing. I want to be the one who hands it back to your Monsignor friend in Torino." Dan insisted. Franco realizing Dan wasn't going to hand it over said, "It would mean more paper work anyway. I'm busy enough as it is. I'll let the Carabinieri decide about Mitcelli."

"Do you think they'll pursue the matter?" I asked Franco.

"I doubt it. The Church won't want it to come out that they had a fake Shroud for sixty years. Mitcelli will probably pay off some high official who can make it all go away."

"Perhaps a guest at one of his bunga-bungas," I offered.

"I'd bet that's why he has them," Dan speculated. Franco agreed.

After several more minutes of us chatting on the sidewalk, the Carabinieri got a call and had to leave. Franco decided he should head home too.

Dan slapped him on the back saying, *"Grazia* Lieutenant Columbo."

Franco laughed and corrected Dan by pointing to me and saying, "No, him Columbo."

I promised to call him before I returned home.

Chapter 58

We checked out of our hotel and began to make our way out onto the highway for Torino when I said, "Oh, no. I forgot about Luiza. I better call her!"

"Marty, you ok? What's going on?" Luiza quickly said as she answered the phone.

"We got the Shroud!"

"What do you mean?" she asked.

"I mean we have it! This evening we went to the house of the guy who bought the Shroud from Russo and Amato."

"How did you do that?"

"It's a long story. When you called before, we were trying to get away from a couple of Mitcelli's men."

"Who's Mitcelli?" she asked.

"Mitcelli is the guy who had it. He's some rich guy who stole it from Sonia Troia."

"Who's Sonia Troia? Marty, are you ok now?"

"Yes. Now we are. We got away from them and we're now heading back to Torino.

"Are you sure? Did you see Franco?"

"Yes, Franco showed up just in the nick of time."

"Oh, Great."

"Luiza, I've got to tell you about Dan's driving. He's a wicked good driver. It was like being in a movie or on TV. We were being chased by the bad guys. They were trying to get beside us to push us off the road. Dan swerved back and forth preventing them from getting beside us. That's when you called."

"I'm glad I did."

"I guess so. It's funny how often you catch me in the act."

"What I did was I prayed for you two. I read Psalm 91 out loud. It reminded me of the Lord's promise to look after us, especially when we're in danger."

"No doubt, it made a difference," I replied. "In fact the way we got away from them was by Dan hitting his brakes so hard that it forced them to zoom past us. Just as they were passing us he turned his wheel to the left whacking them in the rear. The hit pushed their car into a spin causing them to land in a ditch on the side of the road. He did it with such perfect precision. He then hit the gas, and we sped off. Before they were out of their car we were out of there, leaving them in the dust."

"That's amazing. Were you scared?" Luiza asked.

"To be honest, no I wasn't. I was too excited to think about it. It was all instinct and adrenaline. Then as we got back to our hotel these two guys tried to take us back to Mitcelli."

"What happened?"

"Two patrol cars with four Carabinieri showed up."

"Probably because I called Franco at home and told him you might be in danger." she suggested

"Well, it was good that you did. While we were still on the sidewalk these two cruisers came around the corner with their blue lights flashing. Once Mitchelli's goons realized they were stopping for us, they took off running."

"What are you going to do now?" she asked.

"Get back to Torino."

"What about the Shroud?"

"We checked out of the hotel and are driving towards Torino. In the morning we'll call Monsignor Scagnelli," I said.

It was about this time that we were pulling up to the toll plaza at the entrance to the autostrada. Dan looked at me with his hand out but said nothing. As I wrestled with my wallet to get out my credit card Luiza asked, "When are you coming home?"

"Probably right after that. I should head home Saturday or Sunday. That is unless they want to give us a ticker-tape parade."

"Hey Marty, when you get home I might let you chase me around the kitchen, while I call you Maestro," Luiza said softly, perhaps afraid Dan could hear our conversation.

"Then, I definitely will turn down any offer of a parade," I said.

"Call me after you visit them tomorrow."

"I will, Sweetheart. Goodbye."

"I love you."

"I love you too."

After saying goodbye, we drove in silence for a while. Dan was lost in his thoughts, and I was missing Luiza. At a certain point Dan broke the silence, "You know, we may have the real burial cloth they laid Jesus in."

"I don't know. I really don't think it is the real thing. I think it's just a medieval fake," I said.

"Why do you say that?" Dan asked.

"If we had the real burial cloth of Christ, I think I'd be freaking out," I said and then added, "To think a week ago, I never really thought about it. I actually thought it was at the Vatican somewhere. And now to think we might have it here in the back of our car. It's just too weird to think about."

We drove about an hour before we decided to get off the highway and find a place to sleep. By the time we actually got off, we were in Santhia`, a town about half way to Torino. When we headed towards town, we passed a hotel on the way in.

Dan asked, "What about this place?"

I replied, "Let's head in closer towards the center of town and train station. This place looks like one of those hotels that are used by men who find women by the roadside when they're in the mood for a *camporella*, but not in the mood for the grass... I think they charge by the minute."

We found a hotel near the center of the city and decided to pull in. Now that the adrenaline had worn off, I found myself hitting the wall and desperately needed to sleep. I'm sure it was true for Dan, too. We rang the front doorbell and were buzzed in. A half asleep desk clerk met us at the counter with a weak,

"*Buona sera, signore.*" He then asked if we wanted one room or two. I said one room would be ok. Dan quickly added it must have two beds.

"Very well, may I have your passports please?" the clerk asked as he wiggled the mouse to wake up his computer. "Just for tonight?"

"Yes," I replied.

"We do have a room with a double and a single right beside it. Would that be ok?"

"Sure why not," I replied.

"Who gets the single?" Dan asked.

"I don't mind. I'll take the single or whichever bed you don't want...At this point I'll probably just kick off my shoes. I'm not even sure I'll pull down the covers," I said.

"Very well then, it is only one flight up," the clerk said handing us the key, and telling us the room number.

Dan decided he needed a shower; I decided I needed to sleep. The next morning we got ourselves ready and headed down to breakfast. Because of the proximity to the train station, there was a lot of commotion between buses, cars, and pedestrians, which made me want to have my cappuccino outside on the sidewalk so I could people watch.

After relaxing *al fresco,* I went inside to the hotel lobby, sat in an armchair, and called Loretta at her office. I wanted to give her an update on what had happened since we left Torino Wednesday morning. I enthusiastically gave her a blow-by-blow account of everything. From meeting Mitcelli's wife, getting invited to their home and eating horse meat, to Dan sneaking into the library and tossing the Shroud out the window in a trash bag. When I told her about the car chase, I spared no detail.

Chapter **59**

She was fascinated with all my descriptions and would only ask about Dan as I recounted the events to her, like "Did he like eating horse meat? How brave he was to sneak up to the library? How much did he like speaking Russian to Signora Mitcelli?" Then, when I got to the car chase after we left Mariano's studio, she got even more animated and seemed more concerned about Dan than me. In fact, she also made a few comments about how skilled he was to get us away from the Mitcelli's goons, and pushed their car off the road. She even lauded him for doing it in a way so as to not hurt them, though I highly doubted that had been part of his plan.

"He wasn't trying to save them; he was trying to save us. It was by sheer luck they survived," I said almost too sternly.

After I hung up I sat there thinking of our chat. I thought of the scene in the movie 'Father of the Bride.' There's a scene when the father tells his daughter to put on a coat, because it's cold outside. She first refuses, but when her fiancé suggests it, she puts the coat on; she obliges him right away. Her father realizes that she is no longer his daughter but is now soon to be the young man's wife. That's how I felt hanging up with Loretta. She was no longer my little Italian sister; she was now Dan's girlfriend. I just didn't know if Dan knew it yet. Because of my sense of loss, I wasn't in any mood to be tipping him off.

Next I called Sister Bonny to ask her for Monsignor Scagnelli's phone number. As with Loretta, I filled her in on our progress and seeming success to retrieve the Shroud. She said that since last Friday she and the other nuns had been praying for our safety and success. She was glad to hear we were able to discover what had happened to the Shroud and get it back to its rightful owner. She then passed the phone to Sister Grazia who gave me her brother's private cellphone number.

Then I called Monsignor Scagnelli. He answered with, "*Pronto?*" He raised his voice in such a way, to make it a question more than a hello.

"*Pronto* Monsignor Scagnelli; it is Marty Daniels,"

"Ah, Maestro Daniels, It is so good to hear from you."

"I got your cell number from your sister."

"Yes, I see."

"I am calling to tell you about our progress," I said.

"Good, very good, I have been waiting for some news from you."

"Well, I believe we may have gotten the Shroud back for you."

"Is that true? You have been successful in getting it back?" he asked.

"Yes. Last night we were able to get it away from a Milanese industrialist who bought it from Bruno Russo," I said.

"That is marvelous! Will you be able to get it back to us today?" he asked.

"We are in Santhia` and should be in Torino in the next couple of hours. We will come directly to your office as soon as we can."

"Very well, I will be here waiting for you," he said. We ended our call with warm well wishes.

*   *   *

It was about 11 o'clock Friday morning, May 25th 2007 when we walked into Monsignor Scagnelli's office and restored the Shroud of Turin to its rightful owners. Waiting for us with excited anticipation were a few other priests who wanted to meet us. Dan and I wore grins that stretched from ear to ear, and yet in spite of this, the sacred cloth was handed over with some solemn reverence. It was then removed from the office and the Monsignor asked us to sit and relax, "May we get you something to drink? An *arangiata*, an espresso, or of course you Americans love cappuccino?" he asked.

"What's an *arangiata*?" Dan asked.

"Orange dry soda," I said. "But with pulp."

"I think I'll have an espresso," Dan replied.

"I would prefer an *arangiata*," I said.

Monsignor Scagnelli asked us about our adventure to retrieve the Shroud, "I want to hear all about it and spare me no details."

At the Monsignor's request I enthusiastically recounted the events that led to our finding the sacred cloth. We told him of our meeting with Signora Russo at her school and Bruno Russo's poker friends Bergeroni and Amato. We told him about finding out about *il Giardino della Fantasia* club and the role they played in finding the man who bought the Shroud. We explained how the Milanese industrialist had taken off with it with the help of his bodyguard. We explained how by coincidence an artist friend of mine from Milan happened to do some stained glass at their villa and knew Mitcelli's wife. We told the Monsignor how we were given a tour of their home and noticed, what we believed could be the Shroud cleverly kept in a display case. As we retold the story, I observed an excitement in Monsignor Scagnelli eyes as he listened to our description of the events.

Dan spared no detail explaining how, during the get together at Mitcelli's villa, he crept upstairs to the library, switched the Shroud with a painting tarp, and quietly dropped it out a bedroom window, where we retrieved it when we left the party. Then there was the chase. I don't know if we purposely embellished the story or if it really was just as thrilling as we described it, but in the retelling it sure felt real. Monsignor Scagnelli thanked the Lord for protecting us from getting hurt or killed.

Although, I failed to see the humor at the time, when I told him about my wife's phone call in the middle of it all, we all had a good laugh. I told them that when Luiza overheard Dan shouting something to me, it tipped her off that something really serious was happening, she actually said something to the effect of, "Marty, if you got yourself in danger, I'll kill you when you get home." Then something like, "You don't know trouble until I get my hands on you."

I told Dan and Monsignor Scagnelli, "My wife has a gift of words. At times I don't know if she was trying to be funny or what?" We had quite a good laugh over it.

While I was describing the night at Mitcelli's, a secretary who had come into his office decided to sit and stay. He too admitted that ours was quite a dangerous mission, and we all marveled about how doors opened and things happened.

As soon as I finished recounting the events with the two thugs waiting for us at our hotel, and after settling down from another round of laughing, the Monsignor said, "I believe the Lord guided you and had His angels watching over you." I agreed, but Dan just looked at the ground, perhaps not so sure.

Monsignor Scagnelli didn't seem to be in a hurry to ask us to leave, so I ventured to ask about the Shroud and its authenticity.

"Monsignor, what about the Shroud of Turin, is it real? I mean is it authentic?"

Chapter 60

"What do you mean by that?" he asked.

"Is it really the burial cloth of Jesus?" I asked.

"The answer is ultimately a question of faith," he said. "What I mean to say is--it is always about your willingness to believe."

"I'm sorry but I don't get what you mean," I said not quite getting his point.

"What I mean, 'by your willingness to believe', is that no matter how much physical and tangible evidence is presented to someone, he always has to believe it is true. He must be willing to accept the evidence," the Monsignor said. Then he paused to reflect and added, "Sometimes in life we will only have so much evidence; and then you must decide if it is enough for you to believe. Then on the other hand sometimes there is irrefutable evidence and people still refuse to believe."

"I think I know what he means," Dan interjected. "I have done investigations into the shenanigans of both husbands and wives. We documented their 'extracurricular activities' and presented them to their spouses. Most of the time they accept our evidence and make a decision based on what they now know. Some choose to forgive, while others choose to divorce. Then there are always those who refuse to believe and even blame us. They almost accuse us of fabricating the evidence. They refuse to believe what is put in front of them."

"May I share a story from the Gospel of Luke?" Monsignor Scagnelli asked.

"I wish you would," I said.

"It's found in the 16th chapter of Luke's gospel. It's the

story of Lazarus, the beggar, and a rich man. In this story that Jesus told, a certain rich man was unwilling to help Lazarus who was a poor beggar. They both die. Lazarus is taken by the angels to heaven and the rich man, because of his selfish greed, finds himself in the torment of hell. The rich man begged Father Abraham to send Lazarus back from the dead to warn his five brothers."

Dan, interrupting Monsignor Scagnelli, said, "Kind of like the warning Marley gave Scrooge coming back from the grave in 'A Christmas Carol.'"

"Yes, I guess-- kind of like that. Jesus however in this story said Abraham's answer to the rich man was 'They have Moses and the prophets; let them hear them,' but the rich man insisted, 'if someone came back from the dead they would listen to him.' Jesus then said, if they won't listen to Moses and the prophets, in other words, the sacred scripture, they won't be persuaded even if someone should rise from the dead,'" the Monsignor said, concluding the story.

"I think I'm getting your point," I said. "I bet if I went out of here and stopped 20 people on the street and asked them, 'Do you believe Jesus performed the miracles recorded in the Bible?' 15 to 18 of them would say yes they do. Also if I asked them 'Do you believe Jesus rose from the dead,' most of them would say yes they do. The question is why don't they believe in Him, or listen and do what He taught, if He is the most unique person who has ever walked this earth?"

Then Monsignor Scagnelli went on to say, "Like I said, it's not that the evidence is not out there, because it is. They'd rather choose not to believe than trust. I personally have enough evidence to believe the Sacred Shroud is truly the linen that wrapped the body of Our Lord."

"So, you mean you really believe it is His burial cloth?" I asked.

"Yes, I do."

We sat and chatted with the Monsignor about our adventure and about scientific evidence pointing to the Shroud's authenticity for a while longer. He asked when we intended to return home. Dan said he still had a few more days left before he had to get back to Amsterdam. I told him I was supposed to return last Monday. "I have a dear friend who works for a travel agency. I'm going to ask her to help get me home."

"I see. Would you mind telling me her name and the agency?" he asked.

"No, not at all, her name is Loretta Grappelli, and she works at Sancarlo Viaggi."

I noticed him write it down, but made no comment, just wondered why.

"When I studied in Milan as a young man, I lived with her family for the first nine months," I said.

It was about this time that another priest briskly came into Monsignor Scagnelli's office, he first greeted the Monsignor in Italian and then turned towards us and greeted us in English with a strong New York accent. He introduced himself as Father Nick Desmone. He told us he was an American priest studying in Italy. When Dan commented on his accent he said he came from Long Island. He then grabbed a wooden chair off in the corner, pulled it up alongside Monsignor Scagnelli's desk and sat down.

Once Father Desmone was seated, Monsignor Scagnelli said, "Don Desmone is one of the priests helping us investigate this whole affair. He happens to be a former officer in your American Navy and an NCIS agent before entering the seminary and being ordained a priest. He has come here to Italy to study further." Monsignor Scagnelli continued, "Knowing about Don Desmone's background and experience with investigations, we asked him if he would be willing to help us. During his investigation, he found that Grassi truly was the King's aide and with some forensic help, we knew the journal was his and is authentic. I decided to wait until Don Desmone could join us, since he is the one who made this amazing discovery; we want to tell you about. It is a very important development that I was just made aware of last night."

"Father Desmone told us about a development in the case. It's something we never expected to discover and it was almost purely by accident," the Monsignor informed us.

"Really...What is it?" Dan asked.

"You may have noticed amongst the papers we gave to you, there were references to several personal letters Grassi had received from a woman he apparently had a romantic relationship with," Father Desmone told us. "Her name was Donatella Calini. She was one of the maids at the Palace in Torino. Noticing the love letters amongst his belongings, we thought it might be worth our while to try to find Miss Calini. We didn't know if we could find her or if she was even still alive. Anyway, we found out while interviewing some of the surviving members of the Palace staff who were at the palace before 1947, that they thought the two were lovers."

"Yes, we could tell. Marty translated a couple of the letters for me," Dan said.

"I've wished I had a few love letters from Luiza," I added.

"Anyway, while interviewing them, we asked if they knew where we might find Miss Calini. Well, one of the former maids said she knew she was still alive, and also knew she was married. She told us her married name was Rocca. She now lives in Monterossa."

"Monterossa, isn't that one of the Cinque Terre towns?" I asked Monsignor Scagnelli.

"Yes it is. Don Desmone found her and visited her at her home," Monsignor said.

Father Desmone continued, "When asked if Grassi ever told her about any secret missions the King had him undertake, she became very nervous and upset. We had to reassure her that after all these years there would be no harm to her. After calming down, the now 85 year old grandmother of seven explained that Grassi was asked to do some horrible things for the King. It upset him very much, but he saw no way out of it. He feared for his own life, she explained to us."

I was riveted by Father Desmone's explanation, but still was wondering where he might be going with it.

Chapter 61

"She explained it was one evening; they were alone in his room. He was pacing back and forth unable to relax. He said he couldn't keep it a secret any longer or he feared he'd burst. She encouraged him to seek a priest and have him hear his confession, but he said he was beyond redemption, Signora Rocca explained to us. At any rate, Grassi explained to his lover how the King had him find a victim, whom they tortured and killed just like the Romans did with Jesus. Then they used the victim's body to reproduce the Sacred Shroud. Grassi told her how the fake was placed in the Royal Chapel and would remain there until the end of the war."

Father Desmone continued Signora Rocca's story, "She said that shortly after he told her about the switch, he had to leave with the King and go back to the Palace in Rome. She informed us, she never heard from him again. Shortly after the war finally ended and the Germans were out of Italy, she wondered about the fake Shroud in the Royal Chapel. Because she was afraid to say anything and feared no one would ever know it was there. She decided to secretly retrieve the real Shroud herself. She knew from Grassi it was hidden in the back of the King's closet. Knowing the right people, she was able to get the keys to the chapel and switch the real one with the forged cloth, which was still in the Chapel. She made the switch late one night and placed the fake one back in the King's closet just where the other one had been. She never told anyone for fear of going to prison."

"*Aspetta*," I said stopping Father Desmone's story. "Are you telling us that you still have the real Shroud and Grassi stole the fake from the King's closet?" I asked both priests.

"Yes, I am. As incredible as it seems, because Grassi believed he found the real one in the King's closet and wrote that in his journal, we believed the real Shroud was lost when Signora Russo told us her story and gave us her uncle's journal," Father Desmone explained.

"That is incredible," I said with excitement in my voice. Dan stared at the ground and shook his head, contemplating the dangerous adventure we had just undertaken to retrieve *a* fake Shroud. Who would believe it.

Father Desmone, who appeared to be someone who never wasted time, got up and asked to be excused. Realizing we were from the Boston area, he said, "Even though you're probably Red Sox fans, it was a pleasure to meet you. Thank you again for your willingness to help us."

"I take it you must be a Yankee fan," I said.

"You better believe it, pin stripes all the way."

Dan now shaking Father Nick's hand said, "We knocked you off in 2004 after being down three games to none to win the Pennant and then the World Series, ending our 84 year drought."

"Eh, just a bump in the road," Father Nick said with a big grin.

"If you're ever up in the Boston area, let us know, and let's try to get together," I said.

"What! Travel into the enemy territory? Never!" he said.

"Just the same, let us know if you're ever out our way."

"I will," Father Desmone said, and shook our hands goodbye.

It was approaching noon time, so Monsignor Scagnelli asked if he could take us to a restaurant around the corner for lunch. Instead, Dan insisted that we should get going. It was obvious that he was agitated and perhaps even upset.

Monsignor Scagnelli, noticing Dan's restlessness asked us to sit a moment. He then asked Dan to tell him what was bothering him.

"I'm surprised it doesn't kind of piss you off, too." Dan said while looking over at me.

"What you mean?" I asked.

"The fact that we risked our lives for nothing."

"I don't know it was all for nothing," I replied.

"They had the real thing all the time," he retorted.

"Yes, but they just found that out."

"Look I'm not mad at anyone. I just wish it had counted for something," Dan said.

"But it did," Monsignor Scagnelli interjected.

"What do you mean?" I asked.

"While listening to your story, I kept thanking the Lord in my heart for His faithfulness towards you two. I see how His unseen sovereign hand guided you and protected you."

The two of us quietly paused to absorb what the Monsignor just said, until I added, "You know I had planned on heading home until we visited Luca at his studio. Then there was Paola, who just happens to work at Sancarlo Viaggi… Don't forget about Luiza calling during the chase, which caused her to call Franco."

"All a bunch of coincidences," Dan insisted.

"How about the timing of your trip to visit Darla's family and their feelings towards you," I added.

"Faith will always be a personal choice and can never be forced on anyone." Monsignor Scagnelli said. Then quickly added, "I hope you won't mind me praying for you and asking our Lord to open your heart to His love and care for you."

"You can do whatever you want; I just want to get going." Dan curtly said to the Monsignor.

I stared at Dan as if to say, "Why the need to be so rude?"

As we got up and moved towards the door, the Monsignor tried to encourage Dan, "I think the Lord has you on his radar and has plans for you." This seemed to calm Dan down and even raise a faint smile.

After handshakes and a few goodbyes, we made our way out onto the street. I asked Dan, "Why the rush to get out of there?"

"I just wanted to get going," he replied.

"Where do you want to go?" I asked.

"I don't care, anywhere we can get some lunch."

Then I said, "Let's call Loretta and see if she can go to lunch with us…We can update her on this latest turn of events."

"That sounds like a great idea," Dan said.

I called Loretta at her office and asked her if she could go to lunch. She said she really couldn't but she was hoping we could meet her at her apartment around six for dinner. We agreed to that plan. Then she asked us what we intended to do with our afternoon. After I explained to her that we would just hang around until we could meet her at the apartment, she offered to give us the keys to her place so we could wait for her there. After we ate lunch, we headed over to Loretta's office to pick up her keys. While there Loretta told us about an Historically famous cafè only a ten minute walk away. It's *Caffè al Bicerin* in *Piazza dell Consolata.* She explained that they have a famous chocolate and coffee drink that's amazingly good. We told her we'd check it out, which is what we did before heading to her apartment.

          *   *   *

It was just after six when Loretta buzzed to be let in, I was watching Italian TV and Dan was out on the balcony sipping white wine and staring out at the city.

In an attempt to be funny, I pushed the intercom button and asked, "*Chi è?*"

"*Fammi entrare,*" Loretta demanded, not playing along and wanting to be let in.

"*Si si, Va bene.*"

Once in the apartment, I could see Loretta was all excited, "I have some good news for you, Marty."

"What is it?" Dan asked standing just inside the doors to the balcony.

"Monsignor Scagnelli called me and instructed me to change your ticket to Boston to a first class ticket. He gave me his personal credit card number to pay for it."

"What are you saying? Can he do that?" I asked.

"Don't worry; his family has money. They can pay for it," Loretta said.

"You mean it's not the Curia paying, but he is personally?"

"Apparently so," Loretta said.

"But why would he do that," I asked.

"Be quiet and just say thank you," Dan added. "You don't want to stare a gift horse in the mouth."

"What does that mean anyway?" I asked.

"It means you're flying home in style," Loretta said.

That evening Loretta, in her usual manner, cooked us a dinner that was simple, lovely, and delicious. We decided to head back to our hotel early because my flight left at 7:25 the next morning. I felt exhausted still from all the excitement of the past few days.

The next morning, still exhausted from all the excitement, Dan accompanied me to Torino's airport where I was to catch a flight to Rome and then my connection to Boston. While walking up the jet way, I remembered what the desk manager had said back in Boston when I asked if he could put me in first class.

"Not with this ticket! You don't think we're going to put you in first class. Do you?"

On the way to the airport, I asked Dan what he was going to do for the next few days. He said he wasn't sure, but had a few ideas in mind. We had arrived there around six that morning. He had dropped me off at the curb, given me a handshake from his driver's seat and said he'd be by to visit as soon as he got back home.

After getting to the States, Dan told me he had decided to wander around Torino for a couple of hours. He stopped by a pharmacy he found open, and finally made his way over to the building where Loretta lived. He pressed the button next to her name. Loretta saw him on her monitor, and happy to see it was Dan, excitedly said, "*Ciao! Avanti!*" and the door buzzed open.

Shrouded Deception

Acknowledgments

I want to thank a number of family and friends who helped me write this story, some with editing, and others with plotlines and ideas. I realized very early in this endeavor that many are very willing to offer suggestions. Some gave me good ideas, and other's I rejected, but I appreciated all input. Had I not listened to some of the comments, especially from my wife Anna, this story would have been very different. For that I am truly grateful, since I believe the final result is much better than it would have been had I not accepted their input. I feel their perspectives helped my ideas and point of view expand. So I want to thank them and acknowledge their very necessary help.

From the very beginning, I would send the rawest of what I wrote to my Aussie cousin and friend Denis Ryan. He would read what I wrote and offer his tweaks and comments; many of which I liked and added. I asked him if I could name a character after him, as an homage, for all his help. He immediately said, "Make me one of your villains, mate," which I did. My hope is I made him enough of a creep and low life to show Den how much I appreciated his help.

Once the story was written, it needed editing. Being from the Boston area, we use wicked poor grammah, so I needed a lot of help. At my church, I attended a Bible study lead by former teacher and principal, Dwain Robbins.

Showing an interest in my work, he asked if he could read it. After reading it, he offered to help edit it, which he did. As I said, it needed a lot of editing... Thank You Dwain a.k.a. Giovanni Amato.

In April 2011, I met Mardi Hack on a flight to Rome. During the flight, we formed a friendship that we still enjoy today. Like Dwain, Mardi too offered to go over the manuscript and offer her great insights, suggestions and corrections. I am amazed at all the time and effort she put into it. I also wanted to name a character after her too, but Hacketti, Hackoni or Hackelli, just never seemed to work, so all I can do is be very grateful—which I am.

Most of the names in the story are fictional and some are not. Some of the fictional names used are friends and family who helped with the story, such as Ted Casey. Ted is my brother-in-law, Mary Anne's husband. Others are names of family and friends, who I wanted to put in, like my oldest two grandsons. It is a privilege of writing a novel and needing to come up with fictional names.

Then there were the avid readers at my local library. I asked them to read my story and answer a questionnaire with comments. Most were positive and with helpful comments, a couple were scathingly critical, but all were appreciated and helped me improve the story. Finally, my sister Mary Anne came to the rescue and offered her help, which has made this a finished project I am actually pleased with, thank you Mary Anne.

There are several others who helped on various levels and if I try to name them all, I may be slighting some for not mentioning them. Again, I am sincerely thankful for all the help, you all were truly a God send.

A Personal Note

I also want to acknowledge what I truly believe was a journey orchestrated by the One who loves and supports me the most. I'll never be able to fully know nor understand how a simple prayer and desire—to write a novel, became a spiritual journey. Like in the story, I found myself on an adventure with doors opening up that I could have never imagined. As the Psalmist said, "Commit your way to the Lord, trust in Him, and He will bring it to pass." (Psalm 37:5)--Thank you Lord.

A few years ago when, installing windows in a convent chapel in Beinasco, which is just outside of Torino and meeting Sister Mary Boniface Okolo, my wife had the idea of writing an adventure about the *Shroud of Turin*. I had been talking about writing a book for perhaps a few years prior. Should it be a cookbook, a travel around Italy guide, or should it be an adventure, perhaps it's a bit of all three. I'm not sure when exactly she first proposed the idea, but I think it was the night we were sharing a narrow single bed at the convent in Beinasco, Italy. Anyway, once the light flashed on, the ideas flowed from there.

As soon as we got home from Italy I worked out an outline for the story—a bit different from what it turned out, but basically the same. My wife, Anna, works as a nurse on alternating weekends. On those days she comes home about 8AM and lies down to sleep for a few hours. Very quickly I found it was the perfect time to write. They were after Sunday morning Mass, a time when the house was kept quiet, and I didn't feel the need to work out in the studio.

It is my sincere wish that you enjoyed *Shrouded Deception*, were entertained, and hopefully surprised by its outcome. I also hope that it made you think a bit about what I believe to be a most important thing –our relationship with Jesus and his willingness to help us.

Like most people, I have never believed in the authenticity of the *Shroud of Turin*. I thought that it was a hoax perpetrated on superstitious Christians, who believe in the power of relics as a talisman. However, because of this work, I needed to do some research, so I went to the library and took out a few books about the Shroud. Two of the books explained why it is a forgery done by the Masons or DaVinci using their secret arts, while one of the another books explained how and why it might actually be Jesus' burial cloth.

I also did more research, especially studying the scientific discoveries made during the STURP forensic investigations done in 1978. Because of the results of the scientific research done, and taking the time to investigate this, I have now come to believe that it truly is Christ's burial cloth, and the image in the cloth is that of Jesus. My faith in Jesus and His resurrection was formed many years ago, but as Loretta said, at the pizzeria in Torino, "Yes, it is Jesus whom I pray to, but for me the Shroud puts a face on Jesus, and makes him more real."

After all Jesus is the only person who doesn't need His burial cloth any longer—just a thought.

Made in the USA
Charleston, SC
11 May 2016